"IT'S TIME YOU
MET YOUR BRIDE, ANGUS."

A tiny young woman, bound at the wrists, a rope secure about her waist, was being dragged into the hall by a burly armed man. Her mantle was dirty, torn at the shoulder, and her red-gold hair was in wild disarray.

Angus's mouth fell open as the man shoved her to the floor. She lay at his feet.

She pushed herself upright, and with some effort stood proudly. Her full breasts heaved with every breath she took. She stared haughtily at Angus, her nostrils flaring with anger and her gray eyes flashing her hatred of him. Even in her bedraggled state, Claudia Cherveny was the most beautiful woman Angus had ever seen, and from the look of her she'd been treated abominably.

Angus let out a low growl and sprang from his chair. When he grabbed the dagger at his waist, he saw fear leap into her eyes. In one swift movement he cut the bindings at her wrists, startling her. He grabbed her arm in a viselike grip and pulled her close to his side. Eyes blazing he turned to Felix.

"Is this how you show mercy to the enemy, uncle?" Angus asked in a low, menacing voice.

GENTLE CONQUEROR

Mary Ellen Gronau

BANTAM BOOKS
NEW YORK • TORONTO • LONDON • SYDNEY • AUCKLAND

GENTLE CONQUEROR
A Bantam Book / October 1989

ISBN 0-553-28060-0

Published simultaneously in the United States and Canada

---

*Bantam Books are published by Bantam Books, a division of Bantam
Doubleday Dell Publishing Group, Inc. Its trademark, consisting of
the words "Bantam Books" and the portrayal of a rooster, is Registered
in U.S. Patent and Trademark Office and in other countries. Marca
Registrada. Bantam Books, 666 Fifth Avenue, New York, New York
10103.*

PRINTED IN THE UNITED STATES OF AMERICA

KR   0 9 8 7 6 5 4 3 2 1

For Jason

CHAPTER 1

A.D. 987

The noise in the great hall reverberated off the thick stone walls and bounced back to the center of the room. More than a hundred men were crowded around the huge oaken tables, celebrating their victory for the third night in a row. They'd broken into the casks of wine and ale stored in the castle, and slaughtered many head of cattle for their feasts. Frightened serving girls scurried around the tables, desperately avoiding the wild grabs of the soldiers. When a girl was caught, the victor let out a cry of triumph and dragged the wench onto his lap, kissing and fondling her, and laughing at her screams and struggles to free herself.

In the center of the room, between the dais, where the lords reclined lazily, and the tables, where the soldiers celebrated raucously, a troop of jongleurs gamely tried to entertain the noisy throng. The musicians had given up playing melancholy love songs, for anything not a fast jig was rewarded with growls and a cuff on the ear. Some of the soldiers, bored by the jongleurs and musicians, burst forth in competition with spirited renditions of racy little ditties.

When a dancing girl came out, she quieted them some, mesmerizing them with her undulating movements. As the music quickened, though, so did her dancing, and she whirled faster and faster. In the excitement she created, one overzealous soldier let out a bellow and charged her. Picking her up easily, he carried the squirming girl from the hall to the catcalls and roaring laughter of his companions.

Angus McMahon sat on the dais with his long legs outstretched, his powerful arms resting lightly across his middle. A goblet of wine in his hands, he watched the scene through half-closed eyes. To one who might watch him in turn, Angus presented the picture of aloof disinterest. In a way he didn't care what his men did, just so long as they didn't hurt themselves or anyone else in their enthusiasm. But that wasn't why he was so distant. He struggled to stifle a yawn.

God, he was tired. It seemed like years since he'd slept, when it actually had been only a few days since the battle was won and he'd been forced to take catnaps instead of getting a decent night's rest. There were so many details to attend to. Enemies who'd escaped into the hills had to be ferreted out, the disputes that erupted with disturbing frequency between his men and those of his uncle had to be settled, the discipline that he demanded of his ranks must be maintained, and order needed to be restored to the ravaged lands.

His lands. All of this was his now. Through his own ingenuity as a leader and through an agreement with his uncle, he had at last made his way in the world. He had a feeling his uncle had not intended to be so generous with him and grant him these lands as a fief, but he was glad for it.

Angus glanced at the stout, hard-muscled man sitting beside him. Duke Felix Perrin was watching the merrymakers with something close to disdain. Angus still couldn't figure this uncle of his, his mother's brother. He was a proud man, accustomed to doing things his own way. That was why it had been such a surprise when he showed up at the home of Angus's father, ostensibly for a long-overdue reunion with his beloved sister, Heloise, who'd left her home in Brittany to marry the red giant from a strange land. Angus felt there was something queer in the ever-watchful Felix, as though he waited to pounce on any person unfortunate enough to be weaker than he. Angus had witnessed his uncle's cruelty more than once, and on several occasions had intervened on the behalf of those who'd angered him. His eyes glittering with rage, Felix would stare at him, then laugh harshly at what he called his nephew's weakness. But he always placated Angus.

In the many stories he'd told Heloise about the family and friends she'd left behind, it came to light that things were not well at home. There was much strife among the feudal lords, and Felix needed help in retaining his lands as well as in gaining more. So he'd traveled to the isle of Erin to seek the aid of Duncan McMahon and his many sons. What he hadn't counted on was the ever-constant conflicts between the McMahons and the neighboring clans. Duncan could not travel to Brittany with his warriors.

Felix's dilemma presented the perfect opportunity for Angus, the second oldest of five sons. The eldest, Hugh, would undoubtedly take his father's place one day as head of the clan. Angus wasn't jealous of his older brother. He recognized Hugh's ability as a great leader, and was proud of his sibling's prowess. In fact, anyone who would challenge any of the McMahon clan soon found that he had the other members to deal with as well. The closeness of the family was the work of Heloise, who was determined there would be no rivalry among her children.

The younger sons, as they came of age, had the choice to seek their fortunes elsewhere or to stay and serve their father, and then their brother. Within Angus was a fierce determination and a hunger for adventure, and his uncle's plea for help fired his spirit. So together they'd sailed for, what was to Angus, a strange and exciting land.

His father and brother had taught him more than the rudiments of war. The nineteen-year-old Angus was a capable leader who had the total respect and loyalty of his men. They found that he was a fair man, but let any one of them break the rules and he found that Angus's punishment was just as swift and sure as his justice.

Angus sipped his wine, his thoughts turning to the home and family he'd left behind. To the sweet, gentle lady, his mother. Heloise had a quiet dignity that was the stable center of their home, and that offset the blusterings of his father. Hugh was so like their father, while Kevin, a year younger than Angus, was a peacemaker, soft-spoken and kind, and always ready to soothe the hurt feelings of others. Bevan and Conan, the youngest McMahons, were mischievous imps, forever in trouble for their pranks. Thalia, his second sister was fast approaching womanhood, and sweet Gwendolyn, still a girl with the face and gentle laughter of an angel. But most of all he thought of Dorcas, with pangs of guilt and remorse, and felt a great longing to see his other self. His twin.

How he missed her, his fiery, tempestuous sister who was as fierce as he was quiet. Who'd flown into a fury when she learned that Angus would accompany Felix across the sea but she would remain at home.

Angus smiled as he recalled Dorcas that day, striding angrily back and forth before their father, her red hair flowing out behind her, her green eyes flashing in anger. He'd watched with amusement as Duncan forbade his daughter to make the journey, and Felix sat in open-mouthed horror at the idea of a woman willing to place herself in danger at her brother's side.

Finally Dorcas had stopped her pacing and glared

at her father. "And just who will protect my brother's back?" she'd snapped.

Duncan had sighed heavily, and Angus had known from his father's weary expression that he was thinking how difficult it was to win an argument against this child of his.

At last Duncan had said, "His uncle Felix will be there, and I am sending Owen along to see to your brother's needs." Then he'd added with finality, "Your mother and I require your presence here."

But that hadn't been the end of it. Later, Angus had found Dorcas still fuming in her chamber, and had had to listen to a long harangue against men and their silly attitudes. He'd managed to tease her out of her tirade by the time dinner was served, explaining to her that there were enough battles between the clans for her to content herself with, instead of traipsing across the sea to an unknown land to take up arms.

Dorcas was as good a warrior as any man. Angus was proud of his twin, and a little sorry that she wasn't with him. There had been times when he could have used her help at his back. Owen, his father's friend and finest warrior, was a godsend. If not for Owen, Angus felt his life might have been forfeited long ago. And if Dorcas had come...Angus chuckled out loud. His fiery sister would set the castle aflame with her spirit.

"You find the festivities amusing?" came a query.

Angus stopped his goblet in midair and looked at his uncle. "My thoughts are more amusing," he replied. His gaze traveled over the merrymakers. "It would appear that the men are having a good time."

Felix nodded. "Aye, that they are. But I think they are getting restless and look for new sport. As perhaps you are, nephew?" He raised his hand, and the huge oaken doors to the great hall were flung open, crashing against the inner walls.

The sound pierced through the soldiers' drunken haze, and they watched the entrance warily, some with half-drawn swords.

Angus looked from the door to his uncle bemusedly.

Felix leaned closer and murmured, "It is time that you met your bride."

Angus's head came up with a jerk and he stared at the empty doorway. He'd almost forgotten, and he wished his uncle had not reminded him.

Angus had been sickened by the blatant destruction and the senseless deaths that had occurred when their armies had overrun the castle. In the midst of the thick fighting in the courtyard, he'd heard the elated cries that the old lord was dead. He'd assumed that the battle was won, and all others would be taken prisoner. At least those were the orders he'd given his own men. It never occurred to him that the blood lust would be so great that the soldiers would strike down all who stood in their path. If he had known, he would have put a stop to the slaughter. When the fighting at last ended and he'd seen the carnage, he had thought that if his uncle had set out to annihilate those he called enemy, he could not have succeeded better.

Angus quickly squelched that thought, ashamed that the idea had ever entered his mind. Felix had appeared to be so sincere upon his visit to Erin, making it seem that his land was continually besieged by others. Therefore, Angus had been surprised upon his arrival in Brittany to learn that Felix intended to lay siege to his neighbor, Duke Robert Cherveny, instead of waiting for the man to attack him. Angus had felt he could not go back on his word to help his uncle, so he had stayed to fight.

Robert Cherveny had died valiantly defending what was his, as had his wife and two sons, and it had been such a waste. It still wasn't clear to Angus what had happened. The only thing he was certain of was that all were dead except one. Claudia Cherveny had survived the siege.

Felix had rescued the frightened girl before anyone could harm or abuse her. He'd set a guard on her, instructing the men that they were to protect her with their lives, for she was to be a gift for his nephew.

At first Angus had been appalled at his uncle's suggestion that he marry Claudia Cherveny. In his country a woman was courted and wooed. She had to be agreeable to the marriage or there would be no marriage, for a woman was an equal partner in that institution, and had rights of her own.

That was one reason his own sister was not yet married. She had frustrated every male's attempt at wooing her away from her family and into his arms by laughing at him. Unlike her sisters, who looked forward to the marriage bed, Dorcas was scared to death of the idea. So she adopted a cold mien and continued going into battle with the men against her father's weak protests. Heloise threw up her hands in despair at the strange creature who one day could cut a man in half with her sword, and the next be flirtatious and charming. It was clear to her that Dorcas would remain a maid to the day she died.

But the longer Angus thought of his uncle's proposal, the more he became reconciled to it. He was in a strange land with strange customs. Here a woman was not thought of so much as an equal partner, but more a slave to bend to her husband's will. It was not only Felix's persuasive arguments that finally swayed him to agree, however. Angus felt he owed the girl for all that had happened to her.

In their many conversations on the subject, Angus had learned from Felix that the maid was no more than sixteen summers and a comely lass, ripe for the marriage bed. It had been a long time since Angus had felt the softness of a woman, and his body cried out for the sweet taste of soft flesh next to his. He'd closed his eyes in memory of some of his more pleasurable moments with a woman, when he heard a high-pitched shriek and a scuffle. His eyes flew open and he half rose from his chair. Only the staying hand of his uncle made him remain where he was, and he sank back into his seat. A cold sweat broke out over him as had happened when he was a fresh youth going into his first battles. Lord God, was Felix using him? What if the maid was a grotesque cow? When his uncle had laughingly ·suggested he take the girl without the benefit of a priest's blessing first, he'd staunchly refused. Angus was not in the habit of raping virgins, and he'd avoided the maiden like the plague. He was now sorry he'd not taken the time to meet her.

Those soldiers who hadn't passed out from too much drink became hushed, staring at the open doors. Angus, too, could not tear his gaze away. The sight that greeted him struck him speechless.

A small slip of a girl, bound at the wrists, and a rope secure around her waist, was being dragged into the hall by a burly soldier armed to the teeth. Her mantle was dirty, and torn at the shoulder. Her red-gold hair hung in tangled disarray about her bowed head, and she stumbled as she tried to keep herself upright while being pulled along.

The guard gave her a rough shove, and she landed on the floor at Angus's feet.

After a moment the girl pushed herself upright, and with some effort stood proudly before them. Her full breasts heaved with every breath she took. She stared haughtily at the amazed Angus. Her nostrils flared with anger and her gray eyes flashed her hatred of him. Even in her bedraggled state, Claudia Cherveny was the most beautiful woman Angus had ever seen. And from the look of her, she'd been treated abominably.

The guard stared straight ahead, arms folded across his chest, unabashed by the treatment he'd dealt the prisoner. Angus noticed he was not one of his men but one of Felix's.

With a low growl Angus sprang from his chair. He grabbed the dagger at his waist and saw fear leap into the girl's eyes. In one swift movement he cut the bindings at her wrists, startling her. Eyes blazing fury, he grabbed her arm and pulled her close to his side. Then he turned to Felix, who was still sprawled in his chair.

"Is this how you show mercy to the enemy, uncle?" Angus asked in a low, menacing voice.

Felix waved a hand nonchalantly. "I thought something was needed to liven these dull festivities. I merely sought to improve your sullen mood by adding some amusement to the evening. I'd not intended to blacken it further."

Angus's eyes narrowed dangerously. If those few who knew him well could have seen the glint in his eyes, the compressed lips, and the muscle twitching in his jaw, they would have had the sense to back off. But Felix was yet unacquainted with his nephew and continued carelessly, "As you say, she is your enemy, and now as your wife, your possession."

"As you say, uncle, *my* possession. And my possessions receive better treatment than this poor child. Owen!"

His companion, who'd been watching the scene close by, hurried over.

"See that the lady is escorted to her chamber

and that a bath is readied for her. She will need
clean clothes, and then she is to return to the hall
as soon as she is ready. The good priest will then
perform the ceremony."

Owen nodded at his lord's crisp commands.

Without looking at the girl, who barely reached
his shoulder, Angus turned to the assemblage.
"There will be a wedding this night," he an-
nounced, and the men raised a cheer that echoed
through the hall.

With her arms resting lightly on the sides of the
metal tub, Claudia sank lower into the water. She
wearily leaned her head back against the edge,
and gave way to the tears she'd been holding in
check for so long. Up to now there hadn't been
time for tears. She'd been too busy surviving.

She cried for the loss of her beloved family. Her
father, at turns both gentle and stern. Her mother,
sweet and loving, kind to a fault. Her parents had
loved each other with unshakable devotion.

It had not always been so, for Jeanette Marcel
had been forced to marry against her will. With
patience, Robert Cherveny had gradually acquired
his wife's respect and love. That love showed in
the children they raised. Mallory, Claudia's older
brother, who'd protected her to the end. Vail, her
laughing-eyed younger brother, who was still only
a boy, and whom she'd looked upon as something
of a pest with his mischievous ways. She'd loved
them all.

She mourned her loss, and theirs. Tears streamed

down her cheeks, and she didn't bother to wipe them away. Life was too harsh, too unfair. She cried, guilt-ridden that she had been spared. If she'd had the courage, she would have taken her own life, but some unseen hand had held her back. She cried all the harder at the thought of being such a coward.

Her family was now a part of the dust of the earth—a part of the land her father had loved so. Everything was gone. The love and security and devotion she'd known all her life and had taken for granted.

Now, through cruel fate, she was being helplessly plunged into a foreign world with strangers. Strangers who now inhabited these walls, whose slave she had become. It mattered not that she was to be mistress of the hall by the way of marriage to the new lord. He was her enemy, and if she had the power to destroy him, she would. Somehow she would find a way.

There was a loud knock at her door. Claudia quickly splashed her face with water before answering. "What is it?" she asked in a trembling voice. She held her breath, waiting for the intruder to try his luck against the barred door, but the latch did not move as she expected it might.

"My lord Angus requests your presence below, m'lady," a man said.

Claudia's heart sank. "Tell your lord that I will be down shortly," she said.

Her throat constricted with fear. To be tied to a barbaric animal was more than she could bear.

Ideas for ending her life flitted in and out of her
mind. Then a slow smile parted her lips. There
was another whose life would be forfeited this
night.

Claudia surreptitiously watched the man at her
side as the priest recited the vows over them. He
was a powerfully built man with a massive chest
and arms, the muscles bulging beneath his shirt.
Claudia had no doubt that he could crush a man,
or a woman, to death in those arms. When she'd
entered the hall, she'd been aware of everything
about the man who would become her husband.
His massive torso tapered to a trim waist and slim
hips, below which were powerful legs. As she'd
approached him, she'd been astonished by his
height, how far back she had to tilt her head to
stare into his clear green eyes. She elicited the
courage to speak to him then.

"My lord, I think it only fair to warn you that I
do not accept this sham. I will not accede to your
dominance over me."

Unfortunately for Claudia, Felix was standing
close enough to hear. He stepped forward and said
threateningly, "You are in no position to accept
anything. You belong to Angus just as this castle
and the vassals and fiefs belong to him, because *I*
saw fit to bestow these things on him. So accept
your fate. You are now my nephew's property."

Frightened by the cruelty in his eyes and voice,
she stepped closer to Angus. She felt someone
grasp her arm and looked down at the strong hand

that firmly held her. Then her eyes traveled slowly upward to find Angus gazing kindly at her.

"You need not fear me, Claudia. You will come to no harm," he said quietly. He held out his arm to her and she tentatively laid her hand upon it to be led before the priest. She was aware of his hard muscles and shivered slightly. He glanced at her but said nothing.

It was just as well, Claudia thought, for her heart was pounding so loudly, she was sure he could hear it. Her throat became dry. Had he guessed what was in her thoughts?

Angus bowed reverently before the priest. His warrior's instinct warned him he was being closely observed, and out of the corner of his eye he watched the watcher.

Outwardly the girl showed no fear, but he could feel her trembling. She was tiny and frail and he felt an overwhelming urge to put a protective arm around her. She was so young and had seen so much death and destruction. He silently vowed to shelter this child-woman for the rest of her life, and to see to it that from now on she knew only happiness and joy.

He was well pleased with the girl's beauty, and was grateful to his uncle for insisting upon the alliance. What comfort he would derive from those arms. And if he were lucky, they'd have a union not unlike his parents'. He'd been surprised by the spirit she'd shown upon entering the hall, then had been more surprised at the sense of relief he'd felt, knowing he was not to be saddled with a meek, simpleminded maid afraid of her own shadow. He could understand her hate, could even sympathize with it, but it would not last forever. Now more than ever he looked forward to getting to know the woman beside him.

They both answered the priest's queries and repeated his vows, and at last the ceremony was finished. Angus arose first and helped Claudia to her feet. They stared at each other for what seemed an eternity—Angus's green eyes calm and observant, Claudia's gray eyes wide and fearful—before the chants of the men brought them back to the present.

"Long live the lord of the hall. Long live the lady of the hall. Long live the fief of McMahon," came the loud cries.

Angus grinned in sheer pleasure, and Claudia was struck by the boyish charm that emerged, transforming his otherwise sober countenance. His eyes crinkling in merriment, he turned to face the men. He lifted his goblet, and in his rich voice toasted his men. They cheered once more, then returned to the serious undertaking of feasting.

Angus led Claudia to the chair beside his on the dais, and she was aware of a tingling sensation shooting through her at his touch. She almost panicked then. It was with great effort that she pushed down the feelings of apprehension that overwhelmed her, telling herself she must control her emotions lest her plans be discovered.

A figure crept stealthily into the hall and hid behind a tapestry, searching the room with haunted eyes. At last they came to rest on the dais. A sigh of relief escaped weathered lips as the figure watched Claudia pick at the food on her plate, moving it from spot to spot but hardly touching anything. The child was silent and withdrawn. She looked so lost and forlorn between the two giants on either side of her. The figure watched, eyes hard with hatred as the older man leaned forward to whisper something to Claudia. Claudia paled and clutched her hands together in her lap. The younger man frowned and touched Claudia's arm, murmuring something to her. She flinched at the contact. Eyes narrowed, the figure finally started inching along the wall to get closer to the nobles. No one was going to hurt Claudia. No one.

Claudia sat brooding about the night ahead. Every so often a movement on her left caught her eye as Angus reached for his wine goblet, and she was again overwhelmed by the fearful power of him. How was she going to fend him off long enough to do what had to be done? She noticed that he ate very little, yet drank his wine steadily. Each time his cup was emptied, a serving girl promptly refilled it.

She started when Felix leaned over to whisper lewdly in her ear, "If you are so unhappy with your present plight, my lady, mayhaps I can be of assistance. With all your husband has had to drink, he might not be able to fulfill his duty to you. I would be delighted to take his place."

Claudia shuddered and clutched her hands together tightly in her lap to keep from clawing Felix's face. She had suffered enough at that one's hands. The humiliating memory of him entering her chamber at odd moments in the past few days, pawing her while cruelly taunting her, was still fresh in her mind. He'd taken great pleasure in describing the horrible life she would have with his nephew, especially if she displeased Angus. His words left an indelible fear and revulsion within her. She'd never realized what a truly evil person he was.

Duke Felix had always been made welcome at Orgueilleux, for Robert Cherveny was not one to spurn his neighbors, no matter how distasteful they were. She had never particularly cared for the man, especially in the past two years. The way he'd stared at her filled her with unease, so she had avoided him as much as possible when he visited. Who could have known that Felix Perrin would turn with such savagery on those who called him friend. Claudia shivered.

Her preoccupation did not go unnoticed by Angus. He nervously drank his wine, hoping he could get drunk. Having a willing wench in his bed was a completely different matter from having an unwilling wife. She was so tiny, like a frightened bird. What if he hurt her?

He was keenly aware of her fear, and when she suddenly clenched her hands and sat immobile, he leaned forward. He touched her arm tentatively, making her jump. "Are you all right?" he inquired.

"Aye, of course I am," she replied quietly.

He sat back, studying her, and didn't see the cloaked figure creeping toward him, stealthily reaching into the folds of the concealing garment to withdraw a dagger.

His keen senses warned of danger before he heard a muffled cry behind him. Owen shouted a warning and he turned his head to see a shrouded figure holding a dagger aloft, ready to strike.

He leapt to his feet and reached for his sword. He had it raised to strike when Claudia shrieked for him to stop. She jumped in front of him and used all her strength to hold his powerful arm at bay.

Fear shot through Angus, for the cloaked figure was rushing toward them, and Claudia was directly in the way. He used his free arm to shove her behind him and was about to bring his weapon down upon this unknown foe when Owen, who was weaponless, threw himself at the assassin. The impact sent the dagger flying, and propelled the attacker and the rescuer to the rushes. Without a moment's hesitation Owen had his hands about the assailant's throat.

"Nay!" screamed Claudia. With a strength unknown to her, she broke free from Angus and ran to Owen. She clawed frantically at his iron-hard hands and arms to break his hold. "Nay. Please stop," she cried, tears streaming down her face. "No harm has been done, please. Please, don't."

In his anger Owen was beyond hearing and continued to crush the life from his friend's enemy. With his powerful hands still encircling the throat, he lifted the limp head from the floor and started shaking it. The hood of the cloak fell away to reveal an old woman.

Claudia let out a wailing moan of grief and bent over in her agony. "Marian!" Her scream echoed through the hall. Then she dissolved into ragged sobs.

The pressure of Owen's hands lessened as he stared in horror at the still face. He pulled his hands away as though they'd been burnt and sat, legs straddling his victim, breathing heavily.

"It's a woman," Felix said, staring over the sobbing Claudia.

"Is she dead?" Angus asked.

"Nay, my lord, she still breathes," Owen said quietly, shaken by what had almost happened.

Claudia's head snapped up, her eyes blazing in fury. "No thanks to you."

Owen flinched at the girl's attack. "I did not know. I thought only to protect my lord. I could not see that she was a woman."

"Nay! Nor would you stop at my urging," she said scathingly.

Owen glanced away from the penetrating gray eyes, unable to face the hatred he saw there.

"Claudia, we did not know," Angus said, placing his hands on her shoulders to help her to her feet.

She shrank away from his touch and crawled to the old woman. "Marian," she whispered. She lifted the woman's head gently and laid it on her lap, stroking the hair heavily streaked with gray.

"Who is she?" Angus asked.

"My former nurse," Claudia whispered. "She helped to raise me. Next to my mother she is the woman I love most in the world."

"Owen, carry the old one to a chamber above and see that she is cared for."

"Aye, my lord," Owen said. He stood and started to reach for her, but Claudia leaned protectively over Marian.

"No harm will come to her," Angus said reassuringly. When he saw the uncertainty on his wife's face, he added, "I promise you."

Claudia hesitated for a moment before finally allowing Owen to lift the faithful servant in his strong arms. She made to follow him from the hall, but Angus stopped her.

"Owen will see to her."

"Nay, my lord, I will," Claudia said resolutely. "She has cared for me from the day I was born. It is only right that I should now see to her when she needs me."

Angus stared into the calm face streaked with tears. Reading the determination in her eyes, he nodded and let her go.

CHAPTER 2

Angus sat frowning into his goblet of wine. Where before there had been pandemonium in the hall, now there was an eerie silence. Those who hadn't passed out where they sat had quietly taken themselves away to bed down for the night.

Felix had expounded his views on his nephew's softness, his folly at letting the woman live. When Angus did not respond to his uncle's taunts, Felix had left in disgust. If he had known that Angus hadn't heard a word he'd said, Felix would have been even more furious.

Angus was too busy trying to answer the questions running through his mind. Why had the old woman wanted to kill him? Even if she was trying to protect her mistress as Claudia said, why that? Surely she could see Claudia was unharmed. He would never hurt her. She was like a little bird, frail and tiny. From the moment he laid eyes on her, all he wanted to do was protect her.

He scowled as another thought came to mind. Mayhaps it had been a plan that went afoul.

Claudia had been hell-bent on hindering his efforts to defend himself. Had she and the old one plotted his death? He didn't like to think that was the case. Of course, he could ask Claudia outright, but then there would always be that lingering doubt, for they were strangers and too newly enemies. A wry smile touched Angus's lips. That was a fact he intended to remedy.

He sighed and wearily plodded upstairs, still in serious thought. The amount of wine he'd consumed was in no way a detriment, for the events of the evening had had their sobering effect.

Claudia sat beside the bed holding Marian's withered hand. A tear escaped from the corner of her eye to trickle forlornly down her cheek. What if Marian died too? She couldn't let that happen. It mustn't. Everything she loved in the world was gone. She couldn't let Marian go.

A small moan came from the bed as Marian rolled her head to one side and opened her eyes.

Claudia leaned forward and placed a trembling hand on the old woman's face. "Marian, how do you feel?" she asked in a hushed tone.

"I—I'm fine," Marian answered in a hoarse whisper. "I am not dead?"

Claudia let out a relieved little laugh. "Nay, dearest. You are here, with me, and I will take care of you."

"It is I who should be taking care of you."

Claudia smiled and shook her head. "Not now. Later. Now you must rest." She threw her arms around the servant and hugged her. "Oh, Marian, it is so good to see you. Where did you come from? I thought you gone. Where have you been?"

Marian frowned as some unpleasant memories came flooding back. "Hiding. I—I think I was hit on the head. One moment I was standing in the courtyard as it was overrun with soldiers, and the next minute there was blackness. They must have thought me dead. I awoke when it was dark, with a terrible ache in my head I might add," she said peevishly. She frowned as if trying to recall what happened next. "Then I dragged myself off to a dark corner. Humphrey found me and took me to his cottage, where Maud could look after me." Her face puckered suddenly, and her lips trembled. "We have lost the battle, haven't we, m'lady?"

"Yea, Marian, we have. The enemy now holds us in their hands."

The servant looked questioningly at Claudia. "And what of Duke Robert and Lady Jeanette?"

Claudia looked away, "Dead," she answered, her voice breaking, "Both dead."

Marian clutched the young girl's hand tightly. "The boys?"

"Gone."

"Both?" Marian croaked, unable to believe what she was hearing.

Claudia could only nod as a fresh wave of tears flowed down her cheeks.

Marian shuddered and gathered the weeping girl into her arms. "Oh, my poor pigeon. My poor, poor pigeon," she crooned, rocking the girl back and forth as she'd done many years before. "I tried to help you, my love. When I saw you sitting in the hall so pale and frightened with those two giants next to you, I had to protect you. No one is going to hurt my little one. Not ever again." She suddenly pushed Claudia away from her. "What did they do to you, child? Did they harm you?"

Claudia shook her head in answer.

"You looked frightened out of your wits."

"Duke Felix made some very lewd remarks. He—he frightened me with what he said."

"Hmph! No doubt. He's a bad one all right. I warned your father about him. Sitting at Duke Robert's table, eating his food, drinking his wine, and all the while plotting against him.

"And what of the young one on your left? When he touched you, you fair jumped right out of your skin." Marian pushed Claudia's hair back from her face. "No one is going to take liberties with my little pigeon."

"He only inquired after my health," Claudia answered wistfully. "I suppose he thinks he has a right to touch me. He is my husband."

Marian felt as though the breath had been knocked from her. "What?"

"I—I was forced to marry him tonight."

"Why?"

"He is Duke Felix's nephew, and Duke Felix is giving this land to him as a fief. Apparently I go along with the fief," she added bitterly.

Marian's head was spinning because of the girl's

revelations. "But I thought Duke Felix coveted this land."

Claudia shrugged. "I guess we were wrong. For Lord Angus's help, his uncle is giving this land to him. Along with me." She smiled wryly. "I suppose that makes me the spoils of war."

Marian clucked her tongue and gathered Claudia in her arms once more. "Oh, my poor pigeon. If I'd known that you were to be delivered into the hands of the enemy, I would have seen to it that my dagger had met its mark."

"Do not fear for me, faithful one. Before this night is over the enemy will pay threefold for all that we have suffered." Claudia gently guided her servant back against the pillows, and pulled the covers around her. "Sleep well. This night will see the death of my family and the wrong done to you avenged."

Marian was frightened by the hard glint of hate in her mistress's eyes. "Be careful, m'lady. That young one is a powerful man. And not without faithful servants of his own. Do not let the same fate befall you as your dear, sweet loved ones."

Claudia looked into the flickering firelight on the hearth and murmured softly, "Mayhaps death would be my salvation."

"M'lady, you must not speak so."

Claudia turned to look at the old woman and smiled wistfully. "Hush. I should not have let you speak so much. Go to sleep now. Everything will be all right." She touched the inside of her sleeve and felt the dagger she'd hidden there. After the attack on Marian, she'd rescued the weapon from where it fell among the rushes when no one was looking.

As Angus approached the chamber where the old woman lay, he saw Owen crouched outside the door, staring at the wall across from him. He stopped and eyed the man without saying anything until Owen, at last, looked up.

"How is she?" Angus asked, pointing to the closed door.

"The lady Claudia is with her," Owen said quietly.

"And how do you fare?"

"In truth, shaken."

The men stared at each other for a moment in silence. Finally Owen said, "I will be fine."

Angus nodded, then pushed open the door.

The old woman lay in the bed, eyes closed. Claudia sat by her side holding Marian's timeworn hand in her own youthful one.

Angus walked to the bed to stand just behind his wife, but Claudia neither looked up nor acknowledged his presence in any way. He noted the bruise marks on Marian's neck and the easy rise and fall of her breaths. "She sleeps," he said.

Silence greeted him.

"Has she awakened at all?"

"For a time." Claudia turned accusing eyes on him. "She can barely speak."

"I am sorry. We did not know. Owen, and I, acted out of instinct. Owen would never harm a woman, let alone kill one."

"And you?"

"Nay, but I am a warrior. What I did was instinctive."

Her eyes flashed. "Ah, yea, the conquering warrior."

Angus gazed into her hate-filled eyes. "Come. Let us retire to our chamber."

A tremor shook her. She started to protest, "But . . ."

"You will do her no good by denying yourself rest." He held out a hand to her. "Come."

She arose reluctantly without accepting the proffered hand and brushed past him. He followed and shut the door quietly.

When Claudia saw Owen in the hall, she stopped in indecision.

"I promised you that no harm would come to the old one," Angus said quietly, as though reading her thoughts.

Without speaking, Claudia turned and started down the hall.

"Where are you going?" Angus called out.

She glanced back at him, puzzled. "To my chamber."

He smiled indulgently and stepped forward to turn her around. "*Our* chamber is this way."

He guided her along the hallway and opened the door to a large, airy room. A huge bed stood in the center of the chamber. Two enormous tapestries depicting hunting scenes hung from one wall, a large wooden chest for clothes standing between them. There was a comfortable chair in one corner beside a beautifully carved table. A bench sat before the fire that threw out the only light in the room.

Claudia looked around her, her heart pounding furiously. This had been her parents' room. Her gaze came to rest on the bed. The bed where her parents had slept, where she and her brothers had been conceived and born. Where as a little girl she'd found solace from all the bad things that were fearful to a child. And this man who stood shrugging out of his leather vest so unconcernedly expected to lie with her there. To commit his vile acts upon her, for anything he did she would consider vile. He was her enemy.

Something snapped inside Claudia as she stared at Angus's now-bare back, the muscles rippling as he placed one foot on the bench and bent to remove his laced shoes. She furtively reached inside the sleeve of her gown and grasped the handle of the dagger. Pulling it out, she crept forward, arm upraised, never taking her eyes off his broad back. Her throat constricted in fear, yet she pressed on. Just as she reached him, Angus stooped to retrieve something from the floor. She struck, but his movement threw off her aim, and the dagger pierced his left shoulder instead of its intended target beneath the shoulder blade.

Angus bolted upright, wincing in pain. He automatically reached back, his fingers clutching at the weapon. He turned in shock to Claudia, and what he saw there brought him up short.

She stood breathing heavily, her eyes wide pools of anger and hate and fear.

With a grunt, he yanked the dagger from his shoulder, then grabbed her, holding the point of the knife to her delicate white throat. Without releasing her, he thrust her onto the bed, landing on top of her. Blood seeped from his wound, but he didn't notice, too angry with himself for letting down his guard. If only he'd not been so deep in thought.

"With this night's actions all my doubts have been laid to rest," he muttered, baring his teeth. "Hear me, and hear me well, my lady. I am a seasoned warrior who has fought many battles, and who has had many a brush with death. But not even I have had the misfortune to be faced by an assassin's hand, nay, by two assassins' hands as I have this day.

"Mark my words well, for I speak with truth now. For every wound that is inflicted upon me by your hand, or by the hand of anyone faithful enough to do your bidding, five serfs will forfeit their lives."

He watched her eyes grow wide with fear.

"If you value your people, my lady, you will heed my words, for I do not make idle threats. If one drop of my blood is spilled other than on a field of battle, your people will be the first to pay, starting with that old woman down the hall."

Claudia gasped in fright, and a slow smile spread across Angus's face. She was reminded of a mad dog snarling at her.

"And," he added cruelly, "you will be forced to watch as the deed is done. So take care of my person as you would your own, my lady. Many lives depend on it."

Angus released her suddenly. Standing by the bed, he glared at the girl who lay staring up at him, too frightened to utter a sound. He whirled away from her and muttered angrily, "Get to bed."

He strode to a table, clutching his shoulder where blood oozed through his fingers. Throwing the knife angrily down, he picked up a cloth and dipped it into the basin of water.

Claudia quickly discarded her outer garments with shaking fingers, her back to Angus. With her chemise still on, she turned to the bed and pulled back the covers. Her eyes unwittingly went to Angus as he struggled to cleanse his wound and stop the bleeding. She bit her lower lip in indecision, then moved toward him.

As she reached out to him, he jerked away. "Do not touch me," he said fiercely. "I will see to my own needs."

Claudia dropped her hands to her sides, and without saying anything returned to the bed and climbed in. She pulled the covers up under her chin and lay watching as Angus clumsily bound his wound.

Angus sat staring pensively into the slowly dying fire. Any doubts he might have had concerning his wife's part in the old woman's attack had been dispelled. His wife! He grimaced at the thought.

He had been well pleased when he'd first laid eyes on Claudia Cherveny, and had looked forward to learning about her. He'd conjured up pictures of sitting before the fire quietly talking, as his parents did, discussing the events of the day or their children. He wanted to see her smile, hear her laughter. He looked forward eagerly to tasting her soft, sweet flesh. And now—

He shifted in the chair and studied the girl lying in the bed. She still looked small and frail, so guiltless as she lay on her side with the covers tucked under her chin, one hand resting lightly on the pillow. In sleep she seemed like an innocent child, incapable of the hatred he'd seen in her eyes.

Angus grunted and shifted again. The throbbing pain in his shoulder had finally lessened to a dull ache, but to him it would always be a reminder of this, his wedding night, and a lesson to be more wary in the future. He would have to watch his back a little more closely.

A whimper came from the bed and he looked once more at her. Claudia whimpered again and started thrashing her head about on the pillow, then she began to mumble.

He sighed and heaved himself up slowly. Walking to the bed, he reached for her shoulder to awaken her, but stopped, his hand hovering near her. He was startled to see her lashes wet with tears, her forehead beaded with perspiration. Tentatively shaking her, he called her name.

She cried out and bolted upright. She seemed disoriented as she shook her head. Her eyes came to rest on his face, and what he saw there made him frown in concern. He'd seen the same look on fresh youths' faces after their first experience with battle. A dazed, terror-stricken expression, haunted by the horrors of what they'd witnessed. She had the same look.

"Claudia?" he whispered.

Her eyes seemed to focus on him, widening in her panic. Clutching the covers tightly to her, she scrambled to her knees and began to back away.

"Nay, nay," she mumbled, then she started sobbing hysterically.

Angus was bewildered by this sudden change in her. Her fright. Her anguish. He leaned across the bed and grabbed her shoulders, dragging her stiff body to him. "Claudia, stop it."

She cried out in fear, not really seeing him.

He shook her. "Claudia, stop it! Do you hear me? Stop it. It was only a dream, a bad dream."

When his words didn't penetrate, he did the only other thing he thought might bring her out of her trancelike state. He slapped her face.

It had the desired effect of stopping her hysterical cries before they turned to screams, and making her actually see him.

"You had a nightmare," he said quietly. "Do you remember?"

She nodded, then surprised him by laying her head against his chest and sobbing as though her heart were breaking.

At first he was too stunned to move. Then his arms went around her, giving her the comfort she sought. "Tell me," he whispered.

Between sobs she said brokenly, "I—I saw them

all fall. My father, cut down when the castle was over-overrun. My older brother as h-he tried to protect my mother and me. My mother—" Her voice rose to a plaintive cry. "She—she took up Mallory's sword and tried to protect me herself, but her head—Oh, God, all the blood.

"My—my young-younger brother ran outside and was lost to me forever. He was but a child." She spoke so pitifully that Angus's heart was wrung with pangs of guilt. "They're all dead, all dead," she ended, sobbing bitterly.

He said nothing as he gently rocked her back and forth. What could he say to ease her pain? She'd lost her whole family and had had to stand by helplessly to watch the deed as it was done. And he was responsible for her anguish. It was no wonder she hated him and had tried to kill him.

He could no longer blame her for her actions. If their situations were reversed, he would have tried the same thing.

He felt impotent to ease her pain as she wept uncontrollably, knowing that no words could express the sorrow he shared with her. He vowed silently to do everything he could to erase from her mind the horrors she'd witnessed. It would take time for her to learn to trust him, but then, they had a lifetime.

He listened as her weeping quieted, and at last, heard her even breathing. He peered down at her and saw that her eyes were closed. He carefully laid her down and pulled the covers around her shoulders. He sat for a time just staring at the now-peaceful face of his young bride.

Finally he arose, and poked at the low-burning fire until it once more flamed up to throw off the chill in the air. Then he settled into the chair to await the early dawn.

When the first pinkish light of day peeked over the horizon, Angus donned his clothing. He shrugged into the heavy fur cloak to ward off the damp chill in the late winter morn and quietly left the room, glancing once more at his peacefully sleeping wife.

He descended to the great hall and stepped gingerly around the still-sleeping bodies of soldiers to make his way to the kitchen area. The servants were preparing the morning meal for the horde of captors who slept on. They stopped what they were doing to stare in silence at their new master.

"I require something to eat," Angus said in the foreign tongue, blessing his mother for teaching him to speak it.

An aged woman, as broad as she was tall, reached for the ladle in the kettle hanging in the huge fireplace.

"I need something I can take with me," he said, before she could dish out a bowl of thick, bubbling porridge. He spied some fresh-baked biscuits on the table, and picked one up and buttered it. After one bite he thought he'd been transported to heaven. "Did you bake these?" he asked the woman.

She nodded.

He took another huge bite and waved the remains of the biscuit at the cook. "This is the best biscuit I've ever tasted in my life. Not even my own dear mother makes them so well," he said with his mouth full.

The old cook smiled a toothless answer as Angus stuffed his pockets with his prizes. He started toward the door, but before he reached it the cook rushed over with a bowl of hard-boiled eggs, offering them to him. He smiled and snatched up four eggs before leaving. He strolled to the stables, where he saddled his destrier, then rode off to inspect his lands.

Claudia awoke a short time later and looked around her, puzzled. Then the events of the evening before came back to her with stark clarity. She sat up quickly. She was alone.

She jumped from the bed and dressed, then let herself out of the chamber to rush to Marian's room.

Owen nodded in greeting and opened the door for her. As she entered the room, she wondered if the man ever slept. Marian was lying quietly on the bed, and she lovingly touched the old servant's face.

Marian's eyes fluttered open. "M'lady, you are well?" she asked, her voice still quite hoarse.

Claudia smiled. "Aye, I am well. And what of you? Did you get enough rest?"

Marian made a face. "Aye. Too much I fear."

She made to rise and Claudia gently pushed her old nurse back, smiling indulgently. "Nay. You are not to move from here, do you understand me? You still need rest."

"Hmph," Marian sniffed. "I am too old to lie abed all day."

"Nevertheless, you will do as you are told. I am still the mistress."

Marian looked askance at the girl. "And what of the master?" she asked quietly.

Claudia looked her in the eye. "He is well." She noted the relieved expression on Marian's face. "My dagger missed its mark," she murmured.

Marian gasped. "And you live?" she exclaimed.

"Aye, I came to no harm, as you can well see."

"But he is the enemy. Why—"

"I do not know why he did not end my life, but he did not. There is a kindness in him," she added wistfully, remembering the tender way he'd held her as she sobbed.

"Kindness, bah!" Marian snorted.

Claudia felt color rising to her cheeks at her memories of her new husband's strong arms, his kind voice, his warm body. "Aye, a kindness..."

"Do you forget so quickly that he is the one responsible for your loss? Surely you have not been so foolish as to give your heart to him!"

"Nay! Never that. But he is kind in his own way."

She remembered something else Angus had said, and shivered. "And we must not make another attempt on his life. He means us no harm."

There was a rap at the door, and Claudia called for the person to enter. Owen stuck his head inside the room. "If your ladyship no longer needs me, I will take my leave," he said in his deep, rumbly voice.

She nodded coolly, and he backed out of the room.

Marian grunted. "That one is a devil."

"Aye. Mayhaps they are both devils, and we are in hell."

After touring the countryside to see that his orders were being carried out—that the peasants' cottages that had been burned were being rebuilt and the fields were being plowed and prepared for the spring planting—Angus returned to the castle. He sat astride his destrier on a hill overlooking his new home. Rubbing the ache from his shoulder, he stared in awe at the stone watchtower rising in the distance. A partially finished wall surrounded the castle, which was built of thick, impregnable stone.

Orgueilleux. That's what Claudia had called her home. Proud. And it was proud, standing sentinel against all invaders. The castle was totally foreign to Angus, quite unlike his father's home. The McMahon stronghold, like others in Erin, consisted of a wooden wall protecting a village, the peasants' cottages made of wattle with thatched roofs, and the wooden keep that housed the McMahon family. Nothing in Erin that he'd seen matched this massive castle, rising the height of ten men and spreading across an area nearly as large as the entire McMahon stronghold. He knew without a doubt that if Claudia's father had had the forces to repel them, the outcome of the battle would indeed have been different. The man had been plainly outnumbered.

Angus decided that the first order of business

would be to finish the stone wall. If it had been completed earlier, he wondered whether the castle would have been so easy to take.

Mayhaps that was why his uncle had been in such a hurry to attack Cherveny, because he knew that once the wall was complete, there would be no way to penetrate the fortress.

The taking of Orgueilleux still left a bitter taste in Angus's mouth. In the days that followed the battle there had been many times when he'd wanted to turn his back on it all and just ride away. His uncle had been full of arguments as to why he should stay, and had finally told Angus that Orgueilleux was his. Angus had been stunned by Felix's generosity, despite the catch of having to marry Claudia Cherveny. He now felt he'd received the better deal by far, and no longer wondered about the reasons for his uncle's munificence. At the moment his main concern was in breaking down the barriers that existed between his wife and himself.

As he rode into the yard, he saw that his warriors—now called knights in the manner of other lords in Brittany—were hard at work on the training field, as he'd known they would be. He dismounted and took care of the destrier's needs before joining his men. He worked with them well into the afternoon until he was hot and sweaty, and he'd beaten Owen soundly in a round of swordplay. With a companionable arm around his friend's shoulder, he strolled with Owen to the horse trough to clean up.

Angus shrugged out of his leather vest and bent to splash water on his face and neck when he was pulled up roughly.

"That is a new wound," Owen said, touching Angus's blood-soaked tunic gingerly.

Angus grinned. "Aye."

"Are you going to explain how you came by it, or do we play a guessing game?" Owen asked when it appeared Angus would not volunteer any information.

"My new wife is not as complacent as I first thought," Angus said sheepishly.

Owen studied the young man in silence, trying to conjure up a picture of how that tiny woman could have caught Angus so unawares. At last he grunted. "She must have attacked you in your sleep."

Angus nodded good-naturedly. "Aye, that she did. This time."

"This time?" Owen asked sharply. "You expect her to try again?"

Angus shrugged. "Mayhaps," he said, picking up his vest from the ground. He turned and started walking toward the hall.

"Watch your back!" Owen shouted after him.

CHAPTER 3

Angus entered the great hall and looked around.
The tables were cleaned of any evidence of the
previous night's festivities. New rushes had been
spread on the floor, and a welcoming fire blazed in
the fireplace.

He made his way upstairs to his chamber, hoping that Claudia was already there. He'd had time
to think on his long ride, and had much to say to
her. He opened the door and was disappointed to
see that the room was empty. But he was surprised to see a tub before the fireplace, steam
rising from it.

He threw his vest on the chair and shed his
tunic. He was reaching for the blood-soaked bandage to strip it away when the door opened.
Glancing over his shoulder he saw Claudia enter
the room, then stop, as if startled to find him
there. He said nothing but pulled the bandage
free, then threw it into the hearth.

"You suffer a new wound?" she asked.

"Nay," he answered, poking at the tender red

flesh. "'Tis the one you gave me. It opened on the training field."

She slammed the door shut and stood with her arms akimbo, glaring at him.

"Why were you training when you should be taking care of yourself so something like this would not happen?"

He looked into her stormy gray eyes, raising an eyebrow in surprise. "Do I hear a note of concern?"

She lowered her arms to her sides and blinked. "Nay, you do not. Not for you."

He grunted and turned away to inspect his wound once more.

"May I remind you," she said, "of your warning to me that my safety and the safety of my people, are dependent upon your good health? I merely do not wish to see you come to harm in case your henchmen decide to carry out your threats."

He nodded in understanding. "'Tis wise that you heed my words, my lady."

"I simply value life more than you."

Angus studied his wife, her chin quivering but tilted defiantly. Then he said quietly, "I value life, Claudia. In truth, I hate wasteful deaths, but I am a leader of men. A warrior. There is no room for weakness in my decisions. Those who serve me soon learn that my authority is supreme next only to God's, and I do not allow insurrection from anyone, including you. I showed more leniency toward you, my wife, than I would have to anyone else, be they my man or my enemy."

"Why show me any mercy at all? I am your

enemy," she said angrily, turning her back on him to walk away.

In two strides Angus was behind her. He whirled her around to face him. "You are my wife, and subject to my lordship. I value your life. Yea, yours! As I would my own, because it is mine, and I am bound to protect it. That is why your dagger did not find its mark in my hand. This time. It is well that you heed my warning, for once I make a judgment, it stands."

"Aye, I am well aware of that," she answered coldly. "I am your servant. To bend to your will. I will not forget again."

Angus sighed and released her. "You are my wife. I do not wish to face each day as a battle between us, Claudia." He grinned suddenly, showing even white teeth, and Claudia was once more taken aback by his boyish charm. "Even warriors grow weary of fighting." As quickly as the grin had come, it was replaced by a serious expression. "I know that I came here as an enemy. I am from a different culture and background, but I am still a man. I have wants and dreams. I have feelings."

Claudia looked at the floor when she could no longer stand his penetrating gaze.

"Am I to forget the destruction of my life?" she asked in a barely audible whisper. "The death of my family?"

"Nay, but remember the happy times. The joy and love, and thank God that you live. I do."

She slowly looked up, and was disconcerted by the kindness and understanding in Angus's piercing green eyes. She moved away to stand before the fire, her arms crossed as though protecting herself from the cold. "It is hard," she said at last.

"Aye, I know."

Angus watched for a few moments as Claudia stared into the fireplace, as though the answers she sought would be found in the depths of the leaping flames. "At least," he said, "you are making an effort to come to terms with your situation. For that I am grateful."

She turned to him, a puzzled frown creasing her forehead.

He motioned to the tub. "A bath is a welcome comfort after a long day."

"But I—" She stopped and snapped her mouth shut.

It was Angus's turn to stare in confusion. "Claudia? The tub was placed here for my convenience, was it not?"

She tilted her chin in the air and faced the fire again. "As you wish."

He frowned at the straight back presented to him. "Claudia," he said in a low voice, "whose bath is that getting colder by the minute?"

When she did not answer, he stepped closer and turned her stiff form around to face him. "Answer me truthfully."

Claudia stared coldly at this man who would take even this small pleasure from her, and decided to throw caution to the wind. She had no more to lose. "It was for me."

His mouth twitched, then he chuckled softly. "And so it shall be," he stated, grinning at her.

She was startled by his good humor, then grew wary. Why should he yield on this? So far he had taken everything from her, offering nothing in return. She'd received only threats from him, she thought belligerently, his words from so short a time before already forgotten.

"The water is not getting any warmer," he whispered.

The frown creasing her forehead deepened. "But . . . you are here."

He raised an eyebrow in mock surprise. "Aye, and I intend to remain. Shall I help you undress?" His eyes twinkled as his hands slid to her waist to unfasten her belt.

Unnerved by his boldness she thrust his hands away from her and stepped out of his reach. "Nay, I need no help from you!" she cried indignantly. She stood with her fingers intertwining nervously, eyeing him warily.

When she could no longer stand his steady gaze, she said in exasperation, "You must leave this chamber now."

Angus cocked his head to one side, studying the fidgeting girl with interest. "Nay. 'Tis my right to be here. We are wed," he said firmly.

Claudia's eyes darted to the tub with longing. Angus hadn't moved, and she bit her lip in indecision. She could leave the room and let him win, then he would have the bath as he'd planned. But why should she? She'd had the tub filled for herself. It was childish to fight over a tub of hot water, she knew, but he had taken so much from her. Just once she wanted to win a battle.

Her decision made, she tilted her chin defiantly and reached for the belt at her waist. She removed it and flung it on the bed. Staring daggers at Angus, she pulled her tunic off, and it landed in the same spot.

Angus watched in amusement as her kirtle followed savagely. She kicked off her slippers, her eyes never leaving his.

She stood clad only in her chemise, which outlined each delicious hill and valley of her young body, and he feasted his eyes on her. Claudia could not bring herself to remove this last piece of clothing in front of *him!* Not the way he was devouring every inch of her.

The heat of embarrassment rose and spread over her whole body. Feeling shamed and degraded she fought the urge to cry in humiliation as his gaze roamed over her with undisguised hunger.

Angus's breathing grew ragged as he stared at his wife. He hadn't dreamed she would be as luscious as a ripe peach. He waited eagerly for her chemise to fall, and when it didn't, looked into Claudia's flushed face. He was startled to see a tear trickle down her cheek, followed by another.

The desire he'd felt rising in him suddenly cooled at the forlorn expression on her face. He swore under his breath and whirled away from her. He strode stiffly to the window and stood looking out, his hands clasped behind his back, feet spread wide.

With a watchful eye on Angus's back, Claudia let the gown slip to the floor and climbed into the lukewarm water.

Angus released the breath he hadn't realized he'd been holding when he heard a soft splashing behind him. He just stood, staring at the horizon, feeling wretched. He'd blundered once more. He'd thought only to tease her. Instead, he'd hurt her without meaning to. She was such a sensitive little thing, and so beautiful.

He gritted his teeth. She didn't realize the effect she had on him. He wanted her so badly. He had that right. She was his now.

He turned and what he saw made him catch his breath sharply.

The water barely covering her breasts, Claudia sat in the tub, holding a cloth above one white shoulder. Her long hair hung in curly waves to the floor over the edge of the tub, looking like molten gold in the firelight. Her creamy skin glistened where she let the water trickle over it. She was the most beautiful creature he had ever seen.

He took a step forward, mesmerized by her, but halted as her head came up sharply at his movement. Her wide eyes were like those of a frightened doe. A pained look crossed his face at the mistrust he read there. He had no intention of harming her. How could he make her understand that?

He sighed and reluctantly dragged his eyes

away. He spied her chemise lying in a heap on the floor and bent to retrieve it. Out of the corner of his eye he saw her edge to the farthest corner of the tub, away from him. He smoothed out the gown and laid it neatly on the bed.

An unexpected stubbornness entered him as he stared at the discarded clothes. Claudia was, after all, his wife. He strolled casually to the chair and sat down, facing her. They surveyed each other silently, the one wary, the other with a smoldering desire darkening his green eyes.

Claudia sank lower into the tub and looked away. With her mouth set in a tight line, she picked up the sliver of soap and lathered the cloth. Raising an arm she began to wash.

Neither one spoke as she washed her other arm. When she lifted a shapely leg to soap it, Angus caught his breath and shifted uncomfortably. He was desperate to drag her from the tub right then and there, but the time was not right.

In her innocence she really did not know what she was doing to him. Damn her defiance. He felt himself break out in a cold sweat. Not ever had he felt this way about a woman. She was his wife, and yet she was out of reach.

Watching her, he ached with desire. If he didn't force himself to leave, he would shame himself and frighten her. Then the distance and mistrust that stood between them now would never be breached.

With a muttered oath Angus leapt from the chair, making Claudia jump. He swore again as his gaze came to rest on the creamy white tops of her breasts showing just above the water. He grabbed his tunic and pulled it on angrily as he stalked to the door. Without bothering to look at Claudia again, he said harshly, "When you are finished, have more hot water added to that tub and have someone fetch me." He then slammed the door shut on his way out.

Claudia stared at the door in bewilderment. He hadn't seemed angry a few moments earlier. She was relieved that he was gone, but what had she done to make him angry?

Angus led a small group of men toward the copse of trees. The day before, outriders had found themselves in a skirmish with the enemy when they'd come this far and Angus had lost two good men. With Owen and six of his best warriors, he vowed to rout the antagonists and bring them to heel.

He was weary from another sleepless night and found his mind wandering. He'd growled at his men before they had a chance to mount their horses, and not one of them had done anything to merit his anger. He knew he was overly tired and on edge, and it was all that witch's fault. That beautiful temptress. His wife.

He was ready to explode with want of her. It was as if her image had burned with such heat into his mind that no matter where he turned, she was there.

He'd finally had his bath, without the benefit of

Claudia in the room. Then they'd joined his men for the evening meal, but only after he'd insisted she leave Marian's bedside to do so. He hadn't missed her defiant glare as she'd marched from the room ahead of him, nor the scowl thrown his way by the old woman.

During the meal Claudia had been withdrawn and silent, no matter how hard he tried to draw her out. She jumped every time he laid a hand on her. And when she asked his permission to retire, he'd been startled. His permission! Thunderation! She was his wife.

That still made him angry. He'd patiently explained to her that she did not need his permission to do as she pleased in their home, that she could come and go as was her wish.

The men stood to bid her good eve, but she ignored them all on her way out, and that had set Angus's jaw to twitching. Mayhaps she had a right to be angry at him, mayhaps not. But she had no right to treat his men as if they were the lowliest animals on the face of the earth.

By the time he reached their chamber he had cooled down, but Claudia was not there. He was just about ready to go in search of her when he remembered his earlier words. If she wanted to spend the night with that old hag, she could. He would not tell her what to do again.

He'd poured himself some wine and was brooding at the fire when she entered the chamber. He was surprised and pleased to see her, but was careful not to let it show. He'd be damned if he'd reveal to her the effect she had on him. However, she did not hide her surprise at seeing him, and he wondered what she expected. Mayhaps he was meant to spend the night on a pallet in the great hall, or even in the stables.

She hadn't said anything, but sat before the polished brass to brush her hair. He watched her for a moment, noting her stiffness, then turned away. His shoulder was sore and he stood to move his arm, hoping to work out the ache.

"Your shoulder pains you?" Claudia asked.

"Aye," he mumbled. He removed his tunic to peel away the bandage, and heard Claudia gasp. He peered over his shoulder, but could not see the wound very well.

"Sit down," she commanded.

He glanced at her with raised eyebrows, somewhat wary.

"It is infected. It must have the poison removed and a healing balm applied."

Suspiciously, he did as he was told. However, when she reached for the dagger lying on the fireplace mantel, he leapt from his chair. He grabbed her wrist, staring at her with a thunderous expression.

"The wound needs to be lanced," she whispered.

He eased the pressure on her wrist but did not let her go. He could feel her trembling. "Can I be blamed if I fear the dagger will see my heart instead of my shoulder?"

"I have been warned," she answered, lowering her eyes, "and I have considered the consequences should you come to harm. If insuring your safety is the only means of protecting my people, then so be it."

When Angus made no reply, she looked up to find him gazing at her with an unreadable expression.

"If you prefer your servant to aid you," she said quietly, "I will fetch him."

He released his hold on her. "Nay, you do it," he replied as he took his seat once more. "And Owen is not my servant. He is my friend."

Claudia glanced at him but said nothing.

Angus kept a watchful eye on her as she ministered to him, keenly aware of her. Her scent. Her touch. He ached to draw her to him, and yet he feared to do so. His chance was lost when the new bandage was in place and she stepped away, out of his reach.

The only thought in his mind was of her gentle hands as she eased his pain, the sweet smell of her when she was near. He moved toward her as she stood at the window, but when he reached out a hand to touch her arm, she jumped nervously, stiffening like a frightened, cornered animal.

He swore under his breath and turned on his heel abruptly. He'd left the chamber then, and had spent an uncomfortable night in the stables. His horse was a far less pleasant companion, but at least it was not repelled by its master.

He wondered what would happen if he forced Claudia to submit to him. He had never done such a thing in his life. He'd never had to. Of course, there were ways in which he could have her and make her want him too.

And so were the course of his thoughts when the attack came.

A flurry of arrows fell from the sky, striking two of his men. Angus swore aloud for not keeping his mind on the business at hand and shouted orders to the other men. With weapons drawn they spurred their horses into the woods as another volley of arrows flew out of the trees at them, most landing harmlessly on the ground around them.

Angus felt a piercing pain shoot through his right arm as an arrow found its mark. Through the low-hanging branches of a nearby tree, he spied his attacker and charged forward. With a war cry that rent through the forest, he swung his sword above his head, catching the enemy at his legs. He heard a scream, and out of the corner of his eye saw the man fall to the ground. He was trampled by the destrier's back legs as the horse raced by.

Angus was aware of his men engaged in battles ahead of him and headed in that direction. Suddenly he was pulled from his mount by a new foe. Together they rolled on the ground, and Angus heard a snap as the shaft of the arrow that had pierced him broke, caught between the earth and him. He shook off his assailant and staggered to his feet. He switched the sword to his left hand, silently blessing Hugh for teaching him how to fight with both hands.

He saw the momentary surprise on the other man's face at his dexterity, and before the enemy could recover, Angus swung his weapon in a side arc that hacked deeply through flesh and bone, slicing halfway through the man's ribs. He ignored the splattering blood from his foe that covered his chain-mail vest, grunting as he yanked the sword free. He looked around him and saw Owen and the other men riding toward him through the now-quiet forest.

Owen jumped from his horse before it had come to a complete halt and ran to Angus. "Your arm—"

"Never mind that now," Angus said abruptly. "How many were there?"

"Eight. Besides these two, there are four beyond who lie dead. Two escaped." Owen motioned to the arrow protruding from Angus's arm. "That should come out."

"It can wait until we get back to the castle."

One of the other men had dismounted and stood frowning at the dead man lying at his feet. With the toe of his boot he turned the body so it lay faceup. "I have seen him somewhere," he murmured.

Angus and Owen stopped their heated discussion on whether to pursue those who'd escaped or return to the castle to see to Angus's needs.

"What's that, Dennis?" Angus asked.

The young knight looked up from the body. "I'm sorry, my lord. I said that I have seen this man."

"Where?"

Dennis looked down at the corpse and shook his head. "I do not remember, but there is something familiar about him."

Owen grunted. "You know Dennis never forgets a face. Mayhaps this is one of the men he fought in the battle to win the castle. That is why he remembers him."

Dennis shrugged. "Mayhaps."

On the way to the castle, Angus gave orders for the men to return to the wood with a larger force, to bury the dead and to search for any others who might be hiding there.

When they reached the inner yard, Owen helped Angus to dismount and half carried him into the castle. He was worried over the loss of blood, not only from the arrow, but from the shoulder wound as well.

The doors of the great hall crashed open as the two men entered, startling Claudia, who was arguing with a stubborn Marian. The old woman had refused to stay in bed another day. Claudia gasped when she saw the blood that covered Angus, and took a step forward.

"My lady, your lord needs immediate attention," Owen said.

Claudia stared at the arrow, the broken shaft sticking through one side of Angus's arm while the point protruded out the other side, and did not move.

Owen glanced at her and muttered something under his breath as he made his way carefully to the stairs with his cumbersome burden. He feared Angus was going to pass out at any moment.

Claudia started toward the winding stone stairs but was pulled back.

"You cannot think to attend him!" Marian said. "He is your enemy."

Claudia turned to stare at the woman. "He is hurt," she replied, shaking free of the restraining hand. She hurried up the stairs, reaching the chamber just as Owen gently laid Angus on the bed.

"Now will you let me pull it out?" Owen asked.

Angus nodded. "Aye, now," he said.

Claudia lifted her skirts and grabbed her chemise, ready to rend the garment to use as bandages, when there was a shriek behind her.

"Aaaiee! That is one of your best. You must not!" Marian cried, rushing forward.

All heads turned in her direction, and Owen grunted in disgust. "Then find something that will do for bandages and be quick about it," he growled.

Marian raised herself up haughtily, ready to retort, but before she could say anything, Claudia interceded. "Do as he bids, and hurry."

Marian stared aghast at her mistress for a moment, then stomped from the room, grumbling under her breath. Claudia paid her no heed as she moved closer to the bed.

Owen studied Angus's ashen face with concern. "This will hurt."

Angus shut his eyes, then opened them. "Do it," he whispered, grabbing the bedcovers in anticipation of what was to come.

Owen glanced over his shoulder at Claudia. "I will need your help to hold him, my lady."

Claudia reluctantly dragged her eyes from Angus to stare at Owen.

"Lay your body across his lower arm and chest and hold on tightly," Owen instructed gently. "Your added weight should keep him from moving over much."

She nodded and bent down. She had never before been this close to a man she did not know. Though Angus was her husband, he was still a stranger. Her heart thudded as she rested her full weight on him, her hands gripping his shoulders.

He chuckled. "Do not be so frightened, my little pigeon. I have suffered worse wounds."

She started at the use of her pet name. "How— how did you know that?" she whispered.

"What?"

"That...I was always called pigeon by my family."

He grinned up at her. "The name suits you. You don't have to help us, you know. This is the perfect opportunity for you to be rid of me."

She frowned, her lips tightening. "Nay. Your threats have been heeded."

"Threats?"

"Warnings, then. Oh, call it what you will. I will aid you as I would anyone who is in need, even though we are enemies."

"You are not my enemy, Claudia," he murmured, and she grew disconcerted at the soft look in his eyes.

Suddenly he laughed. "Mayhaps you wish to keep me alive so that your dagger alone can thrust its way into my heart."

She gasped at the words spoken so freely in front of Angus's trusted friend. "Nay, but if you die, who is to say that your men will not carry out your orders? I do not care about myself. I wish only to spare my people. Therefore, I will do all in my power to see that you remain with us, my lord."

Behind Claudia, Owen grunted in irritation. "If this arrow does not come out soon, no power in heaven or on earth will be able to help. Hold on," he warned as he began to pull on the arrow.

Claudia felt Angus's body jerk beneath her, and she used all her strength to push against him. She watched as he closed his eyes and grimaced in pain, and was amazed that he did not cry out.

"Get—that—blasted—thing—out," he said in a hoarse whisper, then his head rolled to one side and he was still.

Claudia watched for a sign that he was all right, and gasped when he did not move. "He is dead!" she exclaimed.

"Nay. He has just fallen into a deep sleep," Owen said. "You can get up now."

She turned her head to see Owen frowning at the arrow in his hand before throwing it into the fireplace. A blush crept onto her face at the intimate way she lay on Angus. She eased herself from him just as Marian stepped into the room. With her old nurse and Owen hovering nearby, she bound the wound. When she was finished, she gazed into Angus's pale face, noting his ragged breathing with concern.

"Will he live?" she asked quietly.

Owen shrugged. "He has had much worse. Right now he needs rest. He has lost much blood. If the fever doesn't set in, he should be all right."

CHAPTER 4

Angus charged into battle on his great black
steed, a savage war cry tearing from his throat. All
around him men were being killed by the enemy.
He watched helplessly as his father slid from his
horse, an arrow through his heart. He looked the
other way and saw Hugh fall when a mace caught
him in the back of the head. Turning in a frenzy,
he saw Kevin's head cut from his body.

With an anguished cry Angus spurred his horse
forward to avenge his family, but was brought up
short when he saw Conan and Bevan running
through the bodies of the slain men on the field.
They were laughing merrily, unconcernedly playing
a game of tag.

Hearing chants behind him of "Watch your back.
Watch your back," he spun around to see Dorcas
and Owen riding furiously toward him.

Suddenly Dorcas was lifted from her horse as
though she had wings, and vanished into thin air.

"Dorcas!" he howled in agony as he stared at the
emptiness before him.

Owen continued toward him, a dagger in his upraised hand, still chanting, "Watch your back. Watch your back."

"They are all gone. All gone," Angus shouted, looking wildly about him at the now-empty field where the grasses bent in the soft breeze, and the bluebells rang their tuneless song undisturbed. He stared around him in disbelief, and turned back to the approaching rider.

Claudia's face loomed before him, laughing demonically. He waited until she reached him, and when the first blow struck, he bent over in pain. When the second blow came, he slid to the ground, senseless.

Angus awoke when a cool hand was placed on his forehead to find his sweet mother bending over him. He heard the sounds of a harp in the background, and tinkling laughter. Suddenly Dorcas appeared beside his mother.

"Get up, lazy," she laughed, pulling on his arm. "You cannot idle away the hours in bed."

He winced. Why did his arm hurt? "Dorcas, my sweet," he whispered, "leave me be."

"Nay, you promised to teach me the use of the battle-ax today, and I intend to see that you do. Remember the contest Father has set forth? I intend to compete, and win."

"Father?" he mumbled.

"Come," she cried gaily, "you cannot be a slugabed."

"Dorcas, I am so tired. Help me, Dorcas." He

made to get up, trying to push back the covers, but they were so very heavy.

Someone shrieked, "Nay!" and he felt a great weight holding him down. He fought with all his might to get free, but the thing pressing against him could not be moved.

He cried out, "Dorcas, help me!" Then he was still once more.

Claudia stared down at the sleeping man in the bed. His breathing was shallow, his face flushed with fever. Her own hair and clothes were disheveled from the three sleepless days and nights she had spent by his side as the fever had gripped him. He was like a vulnerable little boy in sleep, and she felt powerless to help him. She had witnessed swift death, but she had never had to watch a man die slowly as now, with this lingering pain and suffering.

Stifling the exhaustion that racked her body, she picked up the bloody bandages she'd just finished changing, then she felt a gentle hand upon her shoulder. She'd forgotten Owen's presence until then.

"You have done all you can, my lady. He is now in God's hands," he said quietly.

Claudia looked blankly into the man's gentle eyes. She was so tired.

"You need rest yourself," Owen said with concern.

She shook her head. "Nay. I will stay until it is over."

Owen studied the girl for a moment before saying, "If you need me, call."

Her gaze was fixed on the sleeping figure as Owen slipped from the room, closing the door softly behind him.

She studied Angus curiously. His bright red hair was tousled, his lips soft and vulnerable, without the harsh lines of displeasure etching them. She'd never noticed before how straight and fine his nose was. His lids were closed over those brilliant green orbs that could bore through her, could inflame in the heat of anger, or crinkle with pleasure at some merriment. They were the most expressive eyes she had ever seen. So quick to change with his moods.

Her gaze roved over him, his powerful arms and chest, the muscles now relaxed. His large frame covered half the bed. He was so big, so strong. How could he be dying? What would become of her should that happen?

Mayhaps if his Dorcas were here, she could save him. It had never occurred to Claudia that someone might have this man's heart. At that thought a pang of something she could not name shot through her. It was just as well, she thought. They were sworn enemies. She told herself that the only purpose in trying to save his life was to insure the safety of her home.

Angus started mumbling again, and she sighed wearily. Leaning over him she frowned. He was shaking uncontrollably.

She tucked the covers tightly around him and touched his burning forehead, brushing back a lock of curly red hair as she did so. She felt a strong grip on her wrist and looked in surprise to find Angus staring at her with fever-glazed eyes.

"Witch!" he said fiercely, "with your haunting face and scheming eyes. You taunt me day and night. You are mine, for now and always. I will take what is mine now."

She could only stare, wide-eyed with fear, as he pulled her to him with unbelievable strength. With her wrist still in a viselike grip, and despite his injury, he brought his other hand up to grab a handful of hair, forcing her head down to meet his. His mouth tore across hers in a savage kiss as he rolled her over him to lie on her side.

Claudia felt as though she were suffocating under his furious onslaught. The room began to swim and she saw spots before her eyes. There was a ringing in her ears. A shiver coursed up her spine when he released her mouth to trace a line across her chin. His hand released her wrist to stroke slowly down the length of her.

"My sweet," he whispered hoarsely. He pressed his body close to hers, his mouth hungrily seeking hers once more.

Claudia was too frightened to move, completely aware of being crushed intimately to the burning length of him, though the covers separated them. His mouth left hers to nestle in the hollow of her neck, while his hand swept up her body to cover one breast.

She didn't know for how long they lay like that when she realized Angus wasn't moving at all. She peeked at him and found him fast asleep. Aware that he was shivering less, and that his breathing was more deep and even than she'd heard it in three days, she moved closer, careful of his injured arm. If her warmth was what he needed to abate the fever, then she was willing to sacrifice her modesty. Besides, she knew that in his delirious state, he thought she was another.

She mused for a long time over the words Angus had spoken in his delirium and wondered what it would be like to be loved so intensely by a man. She had neither loved nor been loved in return. Although her father had spoken of finding her a husband, he'd not gotten around to considering anyone seriously. Due to their own joyous union, her parents had felt Claudia should marry for love alone. Her last thoughts as she drifted into a dreamless sleep was of the woman, Dorcas, who had Angus's heart.

Claudia stirred and opened her eyes slowly to find her husband staring intently at her. She blinked in disbelief at the clarity in his green eyes, and suddenly became aware of her position. Raising herself up, she tried to move away, but Angus tightened his grip on her. Though he was weakened, she was no match for him.

"How do you feel, my lord?" she asked nervously.

His frown deepened, "As thought I'd been beaten while I slept. Have you been up to your old tricks?"

She shook her head, swallowing hard at the

menacing look in his eyes. "Nay, my lord. You have been ill."

"Ill," he scoffed. He started to sit up, only to fall back with a groan.

"Aye, ill. You lost much blood from the arrow in your arm."

He glanced down at his bandaged right arm. "Ah, yea, now I remember."

"You have been in a fever for the last four days."

He stared incredulously at her. "Four days! I must be about my business."

She knelt beside him and pushed against his chest as he again made to rise. "Nay, you are too weak. You must first gain some strength before you leave this room," she cried.

Angus plopped back against the soft pillows, exhausted by his effort to move.

"Are you hungry?"

He nodded.

"That is good. I will get you something," she said, scrambling from the bed. She donned her tunic while Angus took in her lithe form appreciatively, regretting that she covered it so quickly. He kept his eyes on her as she slipped from the room before he let them close in weariness.

Claudia smoothed her skirts and ran her fingers through her tangled hair. She knew she looked frightful, but she was more concerned with seeing to it that Angus got some nourishment than with her appearance.

All eyes turned to the girl rushing down the

stairs, and the hall became hushed. Owen stood up as Claudia grabbed one of the serving girls.

"See that a tray is readied for the master. He will eat now," Claudia said.

The girl bobbed her head in answer and ran off to the kitchen. The men looked at one another, grins of relief spreading across their faces. Then the din of conversation was heard once more.

Two young knights approached Claudia.

"Lord Angus is well?" one of them asked anxiously.

Claudia looked into the boyish face. "Aye, he is well, and in no time will be up and about."

The lad grinned from ear to ear as he clapped his companion on the back. "Did I not tell you that your fears were unfounded, Colin?"

Colin raised a questioning brow. "My fears? 'Twas you who wrung his hands like an old woman and moaned about the prospect of facing his family with the news of his death, Dennis."

"Nay, I was not really worried," Dennis said, affronted by his friend's words. "Except, of course, for facing the Lady Dorcas," he added with a nervous laugh.

Claudia started at the mention of that name. Even Angus's men knew of Dorcas, and they hadn't the decency to keep still in her presence. She was Angus's wife, while this Dorcas was only his paramour. What barbarians they were, crude and unfeeling.

The knight named Colin laughed heartily. "Yea, and afeared you should be. She would literally have had your head on a platter, cutting it off herself without any qualms."

The other man shuddered. "Aye, I know that only too well."

Curiosity pushed aside some of Claudia's irritation. "It seems that this Dorcas is to be feared," she said.

The men turned to her, having forgotten her in their bantering.

"Aye, that she is," Colin replied, "but she is also the fairest damsel in all of Erin. The most beautiful, most splendid creature one can feast the eyes upon. No one can match such unblemished perfection."

Dennis chuckled and placed a companionable arm around his friend. "Methinks you are enamored of the woman. You forget that no one can match her flaming fury save Lord Angus. He is the only one who dares to stand up to her raging anger. Yea, she is truly a beauty, but also a hellion, and I—"

"Enough!" a voice behind them growled. The men turned to see Owen glaring at them. "Do not speak with disrespect of the Lady Dorcas, or it will not be she who sees your head on a platter, but Lord Angus."

"We meant no disrespect, Owen," Dennis said, shamefaced. "We speak more in awe of the lady than anything else. She is a beauteous woman, and a great warrior in her own right. It is an honor to serve her as well as Lord Angus."

Claudia had heard enough. It would seem that

Angus was not the only one enamored of this Dorcas. She had his men under her spell as well, if they revered her enough to serve her along with their lord. She must be very special indeed.

Claudia took the tray from the serving girl who'd been standing quietly to one side and returned upstairs. She set the tray down on the bench that Owen had pulled closer to the bed and sat down. Lifting the bowl of oatmeal porridge, she raised the spoon to Angus's lips.

"I can feed myself," he grumbled.

Her eyes snapped in anger as she let the spoon drop back into the bowl, and set the bowl on Angus's stomach. Tears brimming in her eyes, she jumped up from her seat and strode over to the fireplace. What did it matter? She was forever making him angry. She'd bet her life that if Dorcas were here, he would not be so ill tempered.

"Claudia?" came a plaintive voice behind her. "I spoke in haste. I fear my arm hurts overmuch."

She surreptitiously wiped her eyes and turned. With her face set, she marched back to the bed and took up the job of feeding him.

When he finished, she set the tray aside. With a supportive arm around his shoulders, she helped him to sit up so that she could cleanse the wound on his shoulder. He half sat and half leaned against her while she worked, and when the new bandage was in place, he sighed with relief that he could once again lie down. She then changed the bandage on his arm while he watched her every movement. When she started to move away from him, he grabbed her hand.

"Lie with me," he said huskily.

Her mouth opened in surprise.

"I fear the fever is still with me," he added.

She frowned and touched his forehead. "Nay, there is no fever."

"It comforts me to have you near."

Liar! she thought, jerking free. Scooping up the tray, she started toward the door. "I have much to see to," she said tersely, and slammed the door shut behind her.

Angus's forehead creased in a frown as he watched her leave. How could she have lain with him last night and now act so cold? He stared into the fire for a long time, bemused by the moods of women, before a restless sleep overtook him.

Claudia shivered and curled up in a tighter ball in the chair, pulling the blanket more securely about her. She laid her head back and closed her eyes, wishing sleep would come.

She'd spent most of the day away from the chamber, forcing herself to see to the running of the castle, returning only to feed Angus the evening meal.

He'd greeted her cheerfully and had asked endless questions about what was going on below. She had been thankful when Owen slipped into the room to answer the questions concerning the men, and their progress in routing out the enemy around them. It appeared that the two who'd escaped their clutches had vanished with no trace, but they were continuing the search.

Owen chuckled as he recounted the tale of young Andrew, the young knight Colin's squire, embroiling in fisticuffs with two other squires, boasting that he could best any of them in a contest of arms. The boys had been pulled apart, and the knights decided that if a contest was what they wanted, a contest they would get. So they'd discarded their armor and donned the boys with the battle dress.

Owen rumbled with laughter as he described the scene when the boys sought to engage each other, the too-large helmets slipping around every time they turned their heads. The boys had scarcely been able to move in the heavy chain mail.

His arms flailing, young Andrew had finally fallen flat on his back and the other boys, unable to see where they were going, tripped over him. There they all lay in a heap until the knights, laughing uproariously, untangled them and tried to figure out who was who.

Claudia saw nothing funny in a sport that poked fun at others, and said so.

Owen had a hard time stifling his laughter, but the smile faded from Angus's lips.

"The men meant no harm," he said quietly. "They meant only to teach the boys a lesson. War is a deadly game, and not one for children to trifle with."

The flush of anger rose in her cheeks. "Remember

that the next time your sword finds it way into the heart of an innocent child."

She ran from the room then to find solace in Marian's arms, thoughts of Vail creeping into her mind as she wept against the old woman.

By the time she composed herself enough to go back to the room, Owen was gone. In silence she sat down before the fire and picked up her embroidery, aware that Angus's eyes were on her.

At last he spoke. "Claudia, I am truly sorry about your little brother."

She stared at him in surprise.

"I have three younger brothers," he added. "Although Kevin is closer to my age, Conan and Bevan are but lads. I would feel a great loss should anything happen to them."

She looked away from his penetrating gaze, which seemed to bore through her. How could he read her so easily? She continued to ignore him until he fell asleep.

Now she squirmed in her chair and opened her eyes upon hearing something. Looking at Angus, she saw he was shaking again, and his teeth were chattering.

She got up and stoked the fire, then walked over to the bed. Angus stared up at her, but his eyes hadn't the glazed look of the day before.

"I am so cold," he said, grasping her hand tightly.

She hesitated only a moment before slipping between the covers. Stretching out along the length of him, she held him close. Presently her body heat warmed him, and he slept.

A delicious feeling of languor washed over Claudia as gentle hands caressed her, pulling her ever closer to a warm body. Her mouth turned upward in a smile. Soft lips tickled the hollow of her neck, making her skin tingle. Then they moved down to tease her aching breast, sending delightful shivers through her, setting her on fire.

Suddenly her eyes shot open and she gasped, trying to push Angus away.

He chuckled and raised his mouth to hers, kissing her thoroughly and stifling her shriek. It wasn't the same savagery she'd experienced the day before, but a gentle, persistent assault that left her breathless and feeling faint.

They were still locked in their embrace when they were interrupted.

"Aaiee!" Marian shrieked from the doorway. "Is this how you would cut out this one's heart and feed it to the dogs? Is this how you would repay his cruelty?"

Angus swore soundly, and raising up on one arm, pointed toward the door. "Out!" he shouted, his face as black as thunder.

Marian's chin jutted out mutinously. "I'll not let you harm my innocent babe."

Angus bolted upright, and Marian jumped back a step, her eyes widening at the huge expanse of chest that became visible as the covers fell away.

"This *babe* is *my wife*, you old hag, and I will do

what I will with her, and that goes for you or anyone else under my domain. Now, get out of this chamber and *never* enter here again unless you are specifically bade to do so! It that clear?"

Faced with Angus's wrath, Marian stood immobile. Even Duke Robert, in his finest fit of temper, never equaled such fury. She scuttled from the room only when Angus growled, and made to leap from the bed.

Claudia, too, was paralyzed by his outburst, and when Angus lay back down with a heavy sigh, she rolled away from him and sprang from the bed.

The door opened again, and with a curse Angus sat up to see who dared to intrude this time. Owen stood in the doorway, his sword drawn.

"What do you want?" Angus growled in a black humor.

With shaking fingers Claudia turned her back on the men and tried to tie the strings of her chemise together.

Owen stared bemusedly from Angus to Claudia and back to Angus. He grunted and sheathed his sword. "It sounded like I might have to save your worthless hide once more."

Angus glowered at his friend. "If everyone does not leave us alone, I am going to take a life. Mayhaps the nearest one."

Owen chuckled and nodded. "Shall I stand guard?"

"If I need you, I will call," Angus replied tight-lipped.

Owen shut the door, still chuckling.

Angus lay back and watched Claudia struggle into her tunic. "What are you doing?"

"The day is beginning and there is much to do."

"Claudia, come back to bed."

"Nay, my lord," she said, disconcerted by what had almost happened. "I will get you something to eat," she added, and quickly left.

A string of expletives aimed at her nurse followed her from the room. She had to escape him for a while. He'd aroused feelings in her that she'd never known existed. Her face burned at the thought of what might have happened had not Marian walked in when she did.

Claudia's eyes filled with tears of humiliation. How could he abuse her so, and make her feel so—so... She sighed heavily. She didn't know how she felt. But how could he do those things to her when his heart belonged to another?

When she returned to the chamber, Angus was wrapped in a robe and sitting in the chair before the fire. She avoided his eyes as she set the tray on his lap and turned to go.

"Don't leave yet," he murmured.

She stiffened, then squared her shoulders and moved around the room, tidying up.

Angus watched her as he ate. What was the cause of her change of moods? He'd come so close to having her, he thought, and gritted his teeth in frustration. If it hadn't been for that damned old woman! He eyed Claudia as she stripped the linens from the bed. She was so different from that warm and willing wench of a short time before.

He set the tray on the floor when he was through eating and leaned back, still watching his wife. When she had finished spreading fresh linens over the bed, she approached his chair to retrieve the tray. He seized her arm and pulled her onto his lap, careful to ease her down on his left side.

He felt her resistance and stroked his hand down her arm. He was filled with the heady scent of her. "Claudia, what is it? What is wrong?" he asked gently, pushing back her hair from where it fell in soft waves over her breast.

Claudia felt a lump in her throat and knew that she would not be able to answer even if she tried. She didn't know which was worse, his raging anger or this surprising gentleness. She shook her head, unable to find her voice.

"Talk to me, my sweet."

Anger filled her. How dare he call her by that endearment when in his delirium he'd called another the same thing? She sprang from his lap and stood glaring at him. "Don't call me that. Don't ever call me that without meaning it."

She stalked from the room, leaving a puzzled Angus staring in confusion at the closed door.

Late that night Angus lay in bed frowning up at the ceiling. He'd not seen Claudia since she'd left him that morning.

Owen had been in with his evening meal, and the two had passed the time by playing chess until Angus became too tired. Owen had helped his young friend to bed, and Angus had not asked about nor mentioned Claudia. If Owen found that strange, he did not say so.

She was probably spending the night in that old hag's room, Angus thought. That was fine with him. He didn't know which he wanted to do more. Throttle her, or make love to her—or both. She was without a doubt the most ill tempered, shrewish witch he'd ever known in his life, save his twin. Lord help him if his wife and sister ever crossed paths. There would be no living with either of them. He had his hands full with one or the other of them, but not both. Never both at the same time!

He was still peevishly trying to figure out what he'd done to anger her when the door opened. He peered down the length of the bed and saw Claudia's outline in the doorway. He expelled his breath slowly as she closed the door and walked to the end of the bed to gaze at him. Through half-closed eyes he watched her disrobe down to her chemise, then walk to the chair. She wrapped a blanket around her and sat down, tucking her feet under her. "Instead of getting cramped in that position," he said gruffly, "you may as well make yourself comfortable by sharing this bed."

Claudia jumped to her feet, startled. "I—I thought you were asleep," she stammered.

"How can I sleep when I don't know that everyone under my roof is safe for the night?" he asked tersely.

When she made no reply, he lifted the covers.

"Come, it is cold out there. You will be more comfortable here."

The bed did look inviting, she thought, but *he* was in it. Still she made no move to join him, and he lost his patience. "God's teeth, woman! You are ten times more stubborn than Dorcas!"

She caught her breath in pain, as if he'd hit her. *How dare he mention his mistress to me*, she thought, *without the slightest pangs of guilt*. Without thinking, she reached out and slapped him across the face.

She had only a second in which to regret her rashness before Angus grabbed her and hauled her down onto the bed. Tears filling her eyes, she watched as his hand came up and braced herself for the blow. But it never fell. His hand hovered in the air as an expression of horror filled his eyes.

"Claudia," he whispered raggedly. He lowered his mouth to her cheek, leaving a trail of kisses as light as butterfly wings.

She turned her head slightly toward him, and he captured her mouth with his, moaning in ecstasy when she parted her lips for him. His kiss was like a searing fire, igniting within her the same warmth she'd felt that morning.

She lay pliant beneath him as his lips left hers to kiss away the tears on her cheeks and eyelashes, then returned to her mouth to devour the very breath from her. She shivered with this newfound pleasure. Her arms slipped around his neck of their own volition, and she clung to him as one drowning in a sea of passion.

His mouth released hers once more to slip along her jaw and down her neck. He untied the laces of her chemise and gently moved the fabric aside. Lowering his head, he trailed tantalizing kisses across the soft mounds of her breasts while his hands eased the chemise over her shoulders, baring more of her to him.

He lifted her as he slid the chemise off and let it float to the floor. His breath caught as he gazed at her in the firelight, his eyes darkening with desire. Her skin was like the softest rose petals. His hands cupped each breast, his thumbs arousing the peaks with slow, torturous caresses.

Claudia moaned, tossing her head on the pillow, when his mouth closed around one pink crest, his tongue flicking back and forth across it until it grew taut and strained upward. Then he moved to the other breast to work his magic there while his hand roamed the length of her, lightly caressing her.

A wildfire swept through her body, stealing her senses and making her crave his touch with a shocking fury.

His mouth sought hers once more. His tongue probed her lips and she opened to him, welcoming the warmth of him without any fear. His hand stroked over her hips, then slid down her belly to find that most secret of places.

She sucked in her breath when he touched her hot, throbbing flesh. Her legs closed instinctively, and he raised his head to look at her.

"I will not harm you, my little pigeon," he murmured, smiling reassuringly.

She relaxed at his soothing voice and let him spread her legs. He stroked her, watching her move uncontrollably, her hips rising to his touch. He was amazed at her passion as she cried out her ecstasy, clutching the bedclothes in her frenzy. Her body trembled as sensations washed over her, then she sighed and blindly reached up for him. He kissed her gently.

"I do not understand," she whispered huskily. "What have you done to me?"

He chuckled. "I am teaching you what it is to be a woman." He ran his tongue lightly over her lips, making her shiver. "There is more delight awaiting you."

She stared at him in disbelief. "More?"

He laughed. "Yea, indeed. There is more." He captured her mouth with his once again, taking the breath from her. Then he drew back suddenly. "And what a pleasure it is to teach my little pigeon the art of love. Such a passionate little bird," he whispered against her mouth before he once more kissed her deeply.

Claudia gave herself up to the whirlpool of desire. His mouth moved to her breasts once more to flit teasingly back and forth between them, arousing her to a fever pitch. When she thought she could no longer stand it, he knelt above her and prodded her legs apart with his knee.

He leaned over her and grasped her head between his hands. "This time it will hurt," he said quietly. When he saw her startled look, he added quickly, "But only for a moment, and only this first time. Claudia, do you trust me?"

She continued to stare at him, her thoughts warring with themselves. She did not want this sweet, torturous rapture to end, but she could not trust him either. He was her enemy.

His lips brushed hers, sending enticing shivers through her, leaving her tingling with anticipation.

"You will never feel pain again after this," he whispered against her mouth, "only pleasure. I promise you."

His kiss started as a gentle caress, then grew to the hunger of a starving man. Claudia felt something probe against that place where she'd experienced such ecstasy. Her eyes grew wide and she squirmed beneath him, trying to get free.

He lifted her to him and entered her, muffling her cry with his mouth. A searing pain shot through her, and she felt she'd been torn in half.

After a moment he drew back to look into her frightened eyes. "I'm sorry, my sweet. I tried to make it as easy as possible on you. But now there will be pleasure."

He began moving slowly within her, and she was surprised when the pain left her. At first she lay quietly beneath him, amazed at the sensation of being filled by him. His arms were so strong around her, his body hard and hot as he moved against her. Then slowly she felt a tension building inside her, and of its own accord her body started to move, rising up to meet his as he thrust into her steadily, fully, again and again. The tension squeezed ever tighter, and she sobbed against his shoulder, clinging to him, desperate for the sweet release he'd given her before. And then it was there, sweeping over her in waves of delight. She cried out, and his arms tightened around her as he thrust hard into her once, twice, then his body shuddered and he whispered her name in ecstasy.

They lay silently for a long moment, still joined. As their heartbeats slowed, Angus rolled over onto his side and pulled her close. With his arms still around her and one leg resting on hers, he whispered something she didn't catch, then drifted into sleep.

Sleep did not embrace Claudia so swiftly as a multitude of thoughts skittered through her mind. This was madness. This was heaven. She was now truly a woman. A feeling of guilt overtook her at the knowledge that her enemy had made her so. Her enemy and her husband. Her heart constricted with fear at that realization. She was tied to Angus forever. He could do whatever he chose with her. She could not stop him if he wanted to use her again. A niggling thought crossed her mind that she might not want to.

Angus's even breathing filled the silent chamber, telling her he'd fallen into a deep sleep. It was a long time before she joined him.

CHAPTER 5

Claudia went about her daily chores as one in a dream. She'd never known such contentment. She avoided Marian's eyes whenever the servant was about, feeling a blush creep onto her face under the woman's scrutiny.

She was still lost in wonder at the peaceful night she and Angus had shared. After that first time, it had been just as he said it would be. She'd experienced no more pain, only an extraordinary, exquisite pleasure each time they'd come together. She still blushed to think of how his touch could arouse her so, and she was powerless to halt her own reaction to him.

He had taken her three times through the night, and again this morning, each time awakening her with gentle kisses and caresses. He seemed to know her body better than she herself, for he was able to stoke the fire within her until she was consumed by the flames of passion. There wasn't one inch of her that he hadn't explored.

She knew it was wrong to fall so willingly into

the arms of her enemy, and though she had fought the soul-stirring feelings that engulfed her, her body had betrayed her each time. She was beginning to wonder how such ecstasy could be wrong. Did Angus, in truth, hold some small feelings of tenderness in his heart for her?

So lost in thought was Claudia, she didn't realize she'd ambled into the busy courtyard. The clanging of metal against metal woke her to her surroundings. She gazed disinterestedly at the knights in mock battle, watching two particularly big men in a sword fight. Then her eyes opened wide in astonishment. One of the knights was Angus!

She took a step forward and cried out when he was struck on his left arm by the blunt side of his opponent's weapon. The man lunged forward to press his attack. Angus leapt backward and swung his sword upward, knocking his adversary's weapon from his hand.

"Oh-ho, Lord Angus," the knight laughed with hands upraised. "You make it more and more difficult to win a bout with you, even left-handed."

"Aye, have I not told you time and again how convenient it is to be able to defend yourself with both hands instead of only one," he replied matter-of-factly, sheathing his sword.

"Indeed you have, and were it not for the fact that I am so clumsy with my left hand, I would have you teach me."

"I, too, was clumsy at first. I was fortunate to have Hugh teach me. Though he was oftimes impatient, I was determined to master the skill of it. Kevin is the only one who had not the desire to learn."

They'd removed their helmets, and Claudia saw the young knight gape at Angus.

"You mean even the lady Dorcas fights in this manner?" he asked in amazement.

Angus threw back his head and laughed. "Aye, with a vengeance," he replied, slapping the man on the back.

Claudia caught her breath at the mention of that name, suddenly jolted back to the real world. What had last night been but a mockery? While her husband eased himself into her, his thoughts were of another. Marian had been right. She was twice the fool for letting down her guard. She was nothing more than a prisoner to be used at her master's whim.

She whirled away, disgusted at her weakness. She had just reentered the castle when a hand clamped down on her arm. She turned blazing eyes on her captor and found Angus smiling down at her. The smile left his face at the sight of her.

"Claudia," he asked, "what is it?"

She could only stare back at him, her mouth a tight line. She would not let this enemy humiliate and degrade her. If he thought to find her warm and willing again, he was wrong. She was his wife, but it mattered not to him. His every thought and word pertained to another woman, without regard for her. She'd heard of men like him. Mayhaps this one was like his uncle, who'd married to gain a rich wife, and then sought his pleasure wherever he could find it. She'd been fortunate to witness the devotion and love her beloved father had showered on her mother. Why couldn't she have been lucky enough to have such a love match instead of this sham? She had to admit Angus was very good at deceiving her, and vowed she would not be taken in so again.

Angus suddenly smiled mischievously. "Are you angry because you caught me training when I'd promised to rest?"

An undefined look entered Claudia's eyes. That pompous ass, she thought. He actually expected her to be concerned for his welfare when he'd just flaunted his true love before her. Well, let him think so, for she would not allow him to know her humiliation at the mention of his mistress's name. She could play the game too.

"If you expect me to applaud your bravery, you'd better think again," she said haughtily. "Your foolishness could have opened your wounds, rendering you useless once more and undoing all my hard work."

The lie tasted bitter, and she looked away. A movement in the shadows of the hall caught her attention. She stared in disbelief as a figure slipped through a panel in the wall. It could not be!

Angus laughed at her fierce words. "I am sorry to have upset you so, my sweet. But let me assure you that I am careful. If I do not begin to train, I will grow soft and lazy. I cannot let that happen."

Claudia was still puzzling over the slight form

she'd seen and had missed Angus's reply. "What?" she asked, befuddled, looking at him. She shook free of his restraining hand and moved away, mumbling, "Oh, do what you will, I do not care."

Claudia sat nervously at the table as she supped. Angus seemed not to notice her preoccupation as he touched her, solicitously offering her a tidbit from his trencher, or leaned over to converse with her on some trivial matter.

She was still mystified by the apparition she'd seen that morning. Was she hallucinating now? She'd heard of that happening to people after suffering a great shock. Was her mind playing tricks on her after all she'd encountered?

And now, as if she didn't have enough to contend with, she found herself having to deal with Angus's unwanted attentions. She watched the men around her, eating, drinking, and talking quietly, and prayed for the meal to end so she could escape. She had to speak with Marian. Her gaze roamed over the hall idly, then fixed on a small figure slipping through the same panel as earlier. She gasped aloud, recognizing the person. This was no distortion of the mind.

Angus leaned forward, frowning with concern. "What is it?"

She forced herself to draw her attention from the corner beneath the stairs, her heart pounding. Had Angus witnessed the furtive departure?

"Are you ill?" he asked.

"Nay, my lord, I am just tired," she whispered.

Angus searched her pale face. "Then, mayhaps you'd best retire." He helped her to her feet. Holding her hand in his, he said, "I will be up shortly."

Claudia mounted the stairs sedately, fighting the impulse to take the steps two at a time. She hurried to the end of the corridor, past her chamber, and looked about to make certain she was unobserved. Then she fairly ran up another flight of stairs. Once again she stopped and listened for any sign of being followed. When nothing but silence reached her ears, she stepped past the first door at the head of the stairs and felt along the cold stone wall.

At last her fingers found what they searched for. She pushed against a particular stone and stepped back as the wall swung around. She slipped through the opening and found the latch to close the door on the other side.

She stood in blackness and shivered, wishing she'd brought a torch with her. She felt her way carefully around the edge of the small aperture until her foot touched something. With one hand on the wall to guide her, she climbed a flight of narrow, winding stairs. When she reached the landing she groped in front of her until her fingers came in contact with a wooden door. With a signaled knock that only her family knew, she rapped on the door.

There was a moment when Claudia stood alone in the darkness wondering if she hadn't conjured up the person she'd seen earlier simply because she'd so desperately wanted a connection to the past. At last the door opened a fraction, and a head peered cautiously from behind it. With a small cry the figure moved back to admit Claudia.

Tears of relief sprang into her eyes as she flung her arms around the tiny form. A tight knot formed in her throat and she could whisper only one word. "Vail."

She pushed him away from her and eyed him critically from head to toe. The complete love she felt for her younger brother shone through the tears that now fell freely. She reached out a tentative hand to his cheek, and the anguish she'd experienced at having lost her whole family was replaced with joy at finding she was not truly alone after all.

"You are not a dream," she whispered.

Vail stared wide-eyed at his sister and swallowed hard in a valiant attempt to keep from crying. He flung his arms around her middle and squeezed his eyes shut. "I am so glad you found me," he said huskily.

"Oh, my dearest, I thought you lost to me forever. How glad I am that you are safe. How did you escape?"

In a hushed voice marked with pain, Vail told her how he'd eluded capture and death at the hands of his enemies. Upon seeing his father and older brother slain, a fierce rage had swept through him. He picked up his father's sword and ran outside, dragging the sword along. He ran headlong into a burly fellow with wild black hair and an even wilder look in his eyes.

"The man laughed when he saw me," Vail said quietly. "He was going to kill me. All I could do was stand there and watch as he raised his sword to strike me dead.

"His eyes became odd-looking, as if he were surprised, and just as he brought his sword down to cut me in two, I was pushed out of the way. Then he fell forward, in the spot where I'd been standing, dead. Geoffrey was the one who'd killed him. He shouted at me to get back inside. To hide. When I did not move he shielded me and led me to the secret panel under the stairs and pushed me inside. Oh, Claudia," he said, squeezing her tighter, "I was so scared. I wanted so much to get to you, to see you and talk to you, but I couldn't. There were always too many people around and I was afraid."

She held her brother close, stroking his unruly hair. "I know, dear heart. I, too, have been so very frightened. But now we have found each other. We are no longer alone." She loosened Vail's hold on her and smiled down at him. "Thank God that you are alive and well." Her eyes scanned the room, taking in sparse furnishings. She led Vail to the single bed in the corner and sat, pulling him down beside her. "You have only your mantle for warmth?"

He nodded and grinned happily at her. "Aye, but it is enough."

"What of food?"

"I have been sneaking into the kitchen late at night when no one is about."

"But what if you get caught? There are guards posted."

"I am careful."

"The way you were today? Vail, I saw you not once, but twice. How can we be certain that others did not spy you?"

He shrugged unconcernedly. "If that were the case, I would imagine that this secret chamber would have been besieged by men."

"It is no joking matter," Claudia said sternly.

The grin left Vail's face. "Please do not scold, Claudia. It is just that I get tired of not knowing what goes on below."

Claudia's eyes flashed angrily at this outrage. That she had been taken prisoner and forced to marry her captor, and that her brother had to sneak about in his own home in order to survive was too much to bear.

"I will see that you get some blankets to keep the chill from you and enough food to sustain you."

Vail looked into his sister's face and asked earnestly, "Claudia, could I sleep in my own bed tonight? I could come back here before anyone awakens."

She stared aghast at him. "Oh, my dearest, you must not. You cannot do something that would endanger your life. I could not bear it if I lost you again. Besides, that barbaric *friend* of the new lord, Owen, has moved into your chamber. Nay. At all costs you must be protected. Nothing must happen to you, for you are the rightful heir to Orgueilleux. It is you who will rule here once again."

"But, Claudia, we no longer hold Orgueilleux."

"Nay! As long as there is breath left in me, I will see the enemy on their knees before us."

Vail watched his sister pacing back and forth in front of him. "Even your husband?" he asked quietly.

She stopped her pacing and stared at her brother. "You know of that?"

"Yea, I do. I was there."

"But how?"

He smiled impishly and braced his small hands on the bed. "There were so many people and I am very small. No one noticed me in the shadows." He suddenly sobered. "I am sorry that you had to suffer so at the hands of our enemies. I would like to kill Felix Perrin for what he has done. But at least this Angus McMahon has not dishonored you."

"Nay!" Claudia cried, holding out a hand to silence him. "He knows no honor. He is my enemy."

"But, Claudia—"

"Enough!" She suddenly flung herself at Vail's feet and held him close to her. "Please, do not let us argue. I am so glad that you are alive and that we are once again together. Do not let anything mar my happiness." She pushed him away and smoothed back the curly blond locks from his forehead. "I must go now before I am missed.

Promise me that you will stay hidden, and I will come to you tomorrow."

Vail gave his word, and Claudia left him to slip through the darkness to her chamber.

She hesitated before the door of her chamber, trying to compose herself. As she entered, she saw Angus sitting in front of the fire. He did not speak, but watched in silence as she crossed the room to her dressing table. She stood with her back to him, fingering a silver figurine that had been a favorite of her mother's, not daring to look at him.

At last he broke the silence. "You are feeling better?" he asked.

"Yea, I am," she said.

"Where have you been?"

She was afraid to turn and face him. Though his voice was quiet, it also held a hard note that made her apprehensive. She would have to lie to him. At all costs her brother must be protected.

"I was seeing to Marian's needs."

At the silence behind her, she turned to find Angus staring at her, his face unreadable. "I am fatigued," she said. "I will retire now." When he still did not speak, she moved nervously to the bed and began to undress.

Angus continued to watch her as she slipped between the covers. He knew she lied. He'd been concerned for her and had meant to join her soon after she'd left the hall. On his way to their chamber, he'd passed that old witch, Marian, and she had watched him with glowering eyes.

What was the reason for the lie? He didn't

believe Claudia was plotting against his life again.
He didn't want to believe that. Her recent actions
had proved only her concern for his welfare, hadn't
they? If she just did not distrust him so. They'd
passed the first step in breaching the barrier between them, and Angus knew that if he ever
intended to conquer her suspicion and fear, he
would have to show her his own trust. And
yet... Thoughts of his wedding night and the two
attacks on him entered his mind to torment him.

He joined her in bed and lay on his back,
staring at the ceiling, unable to sleep for the
unbidden notions floating through his head. He
was achingly aware of his wife's slight form next to
him. Her scent wafted in the air, surrounding him
with its heady fragrance. He felt a familiar stirring
in his loins at the thought of her. She was like no
woman he'd ever know. She could be sharp and
unyielding one moment, and in the next could
turn into a passionate temptress. Was she playing
him false? Somehow it did not matter when she
lay with him as now. Every thought flew from his
mind, replaced with his desire for her. When he
was able to ignite the smoldering embers of passion within her and set her aflame with his touch,
all the hate and distrust disappeared, replaced by
their wild craving for each other.

He reached for her as his desire consumed him.
She stiffened. Undaunted, he drew her to him. He
leaned over her and gazed into her wide eyes for a
long moment before his mouth captured hers,
leaving her breathless. His lips left hers to trace a

path along her chin to her ear, and she shivered
when he nibbled on her earlobe.

"I wish you would put aside your modesty and
stop hindering my access to what is mine," he told
her lazily as he removed her chemise, leaving a
trail of searing kisses in its wake. "For you are
mine, you know, by right of conquest." He felt her
resistance and chuckled deeply. "I will prove it to
you now," he declared, and his mouth swooped
down to claim hers once more.

Under his tender assault Claudia could not help
but respond, and gave herself up to the delicious
heat flowing like liquid fire through her body.
Without realizing what was happening, she gave
more of herself to Angus than she had ever wanted
to. But she didn't care. Her need for him was too
great. His hands stroked over her as if she were a
beautiful, sensitive harp, arousing her to even
fiercer passion than she'd felt the night before.
When she thought she would scream for want of
release, he came to her, filling her with a warmth
that spread through her pulsating body, and left
her trembling.

In the days that followed, Claudia went about
her work, sometimes blissfully, sometimes troubled. Marian noticed a change in her young mistress, but when confronted, Claudia told her it
was none of her affair. Only that morning they'd
argued, and Marian's words stood out clearly in
Claudia's mind. She'd accused Claudia of forget-

ting all too quickly what they'd suffered at their enemies' hands.

"Is the new lord so good in bed?" she'd jeered. "Does his very touch make you dismiss the ruin he's brought upon us all?"

Marian's words were too close to the truth, and Claudia puzzled over them as she climbed the secret staircase to Vail's hiding place. When away from Angus, she was filled with the sober rationale of her old self. It was only when they were alone, and he touched her in his special way, arousing her to fever pitch, that she went beyond reason. She would never be able to forget, or forgive, that her husband was the cause of destroying all she knew and loved. She couldn't understand how her body could betray her so when she was consumed with such hate for him.

As long as she kept busy and avoided Angus she was all right. She tried not to think about the nights in their bed, and fortunately during the days she was much too wrapped up in the running of the castle and seeing to her brother's needs to think about anything else. Only rarely did her thoughts stray. Then she had to push them aside quickly or find herself lost in dreams.

She spent as much time as possible with Vail, bringing him blankets, food, and clothing, and any other necessities he needed. When she felt she wouldn't be missed, she stayed with him, and they talked and laughed as in the old days. The only thing to mar their reunion was the knowledge that

Vail's presence must be kept a secret or his life would be forfeited.

Claudia became alarmed whenever he talked of leaving his little hideaway.

"I hate it in here!" he said petulantly when she reached the chamber after her argument with Marian. "I'm tired of hiding, Claudia. I want to see what is going on below."

She tried to soothe him, but to no avail. Her temper was already stretched to its limits, and she lost control, shaking him and ordering him to remain in the secret chamber until she returned.

She was still fuming as she entered the hall, so angry that she didn't see the arm that swept out to grab her around the waist.

"Whoa. Where are you off to in such a hurry?"

She struggled against the strong grip for a moment before glaring up into Angus's smiling face.

"Let me go," she ordered. "Or is it your intention to crush me to death?"

"Nay. But you are in a fit of temper, worse than last night's storm. Tell me what it is that displeases you so and I will vanquish this foe."

"The only thing that displeases me is you!"

Mock surprise entered his eyes. "Surely you jest, my lady. I've not seen you since early this morn in our chamber, and you cannot tell me that you were displeased then. Mayhaps I should take you upstairs to see if I can improve your mood."

She gasped and looked around nervously to see that no one overheard. "Nay. Now you jest, my lord. It is the middle of the day."

He grinned. "What matters the time of day when two people are eager?"

"But I am not," she said decisively, pushing against his chest. "I—I was on my way to the dovecote."

"Ah, my little pigeon is off to see to the flock. Come," he said, placing her arm through the crook of his, "I will accompany you."

"Don't you have something to do?" she asked in irritation.

He cocked his head to one side, as though pondering her question with great thought. Shaking his head, he replied, "Nay."

He did not release her until they reached the pens that housed the birds. With arms leisurely crossed, Angus watched as Claudia scattered feed for the birds who fluttered around her in expectation. She was the most beautiful creature he'd ever seen, with her tilted nose and soft gray eyes. She was smiling quietly as she concentrated on the job at hand. The sun's rays caught her hair in its light, changing it from blond to red, making it appear on fire.

At last Angus spoke. "There are those who could free you from this task, you know."

She threw another handful of feed on the ground without looking up. "Yea, I know, but I prefer to do it. It helps to clear my mind."

"And what worries plague you, my little pigeon?" He saw a frown crease her forehead. "I could help if you'd let me."

Turning away, Claudia stooped to set the pan on

the ground, then straightened, brushing her hands together.

As she started to walk past him, he grabbed her arm to stop her. "I would like to keep your troubles from you."

She looked steadily at him. "The only thing that 'troubles' me is the fact that you claim to be what you are not. The lord of Orgueilleux."

Angus sighed heavily as he released her. "Claudia, what's done is done. I am lord here by right of conquest. Besides, it would not matter if we were here or elsewhere. We are husband and wife. You are subject to me."

Her eyes darkened to the color of slate. "Only because I am forced to do so. I will never belong to you. Never." Her voice rose to a shout. "And if I could find a way to destroy you, I would!"

She suddenly found herself yanked against his hard body. His mouth captured hers in a brutal kiss that demanded everything, and more, from her. Her struggles for release were futile, and she was sucked into a maelstrom of thrilling sensations. As she found herself yielding to him once more, the thought flashed through her mind that even when she was angry with him, she could not deny him.

As quickly as he'd seized her, Angus let her go, and she had to lean against him to keep from falling. She opened her eyes and saw him staring at her. The look in those fathomless green orbs unnerved her. An odd smile curved his mouth, making her back away. Her anger increased at the knowing way in which he gazed at her.

"You will rue the day you ever came here, Angus McMahon," she whispered shakily. Then she whirled and fled from the dovecote and her husband's penetrating stare.

A rider came galloping into the courtyard, but Claudia did not see him. She was unaware of everything save the boiling fury within her, and only when she felt strong arms encircle her waist did she realize the danger. Angus pulled Claudia close to his side and frowned at the reckless rider as the knight pulled up on the reins of his horse, making the animal rear.

"Dennis, what the blazes do you think you're doing?" Angus demanded sharply.

The young man blushed when he saw Claudia and stammered his apologies, then he turned back to Angus to explain his haste. "My lord, while patrolling the west boundaries we came across a herd of deer. Colin bade me return here to let you know." The young knight suddenly grinned. "They would make a great hunt, my lord."

Angus smiled at the young man's enthusiasm. "Aye, that they would. The men are due for some sport. Find Owen and some of the others while I ready my steed."

"Aye, my lord," Dennis replied eagerly, and turned his horse in the direction of the training field.

Angus watched the young man leave, then turned back to Claudia. Her head was bowed as she dejectedly scraped her toe on the paving stones. He opened his mouth to speak, then shut it again. His wife was a constant source of puzzlement to him. One moment she was like a spitting cat, wild and untamed, and the next she was a meek little lamb. Her mouth might spill forth a slew of diatribes upon his head, but she could not deny the burning passions that were unleased each time he touched her. Aye, she spoke of hate, but her body spoke an entirely different language, and Angus was patiently determined to make her his in every way. That was the key. Patience and understanding. A thought suddenly occurred to him. "Claudia, do you ride?"

She stopped her inspection of the ground and looked up. "Aye, but not since..." She let the sentence trail off.

"Would you care to go with us?"

He noticed her surprise, and watched as it turned to suspicion.

"Why would you want to take me?" she asked warily.

He shook his head and chuckled softly. "Because I thought you might enjoy the outing." One shoulder lifted in a careless shrug. "If you do not..." He started to walk away.

"Wait!"

He turned back to find her chewing her lower lip in indecision. At last she said in a small voice, "I would like it very much."

He grinned and took her hand. "Then come, my

lady, we will find a mount worthy enough to carry your fair form."

It was a carefree group that rode across the countryside. The men had become restless in this strange land, away from their homes and families. They looked forward to the diversion of a hunt, for it alleviated the boredom that had settled over them. In their jovial mood they laughed and joked among themselves, and heaped praises upon their lady.

Claudia blushed profusely at the kind words spoken to her, wondering at the cordiality of these men. They were her enemies, yet they treated her with the same regard they showed their lord. With a start she realized that they'd always done so, regardless of her treatment of them. She suddenly felt ashamed of the pettiness of her own actions toward them. Ignoring their friendly greetings and warm smiles, or sending the servants to see to them when one was ill or hurt, instead of going herself as she should. Now that she thought about it, she wouldn't have blamed them had they become sullen and disrespectful in her presence. But they never did. They were always pleasant, as they were now.

Angus smiled indulgently at his men's inane banter and watched his wife proudly as she rode by his side. He took pleasure in the easy way she handled her mount, and his chest swelled as he drank in her grace and beauty, knowing that she was his.

Colin and two other knights greeted the party as

they entered the thick woods. "We've been tracking them for some time, my lord," Colin said, "awaiting your arrival."

"Well, we are here," replied Angus, "and I expect to have a feast this night."

"Aye," Dennis said, "they should be an easy quarry to fell after last night's storm."

"To the hunt!" Angus cried.

The men raised a cheer and galloped off, deeper into the forest.

Angus looked at Claudia. "Will you ride with me, my lady?"

She inclined her head, and together they set off in their own direction. They hadn't ridden far when they spotted a stag standing alone in a clearing, his ears pricked for any sign of danger.

Claudia pulled up on the reins and stared at the magnificent beast. "Such a noble animal," she breathed.

Angus grinned, his eyes never leaving his prey. "Aye, and a nice catch," he whispered, readying his bow for the shot.

The arrow whistled through the air and hit its mark expertly, piercing the animal's jugular vein. Angus laughed in triumph as the stag sank to its knees and keeled over to lie still. He slipped his bow over his head, adjusting it across his chest, and urged his horse forward. The steed refused, tossing its head nervously, and Claudia's mount, too, became jittery, prancing about. They heard a ferocious rustling in the underbrush, and suddenly a boar charged out of the trees at them.

Angus easily brought his horse under control, and calmly drew his sword. He kneed his mount and lunged forward to meet the beast.

Claudia watched in horror as the wild boar and Angus raced toward each other. Just as he reached the animal, Angus veered to the left and thrust his sword through its side. The pig squealed and staggered into the thick brush, where it dropped with a great thud.

In the next second Angus found himself sprawled in the mud. He'd loosed his hold on the reins as he'd leaned forward to strike. When his mount had come in contact with a prickly bramble bush, it had reared. Angus had sailed through the air to land on the muddy ground with as great a thud as the boar he'd just felled. He groaned and raised himself on his elbows, and heard a peal of laughter. He looked up to see Claudia still astride her palfrey, her eyes twinkling, one hand covering her mouth to stifle the laughter threatening to escape. He was stunned for a moment by her gaiety. She was laughing! And she was more beautiful than he'd imagined. He'd dreamed of this moment for so long. Now that it was here, all he could do was stare.

His thoughts were interrupted when his horse neighed softly and nudged him on the back of the head. He cocked an eyebrow and glared at the animal. "You flea-bitten old nag," he growled, "watch your manners lest you find yourself part of this night's fare."

The horse tossed his head and stepped away, as

though it understood. Angus slowly pushed himself up, and once more Claudia's tinkling laugh rippled through the air.

"You dare to laugh at my predicament, my lady?" he asked. He started toward her and grimaced. At his each step there was a squishing sound.

"I do not laugh at you, my lord," she said, unable to hide her smile. "But it was not the animal's fault. He was merely frightened."

Angus stood with hands on hips, surveying his young wife with a mischievous light in his eyes. "Aye, as you should be." Suddenly his arm snaked out to grab Claudia's waist. She squealed as he lifted her from her horse and swung her around in his arms. "Mayhaps you, too, would like a mud bath," he threatened, pretending to drop her.

Claudia felt herself slipping and grasped Angus tightly about the neck. "Nay!" she screamed, holding on with all her might.

He laughed heartily. Still grinning, he murmured, "It would not matter if you were covered with mud. You are the most beautiful woman I have ever known, my sweet."

Claudia's heart hammered in her chest as she watched his eyes darken and his head lower slowly. His mouth suddenly devoured hers, the searing kiss sending shivers through her.

"My lord! My lady!" The cries of the men penetrated Angus's senses, and he reluctantly lifted his head. Owen galloped through the trees followed by several of the knights.

Colin leapt from his horse and rushed forward. "My lady, are you hurt? We heard a scream."

Claudia blushed and struggled to free herself, but Angus only tightened his grip on her possessively. "The lady is not hurt," he said, scowling. He easily placed her back in her saddle and turned to find the men trying very hard to control their laughter.

"Can the same be said for you?" Owen asked, letting out a guffaw.

Angus grunted and motioned to the waiting destrier. "That ungrateful beast decided to dump me after I saved him from being gored." At Owen's questioning look Angus explained. "After I felled that stag, a boar came charging out of the trees. He's over there in the bushes."

Dennis grinned. "This is truly going to be a festive night with your kill and the three deer we caught."

Angus grimaced at the mud clinging to him as he mounted his steed. "Aye, let us get these animals back to the keep."

The destrier showed his displeasure at becoming a pack horse all the way back to the castle, and only when the stag he was carrying was removed did he calm down. After seeing that the animals were taken care of, Angus strode into the hall, where Claudia was in yet another argument with her old nurse over her having joined in the hunt.

"I saw that huge boar they brought in," Marian said in a huff. "What if you'd been in the way? You might have been hurt, or, worse yet, killed."

"But your lady was not hurt," Angus said. "You

have nothing to fear when Claudia is with me. I would never allow any harm to befall her."

Marian raised herself up and eyed Angus critically. "Hmph, it would appear that you cannot even look after yourself, let alone my little pigeon."

A small smile tugged at the corners of his mouth at the woman's brazen tongue. "Merely a minor misfortune with my steed. No permanent damage was done."

"More's the pity," Marian snapped.

Claudia gasped at the woman's audacity, afraid that Angus's temper would flare, but he surprised them by laughing. "Marian, I must applaud your honesty. Someday I hope to acquire the same devotion you show your mistress, then I will truly know peace. But now I am in need of a bath."

"It is being readied for you," Claudia murmured.

With his hand on the small of her back, a still-grinning Angus guided Claudia up the stairs to their chamber.

CHAPTER 6

Angus discarded his clothes hastily, smiling at his wife's carefully turned back, and slipped into the hot water. He quickly washed off the grimy mud and dunked his head under the water to rinse. When he emerged, he shook his fiery mane free of the water and lay back with a sigh.

He watched Claudia move around the room, removing his dirty clothes from where he'd dropped them and laying out clean ones. There was a knock at the door and she opened it. Marian stood uncertainly on the threshold, holding a tray laden with bread, cheese, and wine. She handed her burden to Claudia without a word and scurried off upon seeing Angus in the tub. Claudia set the tray on the table by the bed and busied herself once more with building up the fire. A speculative gleam entered Angus's eyes as he gazed at her slim body appreciatively. The sleeves of her gown were caked with mud where she'd thrown her arms around his neck. When she came close enough, he reached out and pulled her into the tub with him.

Claudia squealed and flailed about in a futile attempt to escape him, but managed only to swallow great gulps of the bathwater instead. When she saw she was getting nowhere other than providing amusement for him, she stopped her struggles and glared at him.

"Why are you trying to drown me?" she asked fiercely.

The grin on his face widened. "I'm not trying to drown you, pet. Your gown is dirty." He grabbed the hem of her kirtle, and in a split second it was off of Claudia and lying in a sopping heap on the floor.

She gasped and tried desperately to stay his hands as they swiftly removed her chemise too. "My—my lord, this is improper," she stammered.

His eyes became smoky as he devoured her creamy flesh with a look that was all too familiar to her. "Nay, Claudia, we are wed. It is not improper. Besides, I need you to wash my back." He picked up the bar of soap and began to lather his hands. "Here, I will wash yours also."

He slipped the soap into her hands and reached around her to start gently washing her back. A delicious warmth spread through her at his touch. She hesitantly followed his lead, placing her hands on his back to soap him. She could feel his muscles rippling as she ran her hands over the broad expanse of warm flesh.

She leaned forward to more fully explore the

length of her husband's back and heard Angus's sharp intake of breath. She stilled her hands and looked questioningly into his intense green eyes, wondering what was wrong.

At the feel of her wet breasts against his chest, Angus was tempted to leap from the tub with her in his arms. He restrained himself, wanting this seduction to last, and instead ran his hands down her arms, leaving a soapy trail behind. He massaged her shoulders, watching her as she closed her eyes and gave herself up to feeling. His hands moved downward to cup her breasts. He lazily ran his thumbs in circles over the rosy crests, tautening them to rigid peaks. Where his hand hovered, he could feel her heartbeat quicken.

Claudia released a sigh of contentment and opened her eyes to find Angus staring intently at her. Their gazes locked as he continued to caress her. A tightness grew and spread within her, down to her belly. Her breathing quickened. She ran her tongue over parted lips, her smoldering gaze never leaving Angus's.

He emitted a low growl and stood up abruptly, pulling her with him. She lowered her eyes and gasped. Angus stood before her in all his brazen glory. She blushed and quickly raised her eyes to meet his amused gaze.

"You have seen me before," he said softly.

"Nay. I—I've not looked."

Stepping from the tub, he lifted her in his strong arms to carry her to the bed. He eased himself down on top of her and pressed his lips to hers to quiet her as she began to speak.

When his mouth left hers to nibble on her ear, she mumbled, "We are all wet."

"Yea. I want you like this. I want you now."

He lifted his head to look at her, and she felt herself drowning in the hot urgency in his eyes. Then he kissed her once more, the sensual on-slaught sending the smoldering embers he'd kin-dled in her spiraling up in flaming desire.

His hands and lips were everywhere at once, stoking the red-hot fire at the very core of her being until she ached with the need for release. Mindlessly, she kissed him in return and ran her nails lightly over the length of his broad back.

He groaned in sheer ecstasy. "Oh, my sweet," he whispered hoarsely, "tell me what you want. Say it."

Claudia was too caught up in the raging fire he was building in her not to obey. "I want you."

"I want you, Angus. Say it. Say my name."

"I want you, Angus."

His mouth crushed hers in a fierce, hungry kiss as he slid into her. She felt herself soaring higher, and she cried out his name again and again as in a wild, uncontrolled abandon he took them both to sweet release.

Angus rolled onto his side, bringing Claudia with him as though he were afraid of losing what they'd just shared by letting go of her. He kissed her temple and smoothed away the hair from her face.

"That is the first time you've called me by my name," he mumbled before falling into a deep and restful sleep.

Claudia lay very still and frowned at the hair-rough chest facing her. She'd said his name only because he'd demanded it. He probably would not have finished what he'd so calculatedly set about doing if she'd refused. The frown deepened. Nay, that was not true.

A hot blush crept over her body at the thought of their lovemaking. She'd called out his name over and over, like some wanton strumpet. Yea, she'd wanted him. He'd made her want him. How could this man kindle such a burning flame within her until none but he could douse the torment in her body? How could she let him do this to her? He was her enemy. The thought angered her and she struggled to free herself, but Angus's grip only tightened.

For fear that he would awaken, she stopped squirming and peevishly settled into her husband's arms. She studied his peaceful face and decided irritably that even in sleep he looked smug and self-satisfied. A tiny scar along his temple drew her attention. She reached out tentatively to run her finger over it, wondering how he'd received it. She'd not noticed it before.

A tiny smile curved his mouth at her touch, and she quickly pulled her hand away. She stared at her husband's tranquil countenance and wondered what it was that he was dreaming of. Mayhaps his Dorcas.

A knot formed in Claudia's throat, tears pricked her eyes, and she didn't understand why. Oh, why did they have to be enemies? Why did his heart have to be taken? Why couldn't she allow herself to feel a warmth for this man who was her husband? Life had been so simple before he came. She'd had a loving family then. Her father had built a strong castle to protect his loved ones, and still this man had come to tear out her heart and ruin her existence. Orgueilleux. Proud. That's what her father had been—proud—and he'd built a proud home. Yet it had been taken from him.

"Oh, Angus," she whispered, "what have you done to me?"

There was still Vail, she thought. Together they would somehow drive this enemy from their home. She sighed. Mayhaps Angus would tire of her soon and go back to his Dorcas. The thought angered her again. Why couldn't he have stayed away? Would she never know a moment's peace again? Someday Vail would rule in his rightful place. Only then would she be content.

Vail! A terrible wave of guilt washed over her. She hadn't given any thought to her brother since that morning when they'd fought.

She bit her lower lip and eyed her sleeping husband. If that little imp decided to make mischief while she was away, she'd throttle him. Claudia tensed. What if he'd left his room and been caught? Nay. If that had happened, Angus would have been informed immediately upon his return. She relaxed again. He must still be safely tucked away in his little hole. Apparently her orders had had the desired effect of making him cautious.

Claudia felt a pang of remorse for having been so rough with him. He must be feeling abandoned and alone by now. She must make peace with him, assure him that she still loved him and had been frightened only for his safety. If nothing else, she was sure that he'd be starved. Her little brother had an astounding appetite.

She cast Angus another look. Barely breathing, she cautiously disentangled herself from his enfolding arms and climbed out of bed. On bare feet she padded silently to the chest. She winced as she lifted the lid inch by slow inch, then pulled from it a fresh chemise and kirtle. She hastily dressed, then tied a plain corded belt around her waist. She picked up a loaf of bread and a chunk of cheese from the tray, all the while glancing furtively at the man still sleeping in the bed, then she slipped quietly from the room.

She grabbed a torch from the wall in the corridor to light her way and hurried to the secret chamber. She tapped out the signal on the door that she, Vail, and Mallory had devised as children, and waited until the bar was lifted to admit her.

Vail shifted from one foot to the other as she placed the torch in a sconce and set the food on the table before turning to him. "I was very bad this morning, Claudia. I am sorry. I know you wish only to protect me," he said, staring at his sister with huge, pleading eyes. "Please don't be angry anymore."

Her face softened at the plaintive note in her brother's voice. She opened her arms, and Vail rushed into them to be held comfortingly. She kissed the top of his head. "Oh, my sweet little one, I came to apologize for being so harsh with you. I did not mean to hurt you, but it frightens me when you speak of leaving here. I could not bear it if anything happened to you."

He lifted his head to look earnestly at her. "I know. But, Claudia, I get so *bored* with nothing to do."

She stroked his hair. "I know, truly I do," she whispered. She smiled suddenly. "Are you hungry?" She indicated the bread and cheese she'd brought and watched Vail's face brighten.

"I'm starved," he answered, breaking away to run to the table. He broke off a huge chunk of bread and took a bite. A slice of cheese followed rapidly as he greedily stuffed his mouth. He turned to plead his case once more, for he'd had all day to think and was determined to bring Claudia around, when he stopped and stared at the open doorway. Angus stared back.

Vail swallowed convulsively, trying to down his food without choking.

Claudia's indulgent smile faded as she realized her brother was staring past her. She whirled and cried out when she saw Angus. She moved in front of Vail as if to protect him. "You will not harm him!" she cried. "Please, my lord, he is but a child."

Angus tore his eyes away from the boy to stare in confusion at his wife. Why would she think he would hurt a simple peasant boy? His gaze strayed back to the lad dressed in the coarse brown woolen garb of the serfs, and he took a step forward.

"Nay!" Claudia cried again. "I will not let you hurt him."

Angus gaped dumbfounded at his wife. He was relieved that he'd found her safely in the company of this boy, but he was becoming angry at her insistence that he meant harm.

As he'd contentedly lain in her arms, he'd been in that netherland between wakefulness and sleep. Her stirring had awakened him enough to know that she was no longer beside him. Just as he was getting ready to call to her, he became aware that she was dressing.

He watched with half-closed eyes as she took the food and left the room. He was immediately out of bed and in his own clothes, all kinds of questions running through his mind. If she was indeed plotting against him, now was the time to find out.

He crept stealthily from the room and had no trouble following her as she lighted the way ahead of them. He was puzzled when she stopped before a stone wall on the floor above their chamber. The puzzlement gave way to amazement as the wall opened and Claudia stepped through it.

He had a little trouble finding the latch in the

darkness, and was becoming more furious by the minute that his wife had duped him once again. When he got his hands on her, he vowed, he'd teach her to scheme against him. He was about to turn around and summon his men to tear the wall out stone by stone when his hand accidentally touched the latch. He was astounded as the wall swung inward to reveal another passageway. The light from the open door above him showed the stairs clearly, and he made his way up them, toward the voices coming from the secret chamber. His anger gave way to relief when he saw the occupants of the room, but now that anger was surfacing to the boiling point once more.

He glared at Claudia. "I do not harm children." Ignoring her, he turned back to the boy and demanded, "Who are you? Why are you here?"

Vail could only stare back at the huge man facing him with balled fists and eyes blazing fury. "Well?" Angus thundered, making both Vail and Claudia jump.

Vail opened his mouth to speak, but no sound would come.

"Can't you see that you are frightening him!" Claudia shouted as she hurried to her brother's side and placed a comforting arm about his shoulders. Her mind whirled for answers that would appease Angus and, at the same time, would protect her brother. "He is but a boy." Her eyes darted to Vail, and she took in his clothing. Of course! "He is a simple peasant boy," she rushed on, "who was frightened by the battle. He—he saw his family slain, and hid. Can you not see that you are frightening him more with your angry blustering and your questions?" She gathered Vail close to her to comfort him, and glared at Angus.

Angus sighed heavily and watched Claudia's grip on the boy tighten. He knew how much she loved her people. She would go to any lengths to protect them, and they depended upon her to look to their welfare. But why was this particular child still being coddled when the battle was won nearly a month ago and peace was being restored?

"Surely you have duties to perform," he said to the boy. "Why are you still in hiding like a thief? Unless—"

"He is not a thief!" Claudia broke in hotly. "I told you, he is but a frightened peasant boy."

Angus snorted in derision. "You told me! Your conduct has hardly been exemplary. Why should I take your word?"

Claudia's throat constricted with fear. He would not believe her. Somehow he knew, yet she had to try to save Vail, even at the cost of her own life. "Please," she whispered, "he is a child. What harm can a child do you? I beg of you, let him go. If you wish to reap your vengeance upon one, then do so upon me. I would rather it were I that was beaten than this innocent boy, for it is I who am at fault. I bade him to hide."

The cloud of anger passed from Angus's face. He had no intention of beating anyone. Why couldn't Claudia understand that he meant to protect her, not hurt her?

"What is your name, son?" he asked quietly.

"My—my name?" stammered Vail.

Claudia's mind whirled. If Vail's identity were revealed, then Angus would have cause to kill him. Before her brother could recover, she quickly answered, "Edward. His name is Edward."

Angus looked the boy up and down. "Edward, eh. Well, Edward, what is it that you do around here?"

"Do?" Vail parroted.

Angus frowned in irritation. Mayhaps the boy was feebleminded, and that was why Claudia felt the need to protect him. "What are the chores that you perform around the castle, boy?"

"But, I don't—" Vail suddenly stopped as Claudia nudged him. He knew that she was protecting him. He'd been surprised when she'd given Angus one of his middle names, and it dawned on him that she'd done it on purpose. If he were to reveal now that he had no specific "chores," Angus's suspicions would be confirmed. He racked his brain to think of something to say.

Claudia once again came to his rescue. "There were many things that he did. He—he helped to serve the meals. He ran errands. He worked with the pigeons and the falcons. He is good with the horses...."

"I am particularly good with the horses, my lord," Vail interrupted, his face brightening. He expelled his breath before continuing. "My lord, I know that you lost your squire in the battle and that you could use another. Mayhaps I could replace him."

Vail ignored Claudia's sharp intake of breath as she stared in horror at him. She was ready to strangle him. She was trying to protect him by keeping him with her, and here he was charging full speed into Angus's clutches.

"Whoa, now, slow down." Angus laughed. From the boy's loquacious speech, it was apparaent he was not addle-witted as he'd first thought. "You are rather young to take on that task, are you not? It would appear that you have many small talents, but squiring..." He shook his head.

"But, my lord, my fa—, Duke Robert was looking for boys to train, and I was chosen," Vail said fervently. It was not really a lie, for his father often chose some of the stronger serfs to train in fighting. And it was almost time for Vail to begin his own training. "If not for, I mean, if, that is—" Vail swallowed back the tears that threatened to escape at the mention of his father. "My training had not yet begun," he whispered.

Angus stared at the bowed head thoughtfully, pain prickling him at the memory of his young squire, Alan. He'd been fond of the boy, and had felt great sorrow at his death. He truly missed him.

"We will see," he said without committing himself. "In the meantime, I suggest that you take yourself from this chamber and bed down in the stables with the other boys. First thing in the morning you can show me what you can do with the horses."

Vail grinned hugely. "Aye, my lord."

"But, my lord," Claudia interjected quickly, "why must he move tonight? He has been here so long, what matters if he stays another night? This chamber is dry and warm, with a soft bed. Surely it can do no harm if he remains here a little longer."

Angus did not miss the boy's fallen expression as Claudia spoke. It was clear to him that the lad was eager to leave this confining place and his mistress's overprotectiveness.

"Nay. It is time he joined the rest of us," Angus replied. He watched the boy's face brighten with anticipation.

Vail broke away from his sister's restricting hold. "Thank you, my lord. I promise you that you won't be sorry. I will prove my worth to you," he said in a rush before running from the room and to his freedom at last.

Claudia swallowed hard and continued to stare at Angus for what seemed an eternity after Vail left the chamber. Why was he looking at her that way? If she had known the course of his thoughts, they would have brought a blush to more than just her face.

She had no idea how alluring she was to him with her hair spread out in wild disarray around her, her eyes wide with wonder and something else that Angus took for fear. He saw the pulse beating nervously in her neck and wondered at it. What cause did she have to fear him? He drew his gaze away from her with difficulty to survey the chamber. It was a round, windowless room with only the small bed and a table on which the half-eaten bread and cheese lay.

It was cold in the room.

His gaze strayed back to his wife standing silently in the middle of the chamber.

Sensing that Angus would not break the silence, Claudia at last spoke. "How did you know?" The words came out in little more than a choked whisper.

"I wasn't fully asleep."

At his reply, her chin came up defiantly and he caught a flash of anger in her eyes.

"When you walked out with the food, I decided to pursue you. I couldn't imagine why you felt the need to go elsewhere to eat, and since you have not felt the need to confide your feelings and thoughts to me, how was I to know but what you weren't plotting my demise with some of your faithful servants once more?"

At this revelation, her eyes darkened to the color of slate. "I would not need any help if I wanted you dead," she said between gritted teeth. "The opportunities have been many to end your life. It is only because of your threat to my people that you live."

"I do not threaten, Claudia."

"Liar! That is all you know how to do. Well, you have us in submission, enemy. For the time being. But hear me well. Someday you will be driven from this land and we will once again have what is rightfully ours."

"You have it all now, Claudia. You are my wife."

"I am your chattel!"

"Enough," he growled, closing the distance between them in two strides and grabbing her roughly by the arms. "I have treated you as an honorable wife and you know it. There is one thing that you had better heed. What is mine is mine. For now and always. I *demand* your obedience to me, and I will no longer tolerate secrets or deceit. You kept that boy and this chamber a secret from me. How many other secrets are you keeping from me?" he demanded, shaking her.

"None," she whispered, frightened by his rage.

"Are all of your people accounted for?"

"Aye."

"Are there any other secret hiding places like this one?"

"You are hurting me!" she cried.

"Answer me!"

"Nay. There is only this one."

Angus released her. "Remember, Claudia, what is mine, I hold." With that he turned and left her alone.

Claudia felt her knees buckle and sank to the cot. The truth of Angus's words had been in his eyes. Dear God, what if he found out who "Edward" was?

She couldn't stop shaking.

CHAPTER 7

Claudia laid the tunic she was embroidering aside for the sixth time and stared into the low-burning fire on the hearth. She cast a nervous glance at Marian, who continued her task of sewing a new chemise for her mistress. Without looking up, Marian said calmly, "Ease your heart, m'lady, he is safe enough."

Claudia gazed incredulously at the old woman. "How can you say that when he is with Angus?" she asked in a hushed, angry voice, glancing around to make certain that no one overheard. "You who've bemoaned our fate, who've showed your contempt, your hate, for our enemy. How can you now sit there so calmly and tell me not to worry!"

Sighing, Marian laid her work in her lap and looked up into Claudia's drawn white face. It was plain that the girl was on the verge of hysterics. It had been all she could do to keep Claudia inside the castle and away from the men all day.

"Have you not taken the precautions necessary to insure the young lord's safety? Our people know

124

what is expected of them and what will befall them if they fail," Marian explained patiently. "Besides, he is not alone. Others watch. If his identity is discovered, the new 'lord' "—her lips curled distastefully on the word—"will not escape harm himself."

Claudia paled as she stared in horror at Marian. "Nay," she breathed unsteadily, "you did not order him killed if he discovered Vail."

Marian cocked an inquiring eyebrow. "You wanted your brother protected at all costs, did you not?"

"Not at the price of Angus's life," Claudia replied heatedly.

"You do love him, then."

"Nay! I do not. But to take his life will serve no purpose other than to bring more disaster upon our heads. You fool! You should know to what lengths his men would go to protect him, for you yourself felt the hands of death upon you. Do you think his men would let any of us live if harm befell their lord? Believe me when I tell you they will not."

Marian drew in her breath sharply. "I did not think . . ."

"Nay, you did not."

Marian's face showed her distress clearly. "But those set to watch were to do only that, unless— unless—the young lord is very clever. I do not think he will give himself away."

"Nor do I," Claudia said, patting the other woman's hand consolingly. She bit her lip in consternation, and then, remembering Vail's jaunty step as he joined the men that morning, fought to stifle a giggle. He would not give himself away. He was having much too much fun in his role as Edward, the little serf boy.

It was Claudia who felt the strain of deceit. After Angus had left the secret chamber, she had run to Marian. She'd quickly explained what had happened, and, over Marian's joyful weeping at hearing that Vail lived, told the woman to let the servants know of his presence and his new role. Vail's secret was not to be given away upon their lives. Even though she'd done all she could, she'd spent a sleepless night worrying about some small detail she'd overlooked. She was as nervous as a mouse by the time the first light of dawn crept over the horizon, and the waiting throughout the day did not ease her conscience any.

"What will you do, m'lady?" a worried Marian asked.

"I have found that honeyed words and a sweet smile can accomplish more than any treachery. Mayhaps I can convince Lord Angus to allow his new charge to spend more time in my company. I am sure there are many ways in which we can put a good strong boy to use. Is that not so?" Claudia asked with a demure smile.

Marian digested her mistress's words before a slow smile lit her face. How many times had she seen that same look creep into Claudia's eyes when she'd wanted something from her father? "Aye, m'lady, that is so."

The women waited until dusk, and when no one

came running to inform them of any imminent disaster, gave up their vigil. Claudia ordered the tables to be set for the evening meal, and Marian took herself off to perform duties of her own.

One by one, two by two, and in small groups the men entered the hall, laughing at some joke or talking quietly among themselves. Their greetings to Claudia were no different from when they'd left that morning after breaking their fast. Without seeming to, Claudia watched the door for any sign of Vail and Angus, but they did not come.

As the hall filled with hungry men, Claudia continued to watch anxiously for her husband and brother. What if Angus had discovered the truth? Horrible images flashed through her mind of the tortures and death her brother might be facing. She blamed herself for putting Vail in danger. She could bear the punishment she knew would come her way. What she could not bear was that she'd surely sent her little brother to his death. Her gaze roamed over the men in the hall, and she thought of how clever they were. They knew. And they were concealing it from her. If anything happened to Vail, she vowed she would personally find Angus's heart with her dagger, and this time she would not miss. That is, if he didn't kill her first.

Claudia was startled from her thoughts when a bellow of rage from beyond the door made her jump and turn her head sharply. Two men-at-arms were forceably leading someone into the hall.

"This is an outrage! I come in peace," the prisoner hollered.

Claudia gasped and jumped to her feet. "Stop that!" she cried, running to where the guards were trying to subdue the man by pushing him into a chair. One of them had a rope with which to bind the captive, but Claudia jerked it from his hands. "How dare you treat a guest so?" she exclaimed, glaring hotly at the surprised guards. She turned back to the man sitting in the chair. "Uncle Theo, are you all right?" she asked with concern.

"This man is your uncle?" one of the guards asked.

"He is the same as my uncle, for I have called him such since I could first talk. How dare you treat a long and valued friend in such a manner!"

"We had no idea, m'lady," said the man with the rope. "We caught him sneaking in the postern door—"

"Sneaking!" she cried, cutting him off. "It is not unusual for him to enter by that door, for he has done so many times in the past. Tell me," she asked, taking a threatening step forward, "did you fear he and his men would overrun the keep by 'sneaking' in the back way? If Duke Theo Archibald wanted to take Orgueilleux he would do it by surrounding the castle to fight face-to-face, not by sneaking in. Now, begone with you, and you can be assured that your lord will be informed of your ill-mannered conduct." She waited until the guards had backed away and were far enough across the hall so that they couldn't eavesdrop before she turned to Theo. "I must apologize for their behavior, my lord. I am ashamed that you were made to feel so unwelcome, but things are very different at Orgueilleux now."

Theo smiled wryly. "It is I who should apologize, my dear. I was sneaking in, as they said."

She stared at her lifelong neighbor and father's closest friend in disbelief. "But why?"

Theo sighed and ran a hand through his dark hair liberally streaked with gray. "Because I did not know what to expect upon my arrival. I have been in Paris, in the company of Hugh Capet, since the winter. I knew very little of what went on here. When I returned I—I heard..." He was watching Claudia closely, and at the change in her expression, he faltered. "It is true, then. My good friends, Robert and Jeanette."

"Aye," she whispered as tears started in her eyes.

"Oh, my poor child." Theo gathered Claudia to him comfortingly. "What you must have suffered. Your brothers?"

"Mallory was struck down when we were overrun, along with my parents, but Vail lives. So much has happened since we last met. There have been so many changes. I am mistress of Orgueilleux only because my enemy commands it. My little brother is forced to masquerade as a serf in order to stay alive." Claudia gasped and her head came up with a jerk. "You will not give him away, will you? He is not known as Vail, but as Edward. Please, I beg you, Uncle Theo, keep our secret."

Theo frowned at her in confusion. "I do not understand."

"There is so much to tell you, and it is all so complicated. I don't know where to begin." She took a deep breath, and in as calm a voice as possible quietly told Theo of the battle that had changed her life forever. Bitterness crept into her voice as she related how Duke Felix Perrin had gloated over his capturing her home, and of how she'd been turned over to her enemy to be used as a chattel. "I was forced to marry Angus McMahon, and now I am tied to him for life," she ended distastefully.

"Is this Angus McMahon anything like his uncle? Does he beat you?"

"Nay," she answered truthfully.

The cloud of worry lifted from Theo's face, and he smiled slightly. "That is good, for I can assure you that it would bode ill for him if he did." Theo's smile broadened. "I am glad that he does not. The man must not be all bad. On the way over I saw fields being planted and new cottages being built. That says something for his character."

"You cannot mean to condone what he has done!"

"Of course not, child. Of course not. It is just that he appears to be doing his best to rebuild Orgueilleux. As your husband, I am sure that he wishes to see the estate prosper." Theo took Claudia's hands in his and studied her flushed face for a moment. "Claudia, years ago your father entrusted me to see to your care, yours and the boys', should anything happen to him. I must think of your best interests. I do not want to see your home completely destroyed so that you have nothing left. Orgueilleux is still yours. Your people look to you for their sustenance. I cannot bring my forces in here to obliterate all that you hold dear."

"It would be worth it to see my enemy destroyed."

"Ah, yea. I have the power to do that, but I would like to meet this man face-to-face who is now your husband."

"Do my feelings mean nothing?" Claudia said hotly. "I was forced!"

"No one said the marriage vows for you, Claudia."

She whirled at the quietly spoken words. Angus stood behind them, staring at them, his face hard. He gazed at his wife for an interminable moment, then his gaze strayed to the tall gray-haired man who kept a protective arm around Claudia. "I heard that we had a guest," he said, studying the stranger.

Theo assessed the young man as thoroughly as Angus stared at him. So this was Felix Perrin's nephew. A multitude of thoughts crossed his mind as he eyed the stranger who'd torn Claudia's world apart. Angus looked nothing like Felix. A shadowy picture entered Theo's head of a tall, muscular man with red hair and a strong, square jaw. The father. But the eyes. Ah, the eyes were the deep, clear green of the mother. A whirlpool of memories came rushing back to Theo. It was true that the young man was Felix Perrin's nephew, but he was Heloise's son.

"I am Duke Theo Archibald of Monticule and a dear friend of your wife's."

"Indeed," Angus murmured, wondering just how close a friend the old man truly was. "If that is so, then I would have expected you to try to see Claudia sooner."

"Duke Theo has been away from Monticule for some time," Claudia explained. "He only just arrived back in the region and was concerned for my safety."

"I see. Tell me, my lord, why is it I did not see your men in the courtyard?"

"For the simple reason that I came alone. In peace."

Angus raised an eyebrow in question as he took the two cups of wine a serving girl held out to him. He handed one to Theo. "Through the postern door?" he asked, taking a sip from his goblet and watching the other man's reaction.

Though the words were spoken quietly, Claudia shivered at the way her husband asked the question. Angus was in no mood to be trifled with, and she spoke swiftly. "Not knowing what his reception would be here, he came quietly so as to make certain that we—that all was well with me."

Angus glanced at her and noted her flushed face and the way her hands played nervously with the folds of her gown. He wondered if he'd caught his wife in the act of plotting against him and quickly pushed the thought aside. Claudia was his, just as Orgueilleux was his. He could not change what had happened. He wished a thousand times over that things could have been different between them, but they were not. Claudia was his wife. He was responsible for her and her people, and no one on earth would ever take her away from him.

"What Claudia says is true," Theo said. "I have been away for a long time, and I did not know what to expect. I did not want to end up as your prisoner, or, worse, find an arrow meet its mark before I had a chance to explain my presence."

"That could still happen."

"Nay," Claudia breathed in horror.

"Surely you are not so dishonorable," Theo said, drawing himself up indignantly.

"Nay. I am not. Not to honorable men."

"Are you insinuating that I am dishonorable?" Theo asked coldly.

"My wife says that you are a guest, yet you arrive without your guard and enter by the back way."

"I can hardly be faulted for using caution where the situation warrants. I return home after a long absence to hear that my good friend Robert Cherveny is dead and that his home has been besieged. Naturally I was concerned for his children."

"As my wife, Claudia is my responsibility now."

"And as her guardian it is my duty to see that she is safe and well. I have not given my consent to your marriage, therefore, I have the right to remove Claudia from Orgueilleux if I choose to do so," Theo said heatedly.

Angus's hand clenched around his goblet. "But you will not. You are only one man. You admit that you came here alone. I have you at my mercy if I so choose."

"My men await my return, and if I do not arrive at the appointed hour, they will come."

A muscle twitched angrily in Angus's jaw. "Then I will fight them just as I will fight you, or anyone else who tries to take what is mine. Claudia is mine."

The only sign of surprise Theo showed was in his narrowed eyes. "She tells me she was forced," he said slowly.

Angus noted the calmer attitude of the other man and forced himself to relax. He took another sip of wine before speaking. "Did she also tell you that we are husband and wife in every way?"

Claudia gasped at Angus's words. She felt the red creep up her neck and into her face as Theo studied her.

"Is this true, child?" he asked.

Aware of the amusement on Angus's face, she forced herself to meet Theo's gaze, but the questioning look in his eyes was too much for her. She wanted to scream at Angus, to slap the mocking smile from his face for humiliating her. It was bad enough that she'd succumbed to the enemy. He did not have to shout it to the world.

"You cannot deny what is true, Claudia," he said in a matter-of-fact tone that set her teeth on edge.

She wanted to. Oh, how she wanted to. A sob escaped from her throat, but the words Angus wanted to hear wouldn't come. She nodded once and heard Theo's sharp intake of breath, then she fled from the hall.

Theo turned burning eyes on the younger man after Claudia disappeared from sight. "Was that necessary?" he spat out.

"A desperate situation calls for desperate measures. Duke Theo, I do not wish to fight you for my wife. You claim to be her guardian. If that is the case, then you have the power to separate us, but I want it understood that I will use my power to keep her. You are obviously concerned for her welfare. So am I. Claudia belongs to me, and no force on this earth will ever take her from me. I just want you to know that."

Theo stared at Angus for a long moment, and Angus could tell by the various emotions crossing the man's face that he was fighting an inner battle with himself. He hoped only that the man would find favor with him and not against him.

At last, his decision made, Theo nodded. "Very well. But I warn you, young man, if you hurt Claudia in any way, you will pay for it."

Angus breathed an inward sigh of relief and inclined his head. "That is fair enough." He suddenly grinned. "And I would like to be fair with you also. We've gotten off to a very bad start. May I suggest that we begin again. I would like to welcome you properly to Orgueilleux. Inasmuch as it has been some time since you've visited Claudia, will you stay and sup with us? I am sure that my wife would enjoy it."

Theo laughed and shook his head. "I am not so sure that she would."

"Oh, she'll be all right. Please, accept my hospitality. I would like the chance to dispel any qualms you may have about my intentions."

"You are a very astute young man," Theo said wryly.

"Not really. I just know how I would feel if our roles were reversed. I want you to know that I intend to see that Claudia is well cared for. I understand your skepticism. I merely wish the chance to put your mind at ease. Surely you can understand that?"

"Aye, that I can. Mayhaps, in time, you can prove your worth to me."

Angus's smile quickly left his face. "I have no need to 'prove' myself to anyone," he said coldly. "I am a man of honor. Once my word is given, it will not be broken."

Theo studied the young man measuringly. There were more than physical differences between Angus McMahon and his uncle. Where Felix was embittered and sullen, with a cruel streak that he seemed to relish, Theo sensed a sparkling humor in Angus, and a genuine desire to be amiable. Theo prided himself on being able to size up people quickly. After all, it was his sharp intelligence that had made him adviser to kings, and what he saw in his first meeting with Angus pleased him. He watched as Angus placed a firm hand on Marian's arm when the woman started to walk past them.

"Marian, inform your mistress that Duke Theo will be dining with us."

Marian shook free of Angus's hold. "Humph, you hurt my lady. You go tell her yourself," she answered huffily, stalking away, and leaving an openmouthed Angus staring at her back.

Angus heard a burst of laughter at his side. "I see that old harridan hasn't changed one bit," Theo said, shaking his head. "She is like a fierce mother wolf protecting her cub and has no use for anyone who hurts it."

"I've not hurt Claudia," Angus growled.

Theo grunted. "See that you don't."

Angus swore under his breath as he stalked across the hall and up the stairs to haul his wife down to dinner.

Still in a foul mood from the impertinence shown by Marian and by Duke Theo's parting words, Angus flung his chamber door open, but stopped short in surprise. Claudia sat near the fireplace, her profile to him. Her red-gold hair framed her face in soft curls, falling about her shoulders in careless abandon. Firelight danced across her relaxed features.

Angus was mesmerized by the sight. She looked like some untamed goddess. Her full attention was held by Edward as the lad regaled her with an account of his first day in Angus's charge, so neither was aware of his presence.

In spite of her bad mood of only moments before, Claudia found herself laughing as Edward told of the recalcitrant mule in the stables who'd first nipped his cap off his head, then, not satisfied with that prank, knocked him into a pile of manure when he bent to retrieve it.

"It serves you right," she said, laughing. "Mayhaps your experience will teach you to heed my advice in the future."

"Oh, I didn't mind, really I didn't. I had a grand day."

Claudia reached for the boy and wrinkled her nose as she hugged him to her. "From the smell of you, I can well guess that was the case. Since I've not seen you all day, I can only assume that it has taken you this long to clean out the stables. 'Tis too bad that you did not clean up yourself as well."

"But I did get most of it off, Claudia."

Angus watched the easy smile his wife bestowed upon Edward and the comfortable manner in which she spoke to him. A pang of jealousy pierced him as he wished it were he instead of this serf boy whom she so easily gathered in her arms.

"On the contrary," he said from the doorway, making Claudia jump. "Edward made quick work of the stables early this morn. In truth, the place was ready for my inspection shortly after I'd finished breaking my fast. The boy has been in my company all day." He grinned. "And I must add, I knew he was there."

Claudia felt a moment's panic while searching her husband's face to see if he knew of the deception, but his smile seemed easy and natural.

"Indeed," she said. "Well, I would suggest that

you get cleaned up, Edward, for the others are waiting to eat."

"That is an excellent idea," Angus said. "Run along, Edward."

"Oh, good! I could eat that whole buck cook is roasting by myself!" Edward shouted, running from the room.

Angus chuckled as he watched the lad's speedy departure before turning back to Claudia.

Claudia laughed as her brother disappeared, and she looked at Angus. The smile slowly left her face. She quickly glanced away, nervous now that she was alone with her husband. The air in the room had suddenly changed, and both she and Angus were acutely aware of it. Now that there were just the two of them, neither one knew what to say.

Angus cleared his throat. "As you said, the others are waiting to eat."

"If it's all the same to you, I would prefer a tray in my room," she said, not looking at him.

"I'm afraid not. I've asked Duke Theo to dine with us," Angus replied in a tone that brooked no refusal.

Claudia leapt from the chair and whirled to face him. Her eyes were like charcoal in her pale face. "How dare you—"

"I dare anything," he interrupted, "to hold what is mine."

"You humiliated me! You shamed me!"

In two swift strides he was in front of her. "I spoke only the truth. What can't you stand, Claudia?

My honesty, or the fact that you yield willingly every time I touch you? You know it is true."

With a low growl he yanked her to him. His mouth crushed hers in a fiery, demanding kiss that sent sparks of arousal spiraling upward to engulf them both in sweet torment. When he at last released her, triumph shone in his eyes. "No one takes what belongs to me. Remember that, Claudia," he warned. "Now, I would suggest that you change your gown while I get cleaned up. Our guest awaits us below."

Claudia's haze-filled eyes slowly cleared. Her quick breathing subsided to a normal pace. As one in a drugged state, she began to undo her gown and noticed that her fingers were shaking. She held her hands out, studying them as if they belonged to someone else.

What was Angus doing to her? What was this strange power he had over her? She had to fight him. He'd taken everything from her. Her home. Her family. She could not allow him to take her heart. If she let that happen, she would betray all that she held dear. Yet she could not help herself when in his arms. His kisses, his touch, were intoxicating and held her spellbound against her will. Somehow she must find the strength to fight him.

She glared at his back as he removed his tunic and walked over to the washbasin. Color stained her cheeks when she realized she was staring openly at him, but she couldn't look away. Her breath caught as she watched him rub the wet cloth over his shoulders, trickles of water sliding down his bare back. She remembered the warmth of his skin, the breadth of his back, when she clung to him as he showed her the ecstasy their bodies could know. She closed her eyes to block out his image, but it didn't help. She could still feel his heat, his kisses that threatened to draw forth her soul, his thighs sliding against hers as he—

Her eyes shot open and she turned away, horrified at her wanton thoughts. How could he do this to her? Would she ever be free of him?

Angus was unusually quiet as he washed himself, lost in his own thoughts, which centered on his day and the boy Edward. He was amazed at Edward's tenacity. The lad was full of energy and good humor. And he was smart. He'd pointed out the need for more farmland on the northern border to enrich Angus's lands, and then brazenly proceeded to give Angus a lesson in rotating fields, and of the defenses needed to protect the area. But when Angus questioned the boy on his knowledge, he smoothly evaded giving a direct answer and managed to sidetrack Angus's thoughts back to the subject of squiring. Angus chuckled as he thought of the many times that topic had been broached.

Claudia turned away from the chest, where she was gathering a change of clothes for her husband. Angus's quicksilver mood changes always surprised her. "You are suddenly in a good humor," she said.

He glanced at her and smiled. "Aye. I was just thinking of the persistence of young Edward."

Claudia bit her lip. "If the boy has done something to displease you, my lord, mayhaps he should remain within the castle."

"Displease me?" Angus repeated, startled. "Nay, he has done nothing to displease me. In truth, I take delight in his company. He is a hard worker, and bright." Angus made a face as he took up a rough cloth to dry himself. "Mayhaps too bright," he mumbled.

"What do you mean?" she asked, her heart skipping a beat.

He stopped drying his arm and frowned. "Claudia, how well do you know Edward?"

"Well enough," she answered cautiously.

"How is it that he is so well informed of the defenses needed to protect my land?"

She laughed nervously. "All of the people on this land are well informed. Besides, Edward spent a good deal of time around my father. I am sure he is only repeating what he overheard."

Angus grunted in satisfaction, and donned his clothes.

They returned to the great hall and found Theo sitting comfortably before the fire sipping wine. He arose as they approached and smiled warmly at Claudia. "Come, child, sit beside me," he said, taking her hand to lead her forward.

She blushed and looked away as she sat down. "Forgive me, Uncle Theo, for not seeing to your needs," she murmured.

"Think nothing of it, my dear. Marian looked after me quite nicely."

"At least the old witch has not forgotten her place when it comes to our guests," Angus muttered, taking a cup of wine from a serving girl.

Claudia stared bemusedly at her husband, but Theo chuckled at Angus's words. She had a feeling she'd missed something, and why had Angus struck out at Marian that way?

Angus led the way to the table. Once seated, he drew Theo into conversation. "Are you often away from your home, my lord?"

"Occasionally."

"You said that you were in Paris. That is very far from this remote area. It must have been something of great importance to take you there."

Theo waved a hand nonchalantly. "A business matter."

"Uncle Theo is as close to King Lothair as to Hugh Capet," Claudia said.

Theo smiled. "Not quite."

"Well, almost. Anyway, you are just as smart as that funny little man, and much nicer," she answered, grinning impishly.

"But not nearly as wealthy. Besides, it would do well not to underestimate Hugh. He is a good and wise man."

"I have heard of this Capet," Angus said. "He is a very powerful man."

"Aye, he is indeed," Theo replied. "The man is faced with many burdens because of that power. While I was staying with Hugh, word came that

Adalberon placed his nephew on the episcopal see of Verdun without consulting Lothair first. The king became so angry that he placed the archbishop's family under arrest."

"Oh, dear," Claudia murmured.

Theo patted her hand. "Oh, he says they are his guests, but he has let it be known that they are not going anywhere, and in retaliation, Adalberon and his supporters approached Hugh with the idea of Capet taking the throne."

Claudia let out a dismayed gasp. "And what of Hugh? Is the king now angry with him?"

Theo shook his head. "Nay. There has never been any question in Lothair's mind of Hugh's loyalty to the crown. Instead, the king's wrath has found its mark on Adalberon's head once more. Lothair has accused the archbishop of treason, and has ordered his trial at which Hugh will preside."

"Oh, no!" Claudia exclaimed.

Angus looked from his wife to Theo. "Why oh, no?" he asked, befuddled.

"Because Hugh Capet is a friend to both the archbishop and the king," Theo answered.

"What will he do?" Claudia asked.

Theo raised his cup of wine, but before taking a drink answered, "He will do his duty to his king, justly."

"I see what you mean by 'Hugh's burdens,'" Claudia said.

"Aye. I am glad that I am only one who will be part of the judicial assembly and not in Capet's seat."

"You will be there?"

"Unfortunately, aye. I leave in a few days for Compiègne. Believe me, I would much prefer to remain here at my estate, but for the moment, I cannot."

"I had hoped that you would be here for a while," Claudia said quietly.

Theo squeezed her hand. "I will not be gone for long, my child, and when I return I will come to see you. You know that should you need me, all you have to do is send word and I will come."

"But of course," Angus said, "there is no reason for my wife to 'need' you, my lord. I provide very well for her."

"I am sure that you will," Theo answered coolly, "but I hope you understand that as your wife's guardian I need to see for myself that that—is . . ." Theo's words trailed off as he happened to look away to the low tables. "God's teeth!" he exploded. "What are they doing to that boy?"

Angus and Claudia turned their heads to see what had caught Theo's attention.

Claudia gasped, but a low rumble of laughter escaped from Angus at the sight of Edward sitting all alone at one end of a long table. A servant hastily set a pewter mug of wine beside the lad, then scurried off to serve the other men, who were clustered together at the rest of the tables, elbowing one another for some much-needed room. Edward sat happily gnawing on a piece of meat, oblivious to the fact that he had no dining companions.

"What is wrong with the boy?" Theo asked strongly. "Why do the others treat him like a leper?"

"'Tis nothing serious, I assure you," Angus said, still chuckling. "Simple a minor misfortune with a mule in the stables. I'm afraid the lad doesn't know what water is."

Theo looked bewilderedly from Angus to Claudia. "A mule, you say? It wouldn't by any chance be the same mean-eyed mule that took a disliking to Vail some time back?"

"Aye," Claudia said quickly. "'Twould seem that the animal has taken a dislike to Edward also."

"Who?" Theo asked, having forgotten that Vail was masquerading as a serf.

"Yonder lad," Angus answered, waving in Edward's direction.

Theo's gaze followed his host's. What Claudia had told him earlier suddenly hit him. He blinked in disbelief at the young master of Orgueilleux, dressed in the filthy garments of a serf, greedily stuffing his mouth in a most uncouth manner.

"A stable boy," he murmured in a soft voice filled with amazement.

Angus laughed loudly. "If only that were true."

"What do you mean?"

"I am beginning to wonder just where that boy's talents really lie. He dresses and acts like a serf. Yet he is very quick-witted, and he's done nothing but hound me to death on the subject of becoming my squire since I encountered him."

Theo raised his eyebrows in surprise. "Are you considering it?"

Angus shrugged. "I do not know. The boy is very young."

Feeling that the time was opportune, Claudia seized upon the chance to get her little brother away from Angus. "My lord, I know that Edward can be extremely talkative, and—and overzealous in his enthusiasm for something he thinks he wants. However, ofttimes he loses interest quickly, and, well, he tends to do half a job."

Angus laid down his eating knife and turned to her. "Are you saying the boy is shiftless?"

"Nay, I am not," she replied quickly. "As you say, he is young and still very much a boy. I simply feel that he needs a woman's guidance."

Angus frowned. "The boy is fast approaching manhood, Claudia. It is good for him to associate with men. He needs that also."

"Yea, he does, but, mayhaps, not so closely. I mean, I could use him around the castle."

Angus smiled as he looked at Claudia with new eyes. He hadn't realized the mothering instinct was so strong in his wife. Mayhaps she needed a brood of her own to coddle instead of showering her attentions on all the serf children. His smile widened at the thought of Claudia with a babe in her arms. His child. He laid a hand over hers and said softly, "You have other boys to help you. Edward seems very enthusiastic to learn the ways of knights. He is strong and shows promise. I need good men to serve me. What say you, Duke Theo?"

Theo glanced at Claudia and saw that she was staring at him with wide, frightened eyes. He knew she sought to protect Vail. If anything happened to the boy, it would destroy her.

He turned his head to stare at the lower table, where Vail sat, and was surprised to find him taking the jibes from the men in a good humor. It appeared he was having a great deal of fun impersonating a serf, and it was as Angus said. Vail *was* quick-witted. What better way for him to come into his right than to have Angus's tutoring? But what if Vail were caught in his little charade?

The thought niggled at Theo's conscience. He did not know what kind of man this Angus McMahon was. He'd made it quite clear that he had no intention of losing Orgueilleux or anything connected with it. And yet Vail should not be denied the right to become what he should.

At last he spoke. "Although the boy is young, he needs the chance to prove his worth in order to become a fine man someday."

Angus smiled and sat back with a satisfied air. "There, you see." He took Claudia's hand and raised it to his lips as she started to speak. "Do not worry. I know you are fond of him." He chuckled. "He is a likable lad. I would not place him in any unnecessary danger and will watch over him."

Claudia could say no more without bringing on Angus's wrath or arousing his suspicions, so she kept silent. But that did not stop her from worrying.

CHAPTER 8

Claudia saw little of Vail in the weeks that followed, and she became resigned to the fact that Angus would not give up his tutelage on his prize. For that was how he looked at "Edward." His prize.

When he was out of earshot of his young charge, he was always praising the boy's hard work and willingness to learn, or laughing at some of the harmless pranks Edward pulled. But when the boy was with him, Angus turned into a hard taskmaster demanding that extra bit of performance to hone Edward's mediocre skills into the best.

The first stirrings of summer were in the air, and with them came a peace to Orgueilleux, and to Claudia. She had accepted her lot in life, but was not wholly satisfied with it. She could not, would not, allow any feelings of warmth to enter her heart for her husband. When he touched her, the fiery tempest he set loose in her soul did not decrease as she hoped it might, but increased to a blazing fury each time they came together. She was unaware that his tender, sensitive handling of her was slowly chipping away the block of stone she'd formed around her heart to keep him out. She stubbornly clung to the thought that he was her enemy, and kept from him that part of herself that would make her one with him.

She felt that if she let go of the talisman of hate and bitterness, and looked upon Angus as something other than her enemy, she would betray the love and devotion she'd shared with her family. Yet she could not overlook the kindness and generosity he showered on her. As much as she tried to ignore it, she felt guilty at not reciprocating in kind. She admitted to herself that whenever she was with him she wanted his arms around her. She craved his lovemaking as a starving person craves food. Yet she was afraid of letting herself feel with more than her body, and because of her torn emotions, she suffered greatly from melancholy.

Besides her own inner turmoil, there was always the shadow of her husband's true love haunting her. Every so often someone would mention Dorcas, and Claudia was pitched further into the bowels of depression. This served only to stiffen her resolve not to get close to Angus. Someday, she was sure, he would leave her to return to his love.

There were times when she would glance up from what she was doing to find him staring at her with a faraway look in his eyes, as though he weren't really seeing her, but something in her stead. Or she would catch him staring at nothing at all with the same remote expression. That set

her imagination in a whirlwind, for she believed
his thoughts were of his homeland and the love
he'd left behind. She knew then that he bitterly
regretted having taken her to wife.

Despite what Claudia thought, to Angus she
was his wife in all things. He confided in her,
raged before her in his anger, shared his amusement over something with her. He instinctively
knew that her reserve toward him was her defense
from loving him, and he was at a loss as to what to
do. He wanted all of her, not just her body because he demanded it.

There was no one to whom he could turn with
the problem. If his mother and sisters were near,
he could have asked them for advice, but they
were too far away. So he did the only thing he
could think of. He was ever patient, hoping Claudia
would eventually display some affection toward
him instead of polite indifference.

As Angus instructed Vail in the execution of his
duties, Claudia was watchful for any sign that her
husband might discover the truth. At first she was
alarmed by the way Vail pestered Angus for the
chance to act as his squire, afraid of the close
contact between the two. Her brother, however,
was determined, and after he'd shown his resolve
by taking care of Angus's needs in small ways, and
by being always underfoot, Angus decided it would
be safer to teach the boy properly.

Claudia began to relax as summer blossomed,
and she realized Angus suspected nothing amiss.
In truth, he seemed fond of Vail, and told her with

delight how well the boy was doing. Claudia was pleased when one evening Vail appeared in the hall to help serve the meal, scrubbed free of the grime that had seemed a part of the boy. She found a moment to ask him how he fared, smoothing back his unruly hair from his eyes.

"Oh, I am fine," he replied, beaming. "Angus is strict, but he is a good lord. There is none better. I have already learned a great deal, and tomorrow he is going to teach me to fight."

At that last statement, Claudia frowned. She did not want to admit that her little brother was growing up. "Are you sure you are ready for that?" she asked.

Vail made a face and looked at his sister with exasperation. "Oh, Claudia, do not treat me like such a babe. A man must know those things."

Angus had been conversing quietly with Owen, but upon hearing the boy speak with disrespect to Claudia, turned to admonish him. "Apparently I have been lax in my teachings. Among them should have been a lesson in courtesy toward your lady," he said sharply. "Firstly, you do not call your mistress by name, nor do you speak in such a tone to her. Secondly, I merely said you would accompany me to the training field. To watch. I never said anything about letting you participate.

"Now, if you cannot conduct yourself in a manner befitting your station, I will find someone who can. Is that clear?"

Vail, realizing his mistake, stared wide-eyed at

Angus. "Yea, my lord," he whispered in a subdued voice.

Angus nodded curtly. "Now, get about your duties, and be careful not to spill anything lest you find your bare back meeting the end of my whip."

"Yea, my lord," Vail breathed, and scurried off.

Claudia sat with eyes downcast, her hands clasped tightly in her lap. "Were you not rather harsh with him, my lord?" she asked in a tight voice.

"Nay, I was not."

She looked up to stare into his blazing eyes. "He is but a child," she whispered, "and he is excited with his new adventures. He meant no harm."

"Those who serve me do so with respect, or they do not serve me. The discussion is now closed, Claudia."

Her mouth involuntarily dropped open. She was finding out what a pigheaded fool her husband really was. She arose and presented a ramrod back to Angus as she marched haughtily from the hall.

Sometime later Angus entered his chamber to find Claudia sitting before the hearth, clothed in only her chemise as she brushed out her long hair. He hesitated momentarily before closing the door, then sighed and moved into the room. He stood behind her chair and ran his hand lovingly down her soft curls. She neither pulled away nor acknowledged his presence, but sat impassively, staring straight ahead.

He'd been too angry at Edward's audacity to go after her or to call her back. He knew that the boy was a favorite of Claudia's. In truth, the way she acted, one would have thought that Edward was of her flesh. Angus finally admitted to himself that he was jealous of the camaraderie between the two. He wished for his wife's smile to fall upon him as easily as it did on the boy, or for her to touch him as willingly as she did Edward without the inducement of their passion for each other. If only she would talk to him as cheerfully and naturally as she did to Edward.

He was glad she was not put off by the boy's low station, but no matter how close she and Edward were, that gave him no right to speak to her the way he did. He must make her see that.

"Claudia," he said softly, "I am sorry I spoke so harshly to you, but I will not permit anyone to speak to you the way Edward did. My men all know better, and so must Edward learn. I certainly would not allow my brothers, Conan and Bevan, to speak thusly, and they are of an age with Edward. Though they have the right to call you by name, Edward does not. He is a serf."

Without looking up she murmured, "He has always done so."

Angus walked around to stand before her. "And you permitted this? Your father permitted this?"

She looked up into his questioning gaze. "Yea. V—Edward is special."

"What makes him so special?" Angus asked, puzzled.

Claudia looked into the leaping flames and

shrugged. "He just is. He meant no harm, nor did I take offense."

"I know that. But you have been too soft in dealing with him. The boy cannot be given free rein. Edward is a serf and must be trained to obey. That is my job, and I will see to it that it is done."

He knelt in front of Claudia. Taking her hands in his, he said more softly, "Mayhaps you need a child of your own to coddle instead of showering Edward with all your attentions."

She stared aghast at him and pulled her hands free. "Nay! I do not want your child," she cried.

A look of pain crossed Angus's face before he masked it with a blank expression. He wearily got to his feet and ran a hand through his hair. "You would rather give your love to a serf boy not of your flesh than to have my babe. You hate me that much," he stated flatly.

She jumped to her feet. "There is no love left in me. You destroyed that when you destroyed all that I ever knew and cared about. You are my enemy!"

"Am I your enemy there?" he yelled, pointing to the bed.

"Yea!" she shouted.

Angus reached for her. With a fistful of her hair in one hand, he hauled her roughly against him. His other arm held her pinned to him as his mouth bruised hers in a violent kiss.

Claudia trembled as shivers of passion snaked through her body from her toes to her head. A tightness coiled in her belly, and she gave in to the glowing warmth spreading through her as her arms went around him to hold him closer.

Angus's mouth left hers to trail kisses over her chin and neck. His hands busied themselves with untying the strings of her chemise to explore her breasts. He bent her back so his mouth could suck the rosy crest of one while his fingers teased the other. His tongue flitted provocatively over the peak, and his teeth pulled gently, tautening the crest, making Claudia moan and cry out in joy. He raised his head and looked at her, his eyes glowing with satisfaction. Then he released her and stepped back.

Shaking with desire, Claudia opened her eyes to stare in bewilderment at her husband. Her lips were full and red from his kisses. Her breasts heaved in growing excitement at the passions he'd stirred in her. She slowly became aware that Angus's eyes were like shards of dark green stone glaring back at her.

"Since you despise me so, my lady, and do not desire my seed within you, you may have your wish," he said in a low, deadly voice. He turned on his heel and left the room, slamming the door on his way out.

A small whimper escaped Claudia. Still trembling with the need he always roused in her, she flung herself on the bed. Angus's scent floated up to her from the linens, mingled with her own. They had fused their bodies and become one in the only way she knew how. She'd insisted that they were enemies. But were they here?

She wanted him desperately. All he had to do was touch her and she melted in his arms. What had she done to him? She'd hurt his manly pride in the worst possible way. She would never again know the warmth of him, his gentle touch. The tears came easily as she cried out her misery.

Although Angus joined her for the evening meal, he did not speak to her. Nor did he come to their chamber all through the long night. The following morn he did not appear to break his fast. Claudia cast anxious glances at the door all through the meal, leaving her own food untouched. She stubbornly refused to ask about her husband, too ashamed to reveal their argument to Angus's men. She knew they would only snicker and jest among themselves. The hall emptied, the servants began to clean up, and still he did not come.

Knowing she needed to keep busy, Claudia at last arose from the table to see to the preparations for the midday meal. All was under control in the kitchen, though. Even the storehouse was well stocked with food, so she could not take her mind off her troubles by tallying the grains and spices and meat to see what they needed. She instructed a pair of serving girls to clean the soiled rushes from her chamber as well as from Marian's and Owen's, and lay fresh ones with sweet-smelling lavender. Still plagued by her tormenting thoughts and the fear that she had driven Angus from her forever, she sought out Marian. She found the woman in the hall, diligently sewing.

Marian glanced up as Claudia sat beside her, then continued her work without saying anything.

Claudia stared at the pile of fine linen beside Marian's chair. Usually the woman did not sew such garments as these. The neat stack of clothes was of excellent quality, as those the knights wore. Claudia picked up a beautifully embroidered tunic and held it up before her. It was for a large man, and not unlike the tunics Angus owned. She lowered the garment and stared at Marian questioningly. When it appeared the woman would not volunteer any information, Claudia asked, "Is this to be taken as a sign of your submission to your enemy?"

The old woman shrugged. "Even the enemy cannot go about naked as the day they were born. Their gold is as good as anyone else's."

"You do this for money?" Claudia exclaimed.

Surprised, Marian looked up. "And why not? Dennis and I came to an understanding."

"Dennis?"

"The young knight always in the *lord's* company." Marian chuckled, thinking of the pleasant young man. He'd neatly tricked her into helping him by feigning helplessness. He had such a boyish look about him that Marian could not stifle her mothering instinct. "He is very good at making a bargain," she went on. "He has no woman of his own to see to his needs. I saw no harm in what I did."

Claudia glanced doubtfully at the pile of clothes. "Nay, I suppose not."

Marian continued her skillful work on the tunic

in her hands. "Besides, if I do good work, he tells others. They come to me. We strike a bargain. They get their clothes cleaned and mended, and I become the richer for it."

Claudia nodded her head slowly. "It sounds reasonable."

"Of course it is," Marian snapped, "and it profits both parties."

"I suppose you are right. There is no harm." Claudia picked up a needle and thread and began to repair a small tear in the sleeve of the tunic she still held.

Marian said nothing, but continued her own work. She had noted the troubled look in her lady's eyes. Earlier that morning she'd been shocked at Claudia's haggard appearance, but she had not asked what was wrong. Her young mistress had taken to telling her to mind her own business of late, and she was not eager to bring on Claudia's wrath this morn.

The women worked in silence for some time as Marian plodded through the stack of clothes beside her. Claudia continued to work on the tunic she'd first picked up, staring into the empty hearth more often than not. Marian tried hard to ignore her lady's moodiness, but finally her impatience got the better of her.

"Claudia, what is wrong?"

Claudia jumped at the sharp tone and turned to Marian. "I—nothing."

"Do not tell me nothing! I know better. I taught you to sew swiftly and accurately, yet you sit there daydreaming and dawdling. I expected you to have finished *his* tunic by now. But if you do not get busy, I will *have* to do it!"

Claudia started at the woman's words and looked down at the garment she held. Of their own volition tears crept into her eyes and rolled down her cheeks. "This is Angus's tunic?" she asked in a plaintive whisper.

"Aye."

"But why did he give it to you? It is my task to see to his needs."

Marian shrugged. "The way you work, it is no wonder the man has nothing to wear." When she saw Claudia's stricken expression, she said more softly, "Mayhaps he feels you have enough to do."

Claudia shook her head. "Nay. He hates me and wants nothing further to do with me."

Marian reached out a hand to take Claudia's. "Tell me what is wrong. Did he beat you? How has he hurt you?"

"Nay. He has done nothing. I fear it is I who have hurt him."

Marian sat back in surprise to study her mistress.

"I—I said something in anger. I have hurt him overmuch."

"What did you say?"

"I told him that I did not wish to bear his child," Claudia sobbed.

Marian winced at her lady's words. She knew that men prided themselves on being able to produce a male heir. Claudia had hit a most vulnerable spot, for she knew her lady's lord was no different from any other man. And the way he'd pursued Claudia, like a rutting stag...

Marian cocked her head to one side as she watched Claudia cry, a thought occurring to her. "It is just as well. You would not wish to bear the devil's spawn."

Claudia's tears stopped abruptly and her head jerked up. "He is not the devil! He is kind, and warm, and gentle. Not—not unlike Papa!" She flung the tunic at Marian and jumped to her feet, then she ran from the hall.

Marian's gaze followed Claudia speculatively. Then she nodded and turned her attention to finishing the task Claudia had started.

Claudia stood just outside the castle door, letting her eyes adjust to the bright sunlight. Wiping the tears from her face, she stepped out into the yard, but she had no destination in mind. She wandered aimlessly until she came to the training field. There she stopped, and watched the men, searching the faces of each. With a sigh of dejection she slowly turned and walked away.

She made her way to the herb garden, telling herself she could at least keep busy there. As she plucked off sprigs of tarragon and thyme, she finally admitted that it had been Angus she searched for. He must truly be angry with her to avoid her this way. And she could not blame him if he did not want to look upon her.

It was true that he was her enemy. He had taken Orgueilleux, and her, by force. He had destroyed everything that she knew and loved.

But he had married her, and he did not beat her or treat her cruelly. He was always kind and gentle with her, so very patient. But how could she bear his child when she knew his heart belonged to another? She frowned. What game was he playing? Why was he toying with her? Being ever kind toward her when she knew he loved his Dorcas. Of course, he was kind to Vail also.

She stooped to pick some weeds, still frowning. Would he be so kind if he knew that "Edward" was her brother? That was the one worry that truly plagued her. No doubt he would kill Vail. How could she bear to have his child then? Mayhaps he would kill her too, she thought ruefully. Then he would have Orgueilleux all to himself. Orgueilleux and his Dorcas. Mayhaps he would bring her here to rule by his side.

Claudia pulled out the weeds viciously, bringing some herbs with them. He would not do it! She would not allow that to happen. If he wanted Dorcas, he could have her, but he would not give her Orgueilleux!

She would go to him. She would bear her child. It had to be so in order to protect what was hers.

She arose and brushed her skirt, then she marched back into the castle. She kept as busy as possible for the rest of the day, pushing all thoughts of Angus from her mind with a firm resolve. Soon enough she would capitulate.

Claudia's fierce activity managed to abate most of her anger. By evening she sat by the hearth in the hall, quietly embroidering. Hearing a commotion without, she raised her head to stare at the door, her heart pounding in expectation. A gasp of dismay escaped her when a man strode into the hall.

Duke Felix Perrin crossed the hall and stopped in front of her. He eyed her up and down disdainfully before speaking. "I see that you have fared well at my nephew's hands," he said, his lip curling in a sneer. "Mayhaps, more than you deserve. I always felt he had a soft streak in him. Must be that barbaric Irish upbringing."

Sparks flew from Claudia's eyes. But that was the only sign of anger she showed as she bit her tongue to keep from lashing out at the ignorant viper standing before her.

"Where is your lord, girl?" he asked imperiously.

"My *husband* is not here at the moment," she answered in a quiet, civil tone. She raised a hand and a serving maid appeared. "See that Duke Felix is taken to a room to freshen up and that something is brought to him to eat." Claudia arose and smoothed out her skirt. She could show good breeding even if this dolt could not, she thought smugly. "I will see that a message is sent to Angus so that he may join you," she said smoothly before walking away.

Wondering how she would find her husband, she ran outside in time to see a small group riding through the gate, led by Angus. He turned his horse toward her as she hurried down the steps calling to him. She stopped and explained breathlessly, "Duke Felix is within."

"Yea, I know," Angus said. "We saw him riding up as we returned. See that he is made comfortable. I will be in momentarily to speak with him." With that, Angus turned his destrier toward the stables.

Claudia's heart sank at the cold detachment with which Angus addressed her. It was obvious he was still angry with her. With a heaviness in her breast she reentered the castle to carry out his orders. There was no point in further bringing on his wrath.

Claudia found Felix seated in Angus's favorite chair by the hearth in the great hall, sipping a cup of wine. He ignored her as she approached, as was his custom in dealing with those whom he felt were inferior to him. She informed him that Angus would be joining him soon, then picked up her embroidery and took a seat on a bench as far away from him as possible.

Felix surveyed his nephew's wife as she quietly resumed her task. She was indeed a beautiful woman. He suddenly regretted bitterly that he'd given her to Angus instead of tasting her sweet charms first. But then, he'd had a purpose in mind.

After defeating Duke Robert Cherveny and gaining Orgueilleux, Felix had known that if he tried to give away Cherveny's lands as a fief to his nephew, who was an outsider, there would be much protest among his peers. He had no desire to fight off everyone in the region. It had taken him too long to come as far as he had, and nothing and no one was going to stand in his way. So he had devised a scheme to make Angus acceptable to the other lords. Angus would marry Claudia Cherveny, and through marriage would gain the land and the respect of the others. With Angus's help, Felix planned to finally attain the wealth and power that was rightfully his.

It had been a sore spot with him to give Orgueilleux to his nephew, but it would be worth it to realize the fruit of his plan at last. Besides, let Angus restore the fields and finish building the wall. Felix could not be everywhere at once. His eyes narrowed thoughtfully and his lips curved in a small smile. The time would come.

Claudia was aware that Felix stared at her. Like a wolf waiting to fall on his prey, she thought. It was an effort to force back the nervous apprehension she felt and remain where she was as his eyes bored into her. Her mind whirled with questions of why this traitorous dog had returned. Could it be that he was planning an attack on another neighbor and needed Angus's assistance once again? If only she hadn't quarreled with Angus. Mayhaps she could have talked him out of such a venture. She didn't have long to wait for her answers as Angus entered the hall and strode forward to greet his uncle.

Angus settled into a chair across from Felix and inquired, "What brings you to Orgueilleux, uncle?"

"A matter of grave importance, I fear. Word has come to me that King Louis is dead."

"What?"

"Oh, dear God," Claudia whispered, crossing herself.

Satisfied that he had their full attention, Felix continued. "I must ride for Compiègne at once where an assembly of nobles is meeting, and I think that you should accompany me. You knew that Lothair had imprisoned the archbishop of Rheims for treason?"

"Aye," Angus said, recalling his conversation with Duke Theo.

"Adalberon is a very powerful man who carried out much policy without Lothair's approval. But he was somewhat... indiscreet for suggesting that Hugh Capet become king through an election. Before Adalberon's trial could take place, though, Lothair mysteriously died. Some say of a stomach ailment."

"Wasn't it?" asked Angus.

Felix shrugged. "Who can be sure? Anyway, Louis was crowned, but he kept putting off the trial. Now he, too, is dead."

"How?"

"He fell from his horse."

"Fell from his horse?" Angus repeated disbelieving. It all sounded very strange to him. His mind whirled as he tried to grasp what his uncle was telling him.

"Aye, and Adalberon is still charged with treason," Felix said in an amused tone.

Angus glanced up to find his uncle staring intently at him. "I do not see your point. So now it is up to the duke Charles to lead the assembly, for he is the heir to the throne by right of blood."

Felix made a face and set his cup down impatiently. "The duke Charles is an inept, bumbling fool. He would make a bad king. The archbishop of Rheims has intimated for years that there should be a change. Now is the time to move. All the grandees of France have been called. Nay, it will not be Charles who leads the assembly, but Capet."

"Then the archbishop is a free man."

Felix grinned wolfishly. "Aye, and the time is ripe for Capet to take the throne."

"But I was under the impression that Capet had always declined when that subject was broached."

"He has always done so in the past, but with all the nobles called to preside over Adalberon's trial, I am certain he can now be persuaded to see the light. If we all let our voices be heard, what can he do? He will have to accept, and Charles will be able to do nothing, for he is too weak. Hugh Capet is a canny leader. He is a holder of many great lands since his father's death. Of course, many of those he had parceled out to his vassals; nevertheless, the man has many powerful friends. The Duke of Burgundy is his brother, and he is brother-by-marriage to the dukes of Normandy and Aquitane. He is allied with the leading members of the clergy. What man is more fitted to the role of king that he?

"It is better that we pay homage to him than ignore the assembly and end up at his mercy because of it, for if we show our support, mayhaps he will leave us to our own devices. After all, he prefers the larger fiefs to this desolate land.

"Showing our support for Capet will have the dual purpose of ridding ourselves of an incompetent ruler in favor of a respected one, and of protecting what is ours."

Angus frowned and leaned forward in his chair. "You speak of treason," he said.

Felix laughed harshly. "Nonsense. This country is so divided now. Do you really believe that Duke Charles can bring unity to the land? I say he cannot. Things will be as they always have been under the Carolingian rule if he takes the throne. The lords will sit on their lands at their will if he calls. At least with Capet there is a chance that they will come when he bids them. I tell you this is for the best. You have not given your fealty to Duke Charles. If you give it to Hugh, you will insure your foothold on these lands and any others you may acquire."

Angus stared thoughtfully at his uncle for a moment. "Mayhaps you are right."

"Of course I am."

Angus arose. "Will you sup with us and stay the night? We can leave—" His words were cut off as Edward rushed into the hall exclaiming loudly that he'd finished the tasks Angus had given him. He came to an abrupt halt in front of Angus and said breathlessly, "If you will disarm, my lord, I will see to your armor."

Angus frowned disapprovingly at the boy, unaware of Felix's surprised gasp, or that Claudia had half risen from her chair, her face a white mask.

"Can you not see that we have a guest?" Angus said sharply. "You have disgraced yourself, and me, by your conduct."

Angus's rebuke was cut off as Felix let out a guffaw and slapped his nephew on the back.

"How delightful to see you bring your enemy to his knees, nephew," he said. Still laughing, he whirled the boy around to face him. "How diabolically clever to remind one and all just who is master here." He chortled, eyeing Vail in the peasant garments.

"The humor in my servant's actions escapes me, uncle," Angus said, scowling.

Felix roared with laughter once more. "Ser-servant! Oh, that is priceless. Perfect. Perfect." His lips curled in an unpleasant smile as he eyed the boy up and down. "My lord churl," he sneered, bowing mockingly.

Vail had been so excited at having had his first real lesson in squiring that his only thought had been of Angus and what he could next do for him. His gaze glued to Angus, and Angus's guest half-hidden from his view, Vail had plunged headlong into his predicament. Too late he'd realized his mistake, and had hoped that Duke Felix would overlook him, for the man did not consider serfs to be human. Now he stood, erect and white-faced. He dared not look at Claudia. His poor sister had tried so hard to protect him. It was too bad that her efforts were for naught, Vail thought with a detached air as he waited in silence for his retribution.

"I do not understand," Angus said, bewildered.

Felix looked at his nephew. The smile slowly left his face, and he grunted. "You do not know."

Angus shook his head.

"Your 'servant' is your brother-by-marriage, nephew."

Angus stared at his uncle and blinked uncomprehendingly.

Vail let out a resigned sigh and turned to face Angus. He lowered himself to one knee, and with his right fist across his heart, stated unflinchingly, "Vail Edward Justin Cherveny at your service, my lord."

Angus sucked in his breath at the boy's words as he stared into the clear blue eyes gazing up at him. One question kept buzzing about in his brain. *Why?*

He whirled around and found Claudia standing, staring at them. Her eyes were like two dark pools of fear.

"Why?" he spat out.

She jumped at his question, but no answer could get past the lump in her throat.

"Why was this knowledge kept from me?" he shouted.

"Please, my lord." Vail's voice rang out clear and steady in the now-silent hall. "My sister sought only to protect me. She—we meant no harm."

Angus turned on Vail in his fury. "You meant no harm! She meant only to protect you! From what?

From me?" He turned and advanced slowly toward her.

Fear rooted Claudia to the spot where she stood. She flinched as Angus grabbed her by the shoulders and shook her. "Why?" he asked again in a low, menacing voice.

"He is all that I have left," she whispered, "I—I was afraid."

"Of me? You could not trust me with your brother's safety?" he asked disbelievingly.

Claudia broke free and glared at her husband. "You have taken all that I love from me. How could I trust you with what I hold so dear, knowing that Vail is the rightful master of Orgueilleux?"

Felix moved forward threateningly. "Look around you, girl. My nephew holds Orgueilleux."

Angus's thoughts skipped back to the night he'd found his wife and the boy together. Now he understood her fright...and he was repulsed to think that Claudia believed him capable of murdering a child.

"It is clear that you do not understand kindness and trust when it is shown you," he said, barely able to control the rage building in him. "Mayhaps my uncle is right. I have been too lenient with you. You need have no fear for your safety, nor for your brother's. You will live. But I tell you this, you will regret it. I have treated you as an honorable wife. It is clear that you deserve no more than the duties of a slave. I am master here. It is my will that is to be served."

He turned his back on her in disgust. "Uncle,

you wish to make haste for Compiègne, so be it. We will ride now. I will not stay here one moment longer to let the foul air surrounding me infect my reasoning, lest I go back on my word and kill this venomous creature."

With that he strode angrily from the hall with his uncle and his men hurrying to keep up with him.

CHAPTER 9

Angus tried hard to focus on the activity around him, but the amount of wine he'd drunk hindered his efforts. That didn't stop him from raising the cup to his lips once more. Somewhere inside his head was a dull, throbbing ache that increasingly worsened at the deafening roar in the hall. He desperately wanted peace and quiet. It had taken days, and an inordinate amount of wine, but he could feel himself slipping into oblivion. Mayhaps then his mind would be at rest and he would no longer have to think, and remember.

If only he did not have to think. Ever since his "wife's" revelation of her trust in him, he'd thought of nothing else. First her confession that she abhorred the idea of bearing his child, then her accusation that he would have killed her brother had his identity been revealed. How could she think that he would murder Edward? Nay. Vail. His name was Vail. That was it. And he was her brother. Angus's befuddled mind tried to sort it all out. He'd told her he was not a murderer of children. Hadn't he? Angus nodded solemnly. Yea, he had. He was sure he had.

Hadn't he told her how he felt about the waste of human lives? Besides, he was fond of Edward. Angus shook his head and frowned at the table. Nay. Vail. But Claudia did not believe that. Could she not see it for herself? Angus nodded once more and took on what he felt was the look of a wise old sage. He'd not even beaten the boy when he'd deserved it. But Claudia shut her eyes to that. She saw only what she wanted to see.

He'd finally come to the conclusion that his wife had bewitched him. How else could he explain his obsession with her? He had stopped looking upon her as his enemy, but she had still considered him an enemy of hers. She tormented his hours, waking or sleeping, and still he was not satisfied. He ached with want of her. Even now, after what he knew, he was racked with desire for her, consuming him from the depths of his being. She was like fire that even after he'd doused her flaming passion, smoldered on to ignite once more into a blazing fury. Would he never know peace? Would that beautiful witch always eat at his guts like a cankerous sore until she destroyed all that he was? He nodded again. He should beat her. It was what she deserved. He shuddered at the thought of marring her flawless skin, so white and soft.

Oh, why was his mind tortured with her image? Why was every other woman he saw pale in comparison? Mayhaps that was the very thing he needed. A woman. Any woman would do. After all, were they not all the same? Then he could exorcise his wife from his mind.

There hadn't been time for that though. He and his uncle had ridden to Compiègne over a week before, where a judicial assembly led by Capet had declared Adalberon innocent of the charge of treason. In turn, a grateful archbishop had conferred the regency on Capet, and a few days later they'd all ridden on to Senlis, where Hugh was unanimously elected king over Charles. Afterward they'd journeyed to Noyon for the coronation, and here they'd remained to enjoy the festivities.

Angus found himself drawn to the quiet man who was now his king. It was hard to imagine that such an ordinary man as Capet had been adviser to kings. Angus could attribute only Hugh's vast experience in battle and his common sense as the cause.

From some of the conversations that Angus had overheard, it was not hard to glean that others felt Capet could be easily swayed, but Angus did not think so. He sensed a strength and wisdom in Capet that would serve the man well.

Some of those who'd elected him had even boasted of how easy it would be to hold another election if Hugh did not meet their standards. They'd done it once; they could do it again. Was there no honor to be found, Angus wondered. Nay, he thought sourly. He'd not found it among these lords, and he'd certainly not found any in his wife! Be damned to Claudia! He took another swallow of wine. He would enjoy himself, and he would forget her perfidy.

The walls of the hall swelled with the roar of high-spirited merrymakers. Angus drained his cup, spilling some of the wine down his chin, and slammed the cup down on the table. He winced at the pounding in his head and once more tried to bring his eyes into focus. A whirling movement in front of him made him dizzy. He blinked several times, trying to clear his vision, and was rewarded when the whirlwind dissolved into a brightly clad figure.

He watched, mesmerized, as the red silk gown swirled higher and higher to reveal bare feet and trim legs, and he remembered another night when he'd watched a dancer. Only then he'd been bored.

His gaze roamed upward to fix on her breasts, almost spilling from the low bodice of her dress as the dancer bent forward directly in front of him. His eyes left the voluptuous swell of bosom to travel upward once more, resting on full lips parted in a sensual smile. A prickly sensation coursed through Angus as he stared into the woman's face. Her features were sharper than Claudia's. Not the soft, feminine womanliness of his wife. High cheekbones and a long, straight nose emphasized her hollow cheeks and jutting chin as she tossed her head back proudly. Her jet-black hair brushed the floor as she arched her back lower and lower before agilely springing up again to stare straight at Angus with flashing dark eyes. He sucked in his breath. Her eyes hypnotized and held his. They reminded him of a cat, strange and foreboding.

Angus was vaguely aware of a chuckle beside him. Felix leaned over and murmured, "Careful, nephew, lest you begin to foam at the mouth with the spell she is weaving over you."

His eyes never leaving the woman's face, Angus answered, "Mayhaps she can exorcise another spell."

Felix eyed the dancer speculatively and nodded. "Mayhaps."

The dancer moved forward slowly, her arms in an arc above her head, stretching the material of her gown tautly over her breasts. She leaned across the table, and, lowering her arms, reached out to Angus invitingly. The scent of jasmine, unlike the sweet smell of wildflowers in spring that wafted around Claudia, assailed his nostrils as she came ever closer, taunting him with her body.

Suddenly Angus's hand snaked out. Snatching her wrist, he dragged her across the table. Black eyes stared amusedly into drunken, haze-filled green ones as she lay sprawled out. She did not try to pull away. Instead, a slow smile curved her lips, and she ran her tongue between her teeth.

Angus hauled her forward. He did not stop until their lips met in a crushing kiss that was greeted with raucous laughter by those around them. He pulled back to look at the woman, annoyed. She was beautiful in a wild sort of way, yet he'd felt nothing. Had the witch spoiled him for any other woman? He would show her. He would not allow himself to become enslaved.

He brushed his hand over a full, soft breast and asked softly, "What is your name?"

"Iona," she answered huskily.

"Well, Iona, I am in need of a woman."

The dancer laughed softly. "You believe in coming right to the point, don't you? No pretty speeches for you."

"Nay. None. What say you?"

Iona lowered her eyes to hide the gleam in them. Men were such terrible fools. At least this one was not full of promises that he had no intention of keeping. She glanced up to find that his eyes had strayed to her bodice once more. 'Twas a pity that he would not get what he desired. She would probably have enjoyed it very much. She shivered at the thought. "Mayhaps we can reach a bargain," she said in a low voice.

Angus started to reach for her again, but she placed a hand against his chest to hold him off. "In private, my lord."

Angus let out a low chuckle and pulled her fiercely to him, scattering trenchers and goblets in her wake. Those nearest him let out with a string of curses upon his head as they scrambled out of the way. He held Iona tightly in his arms and got unsteadily to his feet to leave the hall, unaware of the look that had passed between his uncle and the girl.

Once outside the hall Iona struggled to free herself, but Angus only tightened his grip on her. "Be still," he growled.

"My lord, I am a heavy burden. Please, let me walk by your side as your willing captive."

Angus grunted, then set her on her feet. It was true. She was heavier than Claudia. He swore under his breath. Would he never be free of that treacherous enchantress? He hauled Iona to him and kissed her fiercely.

She broke free and whispered, "Let us be away from here. I yearn for you as you do for me." She tugged on his arm to make him follow.

"My lodgings are near," he mumbled. He halted his steps and looked around in confusion. "My horse."

"If your lodgings are close, let us hurry. We can walk. Come, I will help you." She threw his arm over her shoulder and propelled him away from the noisy hall.

Angus leaned heavily on the girl as she led him down the street, oblivious to his surroundings as he ineffectually pawed her. He didn't notice that she kept glancing over her shoulder.

The city teemed with celebrations in honor of the new king, and they could hear the music and laughter from the houses and inns they passed. Iona turned a corner and led Angus down a side street that was quieter. He was so intent upon capturing the dancer, he was surprised when he was shoved forward. He flailed about helplessly, then felt a stabbing pain in his head. He fell to his knees, half senseless, and another pain pierced his skull. Someone kicked him in the side, then he lay still.

His head swam in and out of the depths of comprehension. Mayhaps if he lay quiet, his attackers would think him dead and leave. Iona. What had they done to her? He could not remember hearing her cry out. He heard voices in the distance, but what they said had no meaning.

"He is not dead," came the soft urgent whisper of a woman's voice.

"Nay, not yet. But he will be."

The silver of a knife blade flashed in the darkness.

What little senses Angus had were alerted by the last statement. He edged his hand underneath him, trying to find the hilt of his sword. Other sounds penetrated as he heard laughter nearby. Was it that of his attackers, or someone in celebration? He did not know, nor did he have the time to wait and find out. He drew his sword and rolled over.

Shouts rang out on the empty street. Angus heard a woman cry out, and caught a glimpse of bare feet and red silk racing past him as he struggled to get up. The sounds of a skirmish came to him, and he finally managed to get to his feet to stand waveringly with sword in hand. He looked about him, puzzled. It seemed that a whole army was facing him, for he was seeing double.

They would not take him. He let out a bellow and swung wildly with his weapon.

"Nay, my lord, it is I, Colin," came a cry.

Angus lowered his sword, and, swaying back and forth, blinked. He squinted at the figures before him until they dissolved into one recognizable as his man. "Hold still," he muttered.

"Are you unharmed, my lord? What did these men want?"

"No doubt a fat purse," Angus said, trying several times before he successfully sheathed his sword. "How many were there?"

"Three. They're all dead. Where is your horse?"

"My horse?" he repeated, befuddled. "I was walking. Iona..." He looked around him. "Where is the woman?"

"You mean the one who ran off as we rode up?"

"Ran off? Why would she..."

Colin glanced at Angus's empty belt. "Your purse is gone, my lord."

Angus swore under his breath as his hand went to the spot where his purse had been. "I have had enough feasting for one night. Let us return to our lodgings." It was a sorry day when there was no woman whom he could trust, he thought peevishly.

The men, who'd been celebrating to the fullest, looked at one another, then heavenward in supplication as they prepared to leave. It was a good thing they'd bought that wine at the last inn. After their lord was abed, they could finish it.

Dennis sat at the gaming table in the hall, a goodly sum of money piled in front of him, concentrating on the next roll of dice. He and Owen had accompanied Lord Angus this evening, and he'd joined in the game of chance to see if his luck would hold here as it had back at Orgueilleux.

He'd watched as Angus took the dancer from the hall and had debated whether to follow his lord, but decided against it. Angus would have been furious to learn Dennis's instincts to watch over his lord had been roused by Angus's drinking. But all Dennis could do was watch as Angus raised cup after cup of wine to his lips.

Of course, he knew why Angus did it. He'd been in the hall at Orgueilleux the day they'd left. Angus had been in a foul disposition since then, and his mood was getting worse. He was as puzzled as his lord as to why the lady Claudia did not trust him. After all, Angus had shown nothing but love and respect for his wife, and for her to treat him so... Dennis could not understand the workings of a woman's mind. He was glad that he'd not yet been snared by that madness called love. The closest he'd ever come was in having an adoring reverence from afar for the lady Dorcas. But he knew, without a doubt, that he was not the man to handle that spitfire. For now he was content to use a woman where he could find her, and not lose his heart.

A voice interrupted Dennis's thoughts. "Come, it is your roll."

He looked up into the broad face of one of his opponents and grinned engagingly. Picking up the dice, he tossed them lightly to land in the middle of the table for another winning play.

"If I did not know that those are my dice, I would swear that you cheat," the broad-faced man grumbled.

Those around the table became quiet and looked nervously at Dennis as he drew his winnings toward him. Was the man deliberately trying to provoke him with such an open insult? Dennis wondered. He knew him to be a poor loser, for the man was one of Felix Perrin's and they'd played together before. Dennis knew that Angus would be very angry if trouble developed between his men and his uncle's. He had no wish to feel Angus's wrath.

"What do you plan to do with all you've won?" asked another player, trying to ease the tension in the air.

The broad-faced man grunted. "Mayhaps he hopes to buy himself an extravagant whore like his lord."

Dennis refused to let the man bait him. Instead, he grinned hugely and agreed. "What better way to spend one's earnings?" he joked.

Amid the laughter the man sullenly picked up the dice. He threw them down forcefully, and lost. But Dennis was only vaguely aware of what went on around him.

His mind skipped in circles as he tried to remember. Where had he heard those same words before?

Suddenly something in his brain clicked as he recalled another gaming table. Only, some of the men had been different. He remembered now where he'd seen the dead man in the forest who'd been a party to the attack on them when Angus had almost lost his life. That man had said some-

thing similar at Orgueilleux concerning the lady
Claudia. That had been on the night of Angus's
wedding feast. And the man had been one of
Felix's.

Dennis scooped up his winnings and prepared
to leave, making his excuses.

"What?" jeered the broad-faced man. "You do
not give us a chance to recoup our losses?"

Dennis patted his purse and grinned. Then he
looked with contempt at the meager pile of coins
in front of the other man. "That is why I am a
winner. I know when to quit," he said before
turning his back on them.

Owen watched the first pinkish rays from the
sun cast a pale light on the horizon, and gradually
change to a brilliant orange and yellow glow. He'd
not slept much since Dennis found him the previous evening to relate his news.

The young man had tried unsuccessfully to find
Angus, and when he encountered Owen, spilled
forth his tale. Dennis had been earnestly concerned for his lord's welfare when, in his search,
he'd discovered Angus's horse still in the stable,
and learned that Angus and the dancer had left on
foot.

If the story had come from anyone else, Owen
might have had his doubts. But he knew Dennis to
be truthful and honest as well as levelheaded.
Moreover, he had a remarkable memory. If he said
he'd sat across from the man in the forest at the
gaming table in Orgueilleux, he had.

The question running through Owen's mind was whether Duke Felix knew of his man's villainy? Mayhaps not. But somehow Owen could not shake the cold feeling of dread that Felix Perrin was a part of what had happened. There had been too many "accidents." It seemed that ever since they'd set foot in this accursed country, Owen had had his hands full in fulfilling his oath to Heloise to watch out for her son.

She had been content only after she'd extracted his promise that he would do everything in his power to see that Angus was safe, even though she knew of her son's skill in warfare. She also knew her brother. Mayhaps there was something she'd neglected to say. Whether that was true or not, the man bore watching. And Angus needed to be told. That would be hardest, for the young man always gave people the benefit of the doubt. When they showed him cause for his distrust, his swift hand of justice swept over the offender ruthlessly. Angus was like his father in that respect.

Owen and Duncan McMahon had been friends since boyhood, and Owen knew the fairness with which Duncan dealt with his people. He knew also that his friend had instilled the same probity in his sons. But he'd witnessed the punishment meted out to those deserving it and he did not, for the world, want to trade places with Angus if his uncle were at the crux of the attacks. Family ties meant everything to the McMahon clan. Owen knew how hurt Angus would be to discover Felix

Perrin's treachery, if indeed the man were behind the assaults on him.

Nay. He must tread carefully. Mayhaps find the truth on his own before laying out the facts, if any, to Angus. He did not want his young friend's anger directed at himself because of false accusations, and with the mood Angus was in of late, that is where his wrath would undoubtedly find its release.

Owen heard a groan and turned from his position at the window. The man on the bed was struggling to sit up.

Swinging his legs gingerly over the side of the bed, Angus moaned and dropped his pounding head into his hands. He felt as though his horse had pranced all over him. He didn't know which hurt worse, his aching body or his throbbing head.

Owen grunted, and moved away from the window to look at him. "It would appear that you are in no shape to travel."

Angus jerked his head up in surprise to find that he was not alone, and groaned again. "Who said I was going anywhere?" he rasped.

"You did, all the way here, last night. You do not remember?"

Angus shook his head slowly, and winced at the heavy, pulsating pain.

"It was all Colin could do to keep you from rounding up all the men and returning to Orgueilleux last night. You reiterated long and loudly on the evils of city life and swore that you would not spend one moment longer than you had to in such a den of depravity."

Angus's lopsided grin gave way to a chuckle at Owen's account of his behavior. "That does not sound like me."

"Nay, it does not. But then, you have not been yourself of late."

Angus grimaced as he arose and walked unsteadily to the washstand. He splashed cool water over his head and turned to face Owen. His eyes were hard in his ashen face. "A great deal has recently changed," he said flatly, throwing the cloth in a corner.

Owen shrugged. "What has changed? You discover that your wife does not trust you?" He ignored the dark scowl that Angus graced him with and continued. "That is not new. The lady Claudia has never trusted you, or, for that matter, any of us. Why should she? She saw her family and home destroyed by us, and she is turned over to you, whom she rightly considers her enemy, and then she is given a few months in which to come to terms with her situation. Would you? Would any of us?"

"She is my wife. I have always shown her the respect she is entitled to as my wife."

"Aye, you have, and you expect her to return your devotion like an obedient servant."

"I love her!" Angus thundered, immediately regretting his outburst as his head vibrated alarmingly. He sought the comfort of the bed and slowly eased himself down.

"I know. But a love that grows slowly is cherished all the more. Angus, sometimes you expect too much from those you love. Lady Claudia is as proud as another I can name. Though she does not have the same fiery temperament of Dorcas, she is just as proud, and she will not yield easily to what she considers wrong."

Angus stared into space. "What am I to do?"

Owen squeezed his shoulder reassuringly. "Give it time. You must have patience, and forgiveness. She did what she had to do out of love for her brother. Would you not do all in your power to protect those you love? She showed much courage, for she knows that you can kill her."

Angus raised his head to stare at Owen. "I will not kill her! Can she not see that I mean her no harm?"

"Aye, she sees it, but she does not trust."

Angus smiled wryly. "You observe much, my friend." A thought occurred to him as he asked, "Have you ever loved a woman, Owen?"

"Aye, Owen replied, his face closed. "But it escaped me. Do not let it escape you, Angus."

Angus arose, and clapping his companion on the back grinned sheepishly. "Come, we must see about the journey home. I imagine that I am not the only one who is not up to traveling."

Angus struggled through the preparations for the trip to Orgueilleux for the rest of the day. It seemed that there were hundreds of details to attend to, and he had to see to them all himself, as the men sought his attention. His head continued to ache and his stomach churned in dissatisfaction at his activity, but he worked unceasingly. He had no one to blame for his condition except himself. His only consolation was in knowing that most of the men were in no better shape than he.

By mid-afternoon he was satisfied enough with the progress made, and decided to seek out Felix to inform him of his plans. He rode through the town, picking his way carefully through the crowded streets on his great black steed. As he neared his uncle's quarters, he pulled up on the reins and stared at a figure moving quickly down the lane in the opposite direction. He called out, but instead of halting, the person glanced back, then hastened off down the street.

Angus swore and spurred the destrier forward, only to be brought up short by the milling crowd in the marketplace. There was no doubt in his mind that the person he'd seen was Iona. He would never forget her catlike features, or her nimble fingers. After he'd pieced the events of the previous evening together, he was sure that it was she who'd robbed him, or that she at least had a hand in it. He wanted some answers.

An angry merchant shoved past Angus, slapping the horse on its hindquarters and angering it. Angus fought to gain control of his horse as the animal snorted and pranced sideways. As the horse reared, he heard someone yelling shrilly. The animal came down on all fours, and horse and rider were jostled to the side. Angus heard a shriek. He saw an old woman falling backward and quickly reached out to grab her before she fell to the ground to be trampled underneath the horse's hooves.

Angus urged the horse slowly through the crowd to an empty spot, clutching the woman as she hung precariously at his side, the tips of her toes dragging in the dirt. He let her down easily once he'd put some distance between the crowd and themselves, and asked gruffly, "Are you hurt?"

"Nay, my lord," she replied in a whining voice. "Well—maybe my arm. A little. And my side is bruised where that brute hit me," she added peevishly, glaring at the now-quiet destrier. "But I am forever in your debt, my lord, for saving me."

"Mayhaps this will teach you not to get so close to a warhorse," Angus said sternly.

"But I had something to show you," the old crone stated, smiling toothlessly up at him.

For the first time he realized that she clung desperately to something. She held out a bolt of fabric for his inspection, and he stared uncomprehendingly while she spread the finely woven wool over her arm. The color was a dark, muted shade of green, with thin gold threads woven through it in a crisscross pattern. Though simple in design, it was an elegant piece of cloth.

"I am a simple warrior. I've no need for such richness among my wardrobe."

"Mayhaps not you, but your lady..." replied the woman slyly.

Angus scowled at the old woman. How could she possibly know of Claudia?

"Mayhaps if she had a gown as rich as this, she would not be so quick to run away?" The woman let her eyes slide to where Iona had disappeared, and jerked her head in that direction.

In the excitement Angus had forgotten all about the dancer. He scowled blackly and tried to move away. "Be gone with you."

A gnarled hand reached out to grab the reins. "I am but a humble weaving woman, my lord. Buying my goods is the least you can do to pay for the damage done to me," she whined.

Angus reached for the purse at his belt and threw it at the woman. Two purses lost in two days, he thought with exasperation.

She caught it easily and held out the fabric to him. He snatched it and watched the old crone cackle as she opened the purse to greedily count the contents.

"I do not know which is worse," he muttered, "being robbed while senseless, or being robbed by your beggary."

The old woman looked up with a gleam of avarice in her eyes and grinned. "You have a worthy bargain, my lord. See if your lady does not think so," she called after him as he turned the destrier and trotted down the street.

Angus was in a foul mood as he and his troops thundered down the road on their way to Orgueilleux. He'd not accomplished anything he'd set out to do that afternoon. He hadn't found his uncle at home as he hoped he might, and had returned to his lodgings to find he'd just missed him. Of course, he might have met up with Felix if he'd not wound his way through the streets of Noyon for a time looking for Iona. He was both perplexed and angered by what he'd found.

As he'd gone into a side street near his uncle's lodgings, a crowd obstructed his passage. Disturbed by the murmurs he overheard, he dismounted, and pushed his way through the people gathered in the doorway of a house.

Sunlight streamed across the sparsely furnished room. It may have once looked austere, but was now a shambles. A table was overturned, as was a bench that had sat before the fire. A chair lay in shattered pieces. The bed had been ripped apart, its straw stuffing scattered about. Vibrantly colored clothes lay strewn all over. But the one thing that Angus could not tear his eyes from was the body lying in a crumpled heap upon the floor. Iona's eyes stared upward unseeingly, and he knew from the unnatural angle of her head that her neck was broken.

His attention was drawn to two soldiers in the room. One was trying to keep the crowd back while the other was on one knee by the dancer, examining the body. He looked up from his task and in a weary voice addressed the bystanders. "Does anyone know who she is?"

Angus drew his gaze away from the still form to stare at the man. "She is—was known as Iona."

The soldier sauntered toward Angus, taking in

his well-cut, expensive clothes. "Was she your woman?"

Angus gazed at the soldier in surprise. "My . . . Nay. She was a dancer. The first and only time I saw her was last night during the festivities."

The soldier grunted derisively. "You remember all the entertainers?"

Angus drew himself up. With his face set in hard lines, he replied coldly, "I remember her. Especially after she separated me from my gold."

The tightness of his mouth and the coldness in his green eyes made the soldier study him with interest.

"What happened here?" Angus demanded. "Why would anyone want to kill the woman?"

The soldier continued to eye Angus. If the woman truly meant nothing to this man, why was he so angry? And why did he speak the language with such a strange accent? The soldier saw that Angus was a man of quality, while the woman . . . Besides, it was hard to say what powerful friends the man might have. But he did have a job to do, thankless though it was. "I do not know why," he answered. "Mayhaps she quarreled with a lover, who in his rage strangled her."

Angus's gaze wandered over the destruction in the room. "Nay," he replied slowly. "Whoever did this was searching for something."

The soldier started. He'd assumed that the wreckage had been caused by the woman's struggle for her life, but now he looked around the room as if seeing it for the first time. His gaze wandered back to Angus. "Mayhaps a stolen purse?"

"Are you suggesting," Angus asked in a deadly calm voice, "that I killed her for a mere pittance in gold?"

The soldier shrugged. "You are the only one who was able to identify her. Mayhaps that is not all you know."

"That's preposterous! I am sure there are others here who could have told you who she was." Angus glanced at the crowd standing around them. They all seemed highly entertained by what was going on, but not one of them stepped forward to speak up.

"Mayhaps," the soldier said, "we should question you further."

"Now, just a minute!" Angus cries as the soldier placed a hand on his arm.

"That won't be necessary," an authoritative voice said from the crowd. "He is not the man who did this."

Angus whriled around to find a well-dressed man staring past him at the body.

"You will vouch for this man, my lord?" The soldier asked.

"Aye, that I will. The man you seek was much smaller, with dark hair."

"How do you know that, my lord?" the soldier asked in an awed tone.

"As I was passing by here, I was almost knocked down by the man I have described. He was running from this house."

"That description could fit over half the town," the soldier answered in despair.

"Aye, it could. Except that this man had an unusually large nose. It was hooked, like that of a bird's beak," the stranger explained, running his fingers in an arc over his own nose. "As this man has so aptly pointed out, I would suggest that you make a thorough search of the premises."

The soldier scratched his head and looked from Angus to the stranger with a puzzled frown. "What am I looking for?"

"Money. Jewels. A woman in her profession must have received a number of costly jewels."

The soldier rubbed his chin before turning to his companion. Together the men set about their task.

It was just as Angus had suspected. There was no money or jewels to be found. He was not surprised by that discovery as were the soldiers. What puzzled him was who would have murdered the dancer. After all, her accomplices in robbing him had been killed.

With the completion of the search, the crowd slowly began to disperse. As the stranger started to leave, Angus caught up with him. "Sir, I wish to express my gratitude for your help. I don't know what would have happened if you'd not stepped forward when you did. Permit me to introduce myself. I am Angus McMahon of Orgueilleux."

"Orgueilleux? In Brittany? I thought Orgueilleux was held by Robert Cherveny?"

"Aye, it was," Angus answered slowly. Was this

another of Cherveny's close friends? "I now hold it, as he is dead. I am the husband of Claudia Cherveny."

"Ah, I do remember something about children. So. You are the girl's husband, eh? As I remember, Orgueilleux is located in a key position within the duchy." The man stopped suddenly and shot Angus a strange look. "Cherveny dead, eh?" When Angus made no reply he asked, "Do you think you can hang on to Orgueilleux?"

Angus smiled. "I have every intention of doing so."

The stranger nodded thoughtfully and continued on his way with Angus strolling beside him. "If you should ever need help in doing so, I hope that you will call upon me for assistance. Duke Robert would have relied upon me, as I would him."

"How would I contact you in the event that I should need your assistance?" Angus asked.

"Ah, I beg your pardon. Fulk Nerra," answered the stranger, extending his hand.

Angus was dumbfounded at the man's revelation. None other than the Count of Anjou had come to his rescue!

All these thoughts and more ran through Angus's mind on the long journey home. The closer he came to Orgueilleux, the more feelings of guilt and anger washed over him. Mayhaps he could have saved Iona if he'd not been stopped by the old crone selling her wares, which brought to light another sore spot with him. He wondered in disgust what he was to do with the bolt of rich fabric.

If he weren't so angry with Claudia, he would present it to her upon his return. But then, she didn't deserve it. At least, not yet.

Although the dagger encrusted with precious gems that he'd found at a silversmith would go to Vail, Claudia's gift could wait. It still irritated him that he was out so much money, but that wasn't Vail's fault. The dagger was a peace offering to let the lad know that it wasn't he Angus was angry with. If he hadn't been robbed twice—for he looked upon that old crone's method of bartering as a form of robbery—he would not be in his present quandary.

Deep down he knew he would give Claudia the cloth, but later. Let her wonder what her fate would be.

He resettled himself in the saddle and wondered what awaited him at Orgueilleux. Would Claudia be the submissive, obedient wife, or would she be a termagant? Her face loomed before him with each passing mile. It seemed that she was always with him. It was as though she'd wormed her way into his heart, mind, and soul, to remain there in a little corner of him. Was it to be for all time? Aye. He knew it would be.

He was suddenly jolted with the realization that he loved her, and recalled blurting out his innermost feelings to Owen only that morning. He did love her. But how could he make her see that?

Owen's words flitted through his mind. *She does not trust*. Angus knew it to be true. The image of Claudia, sorrowful, frightened, mistrusting, came to him. Her sad eyes haunted him. Only once had he heard her laughter, and that had been in jest of him, but he had not minded. He'd never known her smile to fall willingly upon him for him alone, yet he'd seen it for others. With him she displayed a firm detachment. It was only when they were alone that he could break through the barrier she placed between them and unveil the fiery passion within her.

Angus realized with a start that his wife had never come to him willingly. He had always taken her. Not that he'd brutally raped her, but nevertheless, it was rape of a kind. She was always stiff at first, until he'd worn down her resistance and she cried out for release from the sweet torment. He knew without a doubt that she wanted him, because he *made* her want him. Yet there was a part of herself that she kept from him. Angus tightened his hold on the reins. That was the part he wanted. Needed. But how was he to attain it?

Owen was right. He couldn't force Claudia to love him. But would she ever? Would time heal her pain? Would she ever share more than just her body? How long would he have to wait before she trusted him enough to share her thoughts and her feelings? What if she never did? Could he bear it?

Patience. That was not one of his best virtues, he thought wryly. Yet he had to be patient and understanding as Owen advised. To demand

Claudia's love would only drive her further away. He urged the destrier on eagerly as the miles lessened and Orgueilleux neared. The steady rhythm of the horse's hooves beat out one word to Angus's ears. Patience. Patience. Patience. He knew he had to try again, but slowly this time. This time Claudia would come to him.

CHAPTER 10

Angus nodded in satisfaction as Orgueilleux came into sight. The men he'd left behind to see to the completion of the stone wall had done well. The four walls now surrounded the castle and all within in safety. There was no fear that Orgueilleux would be taken by surprise and overrun as it once had been.

The drawbridge was lowered and the portcullis raised as soon as Angus's banner was spied from the watchtower. The weary, dust-stained travelers entered the courtyard to the yapping dogs and the greetings of the inhabitants of the fortress. Angus's gaze fixed on the entrance of the castle, then he looked away again in disappointment. Mayhaps Claudia was inside seeing to their comfort. Then again, mayhaps she was cowering in her chamber afraid to face him. Angus spurred his horse toward the stables as boys came running to assist the knights with their steeds. A lone figure leaning against the wall caught his eye, and he walked the destrier to where Vail stood watching the activity, afraid to join in.

Angus studied the boy who nervously twisted the hem of his peasant tunic. At last he spoke. "You stand idly about when there is work to be done?"

Vail swallowed hard, but did not reply as he stared back apprehensively.

"Both my horse and I need attending."

A light of surprise shone in Vail's eyes as he stilled his hands and expelled his breath. "You— you mean I am still your squire?" he stammered.

"What better way is there for you to learn the ways of the warrior? And who has a better right than you?"

Vail's mouth split in a huge grin as he started to move forward. "Yea, my lord."

But Angus stopped him in his tracks as he called out, "Vail. No matter what ideas your sister has put into your head, I am still the lord here."

Vail shrugged. "I never doubted it. I tried to tell Claudia that she was being foolish, but she is so stubborn. In any case, Orgueilleux would not have been mine. It would have gone to Mallory, and I would have had to seek my fortune elsewhere."

Angus nodded in understanding. "As I have had to do," he said softly. He fished inside his baggage and produced a package which he tossed to Vail. "A memento of my journey," he said.

Vail opened the gift, puzzled, and let out a boyish exclamation of joy at the exquisite dagger, thanking his brother-by-marriage profusely.

Angus grinned, then pointed a finger at Vail. "I trust you have other garments more worthy of adorning that fine piece of workmanship."

Vail looked up from inspecting the knife, and blushed. "If—if they've not been destroyed."

"I believe the lad's clothes are in the storeroom," Owen said, joining them.

"Then see to it that they are taken to his room. From here on in you will dress befitting your station, Vail. I'll not let it be said that my family is beggared. Now, I believe you have work to finish."

Vail could not keep the grin from his face as he stared after Angus, who continued on to the stables. His first instincts about Angus had been right. Now, if only Claudia could be made to see that.

Angus entered the great hall and surveyed the bustling activity in preparation of his return. All under the direction of the old woman, Marian. Where the devil was his wife?

He strode forward angrily. "What do you do here?"

Marian lowered her eyes, for to look upon that countenance was surely looking at the devil himself. She took a deep breath and answered unsteadily, "Seeing to your comfort, my lord, as my lady instructed."

"And just where is your lady?" Angus asked, tightlipped.

"Comforting those less fortunate, my lord. She

and the priest, Father Thomas, have been called to attend one of the serfs."

Angus stared at the woman. His wife was seeing to the serfs—again! He wrestled with himself, trying to decide whether to fetch Claudia back to him. At last he swore under his breath and made for his chamber. "See that a bath is readied for me," he threw over his shoulder as he stalked away.

Claudia walked along blindly, the tears silently escaping, hindering her efforts to see. She hated death. Nora had been such a faithful servant. She recalled the woman clutching her hand and calling her Lady Jeanette. No matter how many times she'd reminded the old woman that it was she, Claudia, Nora still saw her mistress from the past. It had served only to bring back memories that Claudia was trying so hard to bury.

She stumbled on the path and felt a steadying hand on her arm.

"My child, do not weep. It was her time," the priest said quietly.

Through her tears Claudia saw the concern in Father Thomas's kindly eyes, and nodded. "I know, but there is none to mourn her but me," she whispered.

They continued into the courtyard in silence and noted the unusual activity. Claudia looked around her, bemused, then spied Owen coming from the storeroom. She let out a dismayed gasp. Angus was back, and she'd not been there to greet him! She hastily wiped the tears away, and excusing herself, ran toward the castle. What must her husband think of her? It was a good thing she'd instructed the servants in their duties should this happen in one of her absences, she thought as she entered the hall. She heaved a small sigh of relief when she saw that Angus was not about, and hurried up the stairs. Mayhaps she had enough time to freshen up before facing him.

Her heart stopped when she opened the door to their chamber. Nervously, she smoothed the wrinkles from the plain brown linen gown she wore, and straightened the veil covering her hair.

Angus turned briefly from the fire then looked back at the rising flames, swirling the wine in his goblet before downing it. His heart pounded against his ribs as her image leapt out at him. Could it be that he'd forgotten how truly beautiful she was? How could he keep his resolve about her? He clamped his mouth shut in a tight line. Somehow he would. He swore it.

Claudia shut the door quietly and stood just within the room. It was obvious Angus was still angry with her and intended to punish her. He'd had plenty of time in which to think of something. She only hoped it would be quick.

"I trust that you had a safe journey, my lord," she said tremulously.

"Were you concerned for my well-being, my lady?" he asked with raised eyebrows.

"Nay—" Claudia could have bitten out her tongue as she stammered, "I—I mean..."

Angus made a face and turned away from her.
"Never mind. I know what you mean," he said
harshly. He picked up his belt from a chair and
put it on, then slipped his dagger into its sheath.
"The men await us below. As long as you are still
mistress here, I would suggest you conduct yourself as such. Make yourself presentable before you
come down to sup, my lady," he ordered as he
stalked to the door.

Claudia scurried out of his way as he left. She'd
not meant for her words to come out that way. It
was just that Angus was so fierce. She knew he
could take care of himself. She discarded the old
gown she wore for a fresh one and tied back her
hair. Her heart drummed a fast rhythm in her
breast. What had he meant, as long as she was still
mistress here. Did he intend to kill her and set his
Dorcas in her stead? She clutched the dressing
table tightly, making her knuckles white, and shook
off the feeling of nausea that gripped her like an
iron band. Nay. Had he not claimed she would
live? Mayhaps he intended to bring his Dorcas
here to flaunt before her.

Claudia's chin jutted out defiantly. Let him. She
was his wife, and mistress of Orgueilleux. That
would not change. If he meant to humiliate her,
let him try. She would hold her head proudly and
show him that it did not matter.

Dinner was a stilted affair as Angus placed different portions of food in his wife's trencher, then
turned from her to carry on his conversation with
Owen. The only bright spot for her was seeing Vail

dressed in his fine garments once more, his hair
neatly combed for a change, happily serving them.

After supper he proudly showed his sister the
dagger Angus had given him, and she dutifully
exclaimed over its beauty, relieved that her brother had been spared the brunt of her husband's
anger. When she asked to be excused because she
was fatigued, Angus stated that it did not please
him and steered her toward a chair by the fire.
There she silently sat embroidering and fuming, as
Angus and Owen played an absorbing game of
chess. Only when Angus felt the need to retire did
he guide her to their chamber.

Nervously clasping and unclasping her hands,
Claudia watched Angus stride to the bed and
begin to undress. She let out the breath she hadn't
realized she'd been holding. "I—I never had a
chance to thank you, my lord," she said hesitantly.

He looked at her bemusedly. "For what?"

"For your kindness toward my brother."

"Why should I not treat Vail with kindness? I
am no longer angry with him."

She glanced down at the floor, digesting his
words. At least she did not have to worry about
Vail anymore. But what of herself? "Thank you for
that, my lord," she murmured.

Angus's lips tightened in anger as he realized
she'd reverted back to calling him "my lord" instead of using his name. Well, if she found calling
him Angus so distasteful, he would not force her
into it. "The hour grows late, Claudia. Get un-

dressed and come to bed," he said gruffly as he stretched out.

Claudia hastily doffed her garments and lay down beside him. She waited tensely for him to reach out and enfold her in his strong arms. But he continued to lie with his back to her. She was unaware of the torment he suffered as he forced himself to remain where he was.

Claudia was suffering a torment of her own. She had to restrain herself from screaming at him to get it over with. If he intended to take her, then why didn't he? Why was he torturing her this way? Making her wonder when he would strike. It was a long time before either of them slept.

The days passed slowly and Claudia grew more puzzled as time went by. Outwardly she remained the calm, self-assured mistress of Orgueilleux, the only sign of her distress showing in the dark circles beneath her eyes. Since Angus's return, life went on as before. With one exception. He'd not touched her.

Claudia didn't know whether to feel relieved or angry. When she was in his presence, she could feel his eyes upon her. She would look up to find those brilliant green orbs consuming her. In the moment their eyes met her heart would pound frantically, before she finally forced herself to look away.

There was one other difference in her husband since his return. He was no longer gentle in his demands. He now commanded her to do his bidding. But he no longer touched her.

Each night she lay abed awaiting for him to reach out to her until at last, through sheer exhaustion, sleep overtook her.

Whenever she caught Angus staring at her in brooding silence, she could swear she saw a combination of pain and passion on his face. But then, she could have been mistaken. One thing she was not mistaken of, however, was the shock of desire that passed through her when they happened to touch accidentally. A jolt of such potent energy flew through her as to render her powerless.

She asked herself over and over what game he was playing. Why had he not beaten her, or starved her, or whipped her? When she dared to ask him why he'd not punished her as yet, he merely replied quietly that he was not angry with her and felt that she deserved no punishment. Yet she could not stem the anxiety that engulfed her. She was afraid to let down her guard for fear that would be the time she would feel her husband's wrath.

For the most part, Angus seemed content to stay away from her as much as possible. He spent his days outside the castle, in the outlying territories, either checking on the patrols he'd set to guard the boundaries or overseeing the work in the fields as the grain ripened and was nearly ready for harvesting. Vail always accompanied her husband, and Claudia wondered at the camaraderie between the two. It was as though nothing amiss had occurred. It was only in her presence that Angus became stilted and withdrawn, with an angry scowl marking his features.

She was glad, for Vail's sake, that her brother and her husband got along, but for herself, she felt a terrible loss. Bereft on a sea of loneliness, as if she didn't belong. She dared not question her feelings. Instead, she pushed them aside and thought of her parents at such times. If it were not for Angus, her father and mother, and Mallory would all still be with her. She refused to look too closely into her heart to find the reason for her discontent, afraid of the answer.

Claudia poked the needle viciously into her embroidery. Anger smoldered within her. The more she went over the scene that morning with Angus, the more uneven her stitches became, but she didn't even notice.

That oaf! That stubborn, pigheaded—barbarian! That's what he was. A barbarian! Foolish. Ignorant. Stubborn. Stubborn, stubborn, stubborn!

He was lord of Orgueilleux. He was master here. His word was law—as he'd pointed out only too well.

She couldn't understand why he had been so furious. In truth, he had no right, she thought, jabbing the needle through the cloth and jumping when it struck her finger. Tears filled her eyes.

She'd not sought to cause an argument when she told him it was she who'd sent the household guard to rout the thieves burning and looting her land. Nay. It was his fault.

Claudia had been in the herb garden when she heard shouts from the wall. She'd run to see the cause for all the excitement and was alarmed to see smoke billowing up several miles in the distance. Trying to keep her fear from showing in her voice, she'd asked Hugo, who'd been left in charge, if he was not going to ride out to see if something could be done about the fire. Hugo stated that Angus would see the smoke and ride there with his men since they were already out patrolling the area. Or mayhaps they were already there.

"And what if he is not?" she asked. "What if he is to the back of the castle, facing the sea? He would never see the fire. He would never know there was trouble."

She ordered Hugo to take the men and ride out. He tried to reason with his lady, but to no avail. Claudia adamantly stood her ground, and with a sigh of resignation, Hugo did as he was told.

Claudia felt totally justified in her actions. After all, it was her land and her people that were being set upon. Did she not have a responsibility to see to it that all was properly cared for? A lonely tear trickled down her cheek. It was not her fault that Angus spent so much time away from home. If he were where he should be, then she would not have had to make such a decision.

She had tried to explain to him that she was only doing her duty for her land and her people, but Angus had not listened. Instead, he'd shouted at her about her lack of responsibility to the castle.

"What if the thieves had doubled back and laid siege to the castle?" he'd asked. "You could have been raped or murdered!"

It seemed that nothing she did pleased him, she thought, brushing away her tears. Well, what did she care? He hated her. Loathed the sight of her. He could no longer stand to touch her as he once had.

Fresh tears started anew as she remembered his hands caressing her. She closed her eyes, and the vision of him kissing her filled her. His mouth, his hands, left her skin burning, her body trembling until he stilled the fires raging through her. But no more.

She moaned and opened her eyes quickly to push those thoughts from her mind. What was wrong with her. She did not want her husband. He was her enemy. And though he insisted he was no longer angry with her, she knew he considered her his enemy also. Where before he'd been kind, now he either ignored her or chastised her.

The fates had indeed been cruel to her, taking away her family and thrusting her into her enemy's hands. Thank God she still had Vail. But even her little brother was on her husband's side. Vail never missed the opportunity to extol Angus's virtues to her.

Before, she had been afraid to fall under Angus's charming spell, fearing she would betray the memory of her loving family. Since his return from

Noyon, she no longer had to worry, for he showed her no charm. She had no more worries that she would succumb to his touch, either, for he no longer touched her.

Thank God she did not love him! If she did, how would she deal with the knowledge that he loved another... and would be seeing her again? She was sure of that since she'd accidentally found the fine green wool hidden in Angus's chest.

She hadn't intended to snoop, but his tunics would not all fit, and she had only meant to straighten up some so that she could put them neatly away. That was when she'd found the luxurious cloth. She knew it was too fine to adorn anyone other than a woman, except mayhaps someone of Felix Perrin's nature. The man was a veritable peacock when it came to clothes. But Angus was no peacock. He cared naught for clothes, only that they be clean.

A pang of jealousy had touched her as she stared at the beautiful fabric. Angus had thought to bring her brother a present, but he'd brought nothing for her. Instead, he'd hidden the green cloth away. That left only one conclusion. It was for Dorcas. Mayhaps, even now he'd sent for his mistress to join him.

Claudia was filled with such hate for them both. How could he humiliate her like that? If there were some way that she could prevent it, she would, but she felt so helpless and alone.

Her troubled thoughts were interrupted as the door to her chamber was flung open with a crash.

She jumped up and turned frightened eyes on the intruder. The fright was replaced by astonishment as Angus, with an arm thrown over Owen's shoulder, was herded into the room and laid gently on the bed.

Claudia hurried to the bed and gasped as Owen cut away the bloody breeches on one of Angus's legs. "What happened?"

"We came upon a band of outlaws," Angus said, "looting the new farms this morning. One hut was burned to the ground, and all were killed before we reached them." He winced as Owen poked at the flesh on his leg.

"Who...?"

Before she could finish the question, Angus looked up into her wide, frightened eyes, and answered, "Raymond and his wife and son." He watched his wife's face drain of color and turned away. He could not bear to look into her confused, questioning eyes. As it was, he blamed himself for not arriving in time.

Claudia noted the pain on her husband's face and pushed Owen aside. She gently examined Angus's wound, but before she could finish, he grabbed her hands to stop her. "Owen will see to me," he said through gritted teeth.

She stared into his hard green eyes and dropped her hands. "As you wish, my lord," she said, turning her back on them. Could he still be angry with her because of this morning? Nay. It was more than that. He could not stand for her to touch him. He truly hated her.

Out of the corner of her eye she watched Owen's clumsy ministrations, and heard Angus cursing the man under his breath. It was obvious that these men knew how to kill and main without difficulty, but they knew nothing of healing. When she could no longer stand to hear Angus's complaints, she pushed Owen aside and in a firm voice told him to get out. Owen was only too willing to leave, ignoring Angus's pleas to stay.

Claudia turned on her husband, snapping, "Stop acting like a babe! This is not going to hurt nearly as much as that clumsy oaf's efforts."

Angus shut his mouth in surprise and lay still while she cleaned his wound and stitched it. Her sweet scent floated up to him as he watched her closely. Claudia was so engrossed in her task that she didn't see the softening of his eyes as he drank in her every detail. She was so lovely, he thought. He was hard pressed to keep his hands off her. God, didn't she know what she did to him?

He was sorry more times than he could count that he'd made his resolution not to touch her. The only way he could stick to his word was by leaving the castle. He was miserable. He wanted her so badly.

He shifted uncomfortably as he thought of her soft body yielding to him, of her creamy white flesh hot against his. He clenched and unclenched his fists and gritted his teeth. His breathing became ragged at the memory of the passion he could unleash in this woman who was his wife. His own passion grew just thinking about the things he'd like to do to her. To make her cry out her need for him. She was so close. All he had to do was reach for her.

Claudia glanced up and saw Angus's white face. The pain in his eyes surprised her. "Do I hurt you, my lord?" she asked with concern.

"Yea. Nay, just get it done," he answered harshly.

She bent to her task once more, trying to be as gentle as she could.

Angus felt her cool hands on his burning flesh, and to him it was as if she were leaving her imprint there. At last she finished and looked at him. She was dismayed to see he still wore the same expression of pain.

"Do you hurt badly, my lord?"

"Yea, Claudia, but it is not a wound of the flesh," he answered raggedly.

She tore her gaze away, only to have it fall on his manhood, which had hardened and bulged beneath the confining breeches. Eyes wide, she looked up to find him still staring at her. Her heart pounded furiously, and she found herself blushing hotly. But she did not move. She felt weighted to the spot by the intensity in his eyes.

Angus reached out one large hand to cup the back of her head. He eased her forward to within inches of his face. She could feel his breath on her cheek, and she tingled with anticipation, her lips parting slightly as his mouth sought hers in a gentle assault. A tiny spark ignited deep within her, waiting to be fanned into the consuming fire they both knew was there.

Angus moaned, and crushed Claudia to him as her tongue tentatively caressed his. He started to undress her slowly so as not to frighten her, and was surprised when he felt her fingers at the lacings of his tunic. His heart leapt with joy. She was as eager for him as he was for her. They divested themselves of their clothes quickly, and he pushed his trembling wife to the bed. He gazed down at her, the fires of passion lighting his eyes as he took in her lithe form from head to toe.

Claudia's breasts heaved in growing excitement. She bit her lip as Angus continued to stare at her. He made no move toward her. What if he didn't want her after all? Nay, she could not believe that as she boldly gazed at his hard male body. Still, he was motionless. They were enemies, a little voice whispered, but she pushed it aside. It did not matter when he looked at her this way. She wanted him. She needed to feel him inside her. She gazed into his face, and when their eyes met, she held out her arms to him.

Angus sucked in his breath sharply. She was inviting him to join her at last. He lay down beside her and kissed her hungrily, at last finding a release for all the passion stored within him for so long. His hands moved in feathery patterns over her body, his mouth following.

Claudia ran her hands over Angus's well-muscled arms. She moaned and arched upward when his mouth covered her breast. Clutching his back, she felt the powerful muscles rippling beneath her fingers, and was amazed that for all of his strength,

Angus could be so gentle with her now. She raked her nails lightly over his back, and felt him shudder under her touch.

Groaning her name, he covered her body with his. He slid into the depths of her easily, glorying in the warmth that engulfed him, welcomed him.

He could love his Dorcas and hate her, she thought, closing her arms around him, but at least he wanted her. And she wanted him. She needed this. This passion that flared from the very core of her, bursting into a raging fire that would be snuffed out ever so slowly, giving her a sense of peace and contentment. Aye, she wanted her husband. If only for a time, she could forget that they were enemies and pretend that there was true love and devotion between them.

She eagerly met him thrust for thrust, reveling in the feel of him, the warmth spreading through her body. She felt as though she were floating outside herself as waves of tingling sensation engulfed her, sucking her into a whirlpool of sensual excitement.

She felt herself spiraling ever higher, losing herself to all but the reality of the moment. At last she cried out as each delicious wave of sweet release washed over her. She knew that Angus joined her and wondered fleetingly if he knew the same unparalleled ecstasy that filled her, before floating back to a languorous peace that left her completely sated.

She sighed as Angus rolled onto his side and pulled her with him, nestling her in his arms. She lay for a time listening to his even breathing. Finally, she looked up into his soft features reposed in sleep and pulled the covers about them more tightly. Then she snuggled closer and closed her eyes.

CHAPTER 11

Claudia hummed a gay little tune under her breath as she sat by the fire in her chamber. Her gown lay in a discarded heap upon the bench in favor of the comfort of her chemise. She pulled the brush through her thick hair, making it crackle with freshness.

Ever since the day Angus had been wounded, she'd known peace. The dark circles beneath her eyes had disappeared, and she'd taken on a healthy glow. Her husband's absences from the castle had become less frequent, and through an unspoken truce, their time together had become tranquil.

Claudia refused to dwell on the reasons for the peace she felt. It was enough that she gave her body to Angus freely, for he gave in return. Any guilt that crept into her when she thought of all she'd lost was quickly pushed aside. Angus wanted her, and she needed him. She tried to distance herself from their time in bed by telling herself it was not Claudia of Orgueilleux in Angus's arms. They were simply a man and a woman with an overpowering, helpless need for each other. Or, sometimes she pretended that Angus truly loved her, and that she cared deeply for him. If she were honest, she would admit that she wished it were so, but Claudia would not allow that notion to steal into her thoughts.

She glanced over to the window where Angus stood looking out on the horizon. One booted foot rested on a stool, and one powerful arm lay casually across his knee as he stared into the distance. She thrilled at the sight of him, relishing the thought that in a little while she would be encircled in those arms.

She pulled the brush lazily through her red-gold tresses as she studied her husband. She felt an overwhelming urge to go to him and push back the lock of hair that the nighttime breeze had teased down onto his forehead. But his pensive expression stopped her, and she frowned. Angus had been awfully quiet ever since they'd entered their chamber. She wondered what he was so earnestly contemplating.

She arose and joined him at the window. Without looking up, he reached out an arm to pull her close. She stiffened at first contact but relaxed against him when he absently kissed her forehead. She was surprised by the naturalness of his act, and even more surprised to find that she liked it.

"You seem troubled, my lord."

Angus peered down at his wife, then out the window once more. "Nay, not troubled. Just deep in thought."

Wondering if it was his Dorcas he thought of, she was overcome with a sense of dread. She tried to pull away, but Angus straightened and pulled her in front of him, pinning her with both his arms.

His lips brushed the top of her head as he mumbled, "I was just thinking of the green rolling hills of Ireland. My home. My family."

Her heart stopped, her worst fears realized. She swallowed, and asked quietly, "And what else?"

Angus rubbed his chin in her soft curls, inhaling her sweet scent. "Ummm. Nothing."

Suddenly Claudia did not want to know. If his thoughts were filled with his love, he would not tell her anyway. "You've not told me about your family."

He gazed down at her once more, puzzled. "Aye, I have."

"Nay, you've not. Only that you have two little brothers close to Vail's age."

He grinned, thinking of his brothers. "That would be Conan and Bevan, and two more mischievous youngsters there are not." A rumble of laughter escaped him. "I hate to think what would happen if those two and Vail ever became acquainted. What one wouldn't think of, the other two would. Our days of peace would be at an end."

Claudia smiled, too, conjuring a picture of three hellions to contend with instead of just one. "You mentioned another brother?" she prodded.

"Aye. Actually there are seven of us. My sisters

are three of the fairest women ever, save you"—he kissed the tip of her nose—"and I've two more brothers. Kevin is a year younger than I and the quiet one. He is the peacemaker in the family. Though he fights when he has to, his heart is not in it. Now that I am so far from home, I fear for his safety. Hugh and I used to watch out for him.

"Hugh is the eldest, and will one day take our father's place as head of the clan."

Claudia noted the lack of animosity in Angus's voice and said as much.

"Why should I be jealous?" Angus asked, shrugging. "It is as it should be. Hugh is firstborn. Besides," he added, grinning, "he would throttle me easily for suggesting it was not his right, and I have no wish to cross swords with Hugh. You think I am a giant, you should see him." His eyes twinkled at the disbelief on Claudia's face.

"Aye, it is true. He stands a head taller than I, and is twice as broad." He laughed as her eyes grew wider in amazement. He squeezed her to him playfully and kissed her. "I am glad that things worked out as they did," he said, his mouth just barely touching hers, sending chills through her. "I have everything I would ever want or need right here."

His mouth pressed firmly against hers. His nimble fingers untied the strings of her chemise and pushed it over her shoulders to drop to the floor.

Claudia shivered and clutched Angus to her as his mouth slid to the base of her throat. All her earlier thoughts fled, replaced by the desire he roused in her. She bent backward in his arms to give him easy access to her as his mouth closed over one soft breast while his fingers played with the other. With his teeth he pulled at the peak then sucked the rosy crest until it hardened to an exquisite sensitivity. His tongue swirled over the tip until the tautness Claudia felt there worked its way to her belly, tying it in knots.

She clung to him, moaning in ecstasy, clawing at his back. She wanted to feel his flesh against hers.

He scooped her up in his arms effortlessly and carried her to the bed. After laying her down he started to move away to take off his clothes, but she pulled him to her. Kneeling on the bed, she lifted his tunic over his head. Her eyes turned a smoky gray as her hands roamed across his broad chest and arms. Her mouth followed, her tongue leaving hot, moist trails across his skin. She undid his breeches and hooked her fingers inside to push them lower. Her mouth moved over his taut stomach, following the way of her hands.

Angus lay very still, astonished by his wife's ardor. He sucked in his breath sharply as her hands and mouth slid lower still. She dropped stinging kisses on his thighs and traced her tongue over his knees while her hands sought to remove his boots and divest him of his breeches.

Claudia sat back on her haunches, her fingers running lightly over his legs, and looked at him. His eyes seemed to be smoldering and his chest rose and fell in a fast rhythm. Her gaze moved lower to his proud shaft, pointing as a beacon to welcome her womanhood.

She suddenly wondered what it would feel like to touch him, to taste his manhood as he'd tasted her womanhood. She ran her hands up his thighs and caressed the area on either side of his shaft. Angus trembled. He moaned and she looked at him in wonder, startled to realize that she had the power over him that he had over her.

She bent forward and took him in her mouth. She felt him shudder, and was overcome by a heady sense of power that she could give him such pleasure. She made swirling patterns with her tongue, stroking and licking, until she heard a low animal growl and was yanked upright.

Angus lifted her onto him, his manhood piercing her to the core, and with his hands on her hips helped her move. She was amazed at what they were doing, but soon became caught up in the rhythm. Tiny licks of flame started at that hot place where they were joined, and built to an uncontrollable blaze.

Angus caressed her body as though worshipping a goddess. He was ever surprised by this woman, ever awed by the passion she gave to him alone. He felt a fierce pride and jealousy of his wife at that moment. She was his. He sensed that they were not yet complete, but someday they would be.

He watched Claudia close her eyes and arch her back. Her hands clutched his shoulders, and she cried out as the red-hot flames of passion that licked at her very soul were extinguished. Angus let himself flow into her, and together they spiraled downward to the earth once more.

Claudia laid down on Angus and nestled her head against his shoulder. Soon their heartbeats slowed to a steady rhythm and they slept.

Claudia felt a haze of sensuous languor enwrapping her. Her womanhood fluttered with a sweet, frightening rapture. She moved lazily with the rhythm of her dream and sighed.

Suddenly her eyes flew open and she found herself looking into green eyes, crinkled in amusement. She gasped and started to sit up, but Angus held her fast. He gyrated beneath her, and the flutters turned to a throbbing sensation that she could not ignore. Her breathing grew ragged as Angus reached up to run his tongue over her breasts. She felt him swell further within her and reveled in the way he filled her.

His mouth captured hers in a kiss that stole her breath. He thrust his tongue into her mouth, and she touched it with her own in response, then raked her teeth over it as he started to withdraw. She was rewarded by his moan as he drew back to stare at her wonderingly.

Claudia pushed herself upright to sit astride him. Her eyes smoldered with passion as she raked her hands over his chest. She was soaring higher and higher to a place outside herself. She moaned with the ecstasy of fulfillment as Angus joined her at the pinnacle of bliss, before they slowly descended to a languid contentment.

She sighed and fell atop him, exhausted. "We fell asleep like this?"

"Aye," he chuckled. "A very pleasant way to go to sleep, is it not? And an even more pleasant way to awaken."

Claudia raised herself up on an elbow to look at him. "Well, now that we are awake, we had best arise before someone comes in search of us," she said wryly. "The sun is already high."

Angus smiled up at her and pushed a strand of damp hair back from her face. "What if they do? We are married."

She gasped. "We cannot be found like this!" she cried incredulously. "A wife does not act so—so..."

"Brazen?" he asked, chuckling.

"Yea. Nay!" she cried exasperatedly, rolling away from him.

His laughter was cut short when a pillow hit him square in the face. Still grinning, he lowered the pillow to peek at his wife, who stood like some wild, untamed thing, glaring at him. His countenance sobered as he placed the pillow on his stomach and took in her slim form. God, how she stirred his blood. Suddenly his eyes twinkled with amusement, and a smile played about his lips. "I did not hear any complaints last night, or this morning when you ravished me."

"I did not ravish you," she sputtered. "You took advantage of me, just as you always do."

Angus arose swiftly and crossed the room to her, shaking his head slowly.

A thrill of excitement shot through her. Her heart pounded furiously as she openly admired his powerful body. He was so big.

"Nay, Claudia. We took advantage of each other. That is as it should be. There is nothing shameful in that." He raised her lowered head to meet his intense gaze. "You give me great pleasure, and I know from your response that I pleasure you. What makes it even better is that we are husband and wife. It is *no one's* business what goes on in this chamber."

Her tongue came out to wet her dry lips. "Well, everyone will certainly know, since the sun is already high. No lord of Orgueilleux has ever slept so late. Our actions will set tongues wagging."

"No lord of Orgueilleux has ever had such a temptress for a wife," Angus countered, grinning from ear to ear.

Claudia turned her back on him and began dressing. "You're impossible. We cannot spend the whole day in bed."

His arms went around her. He parted the front of her chemise and began fondling her breasts, whispering in her ear, "We can if you wish it."

Claudia fought to control her fluttering heart. She whirled about to face him, ready to retort that she did not wish it, but one look at the tenderness in her husband's eyes stopped the words from spilling forth. She pursed her lips and shook her head. "Get dressed," she said softly.

Sighing, Angus dropped his hands and shrugged. "You are cruel to set my soul on fire only to douse me with that cold rationale of yours. Alas, my lady, you are a hard taskmaster, making me provide for you and all within my domain, without the slightest feelings for the passions you've unleashed within me."

She dropped her gown over her head and turned to face him. "What do you call last night and this morning?" she quipped as she brushed past him.

Angus was still chuckling as the door closed behind her. He decided that today was one day that he would stay within the castle.

Hugo ran toward the training field, his breath coming in short gasps. He was no longer as young as he used to be. All this commotion just went to prove that. But Rodney said to fetch Lord Angus, so that's what he would do.

Hugo couldn't understand all the fuss and bother himself, but Rodney said one couldn't be too careful. That's what Owen said, anyway. At least, that's what Rodney claimed. As he closed the distance between himself and the training field, his breath becoming more labored, Hugo thought resentfully that Rodney was just using Owen as an excuse for something he'd made up on his own. If nothing more than to inconvenience him!

"Lord Angus. Lord Angus," called the older man breathlessly.

Angus sheathed his sword and sauntered over to the old warrior to find out what was so urgent.

"Rodney bade me tell you that riders approach, my lord," Hugo wheezed. If anyone was going to get the blame for interrupting Lord Angus, it was not going to be him. "Of course, I told him that it was foolish to disturb you. It is only Duke Felix."

Angus's mouth twitched in amusement. Had Hugo and Rodney turned into a couple of old women? Ever since his return from Noyon, those two had taken to informing him of everyone who came within view of the watchtower, whether they were visitors or not, with a zeal that left him totally perplexed.

He thanked his man and bade him to let Claudia know so that refreshments could be laid out for the guests. He shook his head, still grinning as Hugo puffed his way back to the castle before strolling to the courtyard to greet his uncle.

Felix dismounted and brushed himself free of the dust from the road.

Angus clapped his uncle on the back companionably. "Come inside so that you may rest and quench your thirst," he said, leading Felix toward the castle.

Once he was comfortably settled in the great hall with a cup of wine in his hand, Felix came right to the point. "I need your help once again, nephew."

"In what way may I be of service?"

"It is time that I taught Duke Theo a lesson. The man has been a thorn in my side for years."

Angus smiled wryly. "So you've mentioned in the past. How may I be of help?"

"That knave has raided my lands for the last time. I intend to take his keep," Felix replied heatedly.

Angus leaned back in his chair and frowned. "Why do you tell me this? From what you've said, this feud between you and Duke Theo has been going on for years. It is a personal matter. I've no quarrel with the man."

Felix's eyes narrowed as he sneered. "Does family honor mean nothing to you?"

"Of course it does, but—"

"But nothing! Do not be too sure that you are going to be left alone. You have already lost much with that fire some weeks ago."

"How did you know of that?" Angus asked, startled.

"I was out hunting and saw the smoke. I rode over, but there was nothing left to do by the time I arrived."

"Surely you aren't suggesting—"

"Aye, I am," Felix declared.

Angus shook his head in disbelief. "But why? Why would he do such a thing? The man holds no grudge against me." Even as he spoke, his thoughts were on Duke Theo's warning to him. Had the man decided to plunder his land after all? Had Claudia had a hand in it? Nay. Angus could not believe that.

Felix's mouth twisted in a grimace. "You have the Perrin blood, don't you?"

"I cannot believe that that alone would be enough to do murder of innocent people," Angus said.

Felix held his breath, studying his nephew's face carefully.

At last Angus looked at his uncle and said tersely, "There is only one way to find out if what you say is true. I will confront the gentleman."

"Nay, you cannot!"

"Why?" Angus asked in surprise, taken aback by Felix's vehemence.

"What will you do?" Felix scoffed. "Ride into his stronghold and ask him if he has been raiding your land and setting fire to your serfs' huts? Do you really think that he will tell you the truth? 'Of course, it was I,'" Felix mimicked. The scowl on his face deepened. "More than likely you would find yourself locked up in his dungeon. The man is a liar, a cheat, a thief. Besides, this is the opportunity I've been waiting for to lay waste to his holdings. His lands lie between yours and mine. If I can take his keep, everything from your southern boundary to my northern will be Perrin land."

Angus raised his eyebrows at his uncle's words, but relaxed as Felix amended, "Land belonging to our family."

Angus nodded. Felix was right. He could not simply walk into the man's home and accuse him outright. But he would find the answers he sought. "I will help you," he said thoughtfully. "But only on the condition that we talk to him first. If he cannot prove that he was not behind the raids, then we will fight."

For the next two days Claudia watched with

anguish as Angus supervised the men and the loading of supplies. No matter how much she pleaded with him, he would not change his mind. She realized that theirs would always be a life of discord. The shadow of what he was would forever hang like a dark cloud between them. He was her enemy. He'd come to ravish the land, and she'd given herself to him wantonly. She would never be able to forgive herself.

Claudia was too angry and hurt to allow Angus any access to her when she discovered what his purpose was. She'd run to Marian's room, and when he'd broken down the door in anger because she would not heed his pleas, she'd held a dagger on him to ward him off. And though they'd both known he could disarm her easily enough, he had not. Instead, he'd stormed from the room, telling her in a deadly calm voice to stay out of his way lest he break her in two. Claudia had cried bitter tears in the old woman's arms, vainly seeking comfort.

She'd spent the entire day within the castle and away from her husband, knowing that this was the day he would leave her. After the midday meal she retired to her chamber to sort through Angus's clothes to see what needed mending. She knew Angus was making one last trip around the estate to see that everything was in order, and she hoped to be out of the chamber before he returned, should he chance to come up there.

She had piled several tunics and breeches on the bed when the door opened. She whirled around, her heart stopping. As if her thoughts had conjured him up from nowhere, Angus stood in the doorway.

He paused momentarily before closing the door. A scowl creased his forehead as he approached her. Claudia swallowed hard and backed away.

Angus stopped in mid-stride when he saw her movement. He held out his hands beseechingly. "Claudia, don't make me go this way."

"I bid you stay."

"I cannot. My word is given," he answered firmly.

"Your word!" she shouted. "To destroy. To wreak havoc. To plunder. To kill!"

"Nay!"

"Yea! And for what? To do harm to a man who loves me as his own. A man who has done nothing to you..."

"Are you so sure? There is reason to believe that Duke Theo may be responsible for the attacks on my land."

"Nay, he is not. To what purpose? He does not know you. He knows me, and he would never harm me or mine. That is your uncle speaking.

"My father welcomed both Duke Theo and Duke Felix into his home. He knew of the trouble between them, but he remained neutral. It was not Duke Theo who attacked Orgueilleux."

"Enough!" Angus bellowed, his face a dark mask of fury. "My word is given. I will find the truth."

"Before or after your sword finds Duke Theo's heart?" she asked caustically.

Too late the words were out. Before she knew what was happening, Angus grabbed her and started shaking her until she thought her head would roll from her shoulders.

He is going to kill me, she thought dispassionately. Something in her snapped as she was shaken senseless. She'd already thrown caution to the wind. She began kicking Angus. Striking back. She was a Cherveny. If she was going to lose her life, she would not stand idly by and be a coward.

She fought with all her might, but Angus had her arms pinned behind her back, forcing her body against his. Tears of frustration coursed down her cheeks as she gasped for breath. She leaned listlessly against him, defeated and angry, resentful of his strength and her weakness.

Suddenly his mouth claimed hers in a fierce kiss. She seemed to fall into a black void as his tongue plundered the recesses of her mouth. She felt her knees buckle, then she was floating. Without knowing how it happened, she found herself lying on the bed unclothed. Angus divested himself of his garments. His hands and mouth worked their magic on her, leaving no spot of her flesh untouched. She tried desperately to resist him, but even with his harsh treatment of her, her body betrayed her, crying out to be assuaged of the aching need she had for him.

She felt she was drowning in the rising excitement. Wave after wave of pulsating pleasure washed over her as Angus took her with him to the fiery depths of passion.

They lay panting heavily, each feeling the pounding heartbeat of the other. At last Angus raised himself up to look at her. His hands still pinned her wrists above her head. His desire-filled eyes mirrored what was in hers, and he started to open his mouth, ready to apologize for his rough treatment of her. He stopped when he saw tears start in the corners of her eyes. Unable to bear the pain he saw there, he took her face between his hands and kissed her gently.

"Claudia, my sweet, forgive me. I did not mean to hurt you. You are mine," he declared passionately. "I need to feel you are a part of me. Do not send me away angry."

Her eyes fluttered closed, then opened again to the stored-up tears. "Then do not go," she urged brokenly.

Angus's features darkened with anger. "Do not ask that of me," he snapped, jumping up quickly. He strode to the fire and stared into the glowing coals. He ran his hand through his thick hair before turning around to face her.

All the pain and anguish she felt for what her husband was about to do showed in her eyes. Angus had to arm himself against the look on her face before he went to her. He was a warrior. She was only a woman and did not understand the ways of a man. His mother would not have dreamed of asking his father to remain at home where there was a question of honor or retaining what he'd fought so hard to build. Why couldn't Claudia understand?

"We have been over this subject many times," he said as he began to dress. "Do not meddle in things you know nothing of. My word is given."

Claudia winced at the finality of his words, but said nothing. Angus was her husband. The protector of Orgueilleux. Yet she felt her heart being torn in half. She had to hold herself from him. He was her enemy, this man who could so easily set her soul on fire. It would have been better if he had never come here. Mayhaps he would die in the coming battle.

Tears brimmed in her eyes, and she fought hard to hold them back. It did not matter that they were enemies. She could not wish his death. She could not.

"I came to tell you that we are leaving now," he said. "Will you come downstairs?"

The tears that she'd tried valiantly to hold back escaped down her cheeks as she shook her head in answer.

Angus muttered an oath under his breath and strode to the bed. He pulled Claudia to him so roughly, the covers she'd been clutching to her fell away. His mouth came down on hers hungrily, tasting the sweet nectar of her lips while his hands roamed possessively over her naked body.

"You are mine," he whispered hoarsely. He held her away from him to drink in her beauty one last time. His eyes smoldered with desire as he raked her form. "All I will ever ask of you is to be here, awaiting my return, for my pleasure. Never, never again hold yourself from me, Claudia. You will regret it if you do."

He released her so suddenly that Claudia had to catch herself in order to keep from falling. Then he was gone.

CHAPTER 12

Claudia clutched the covers to her more tightly, as though she were wrapping herself in a cocoon. Her heart felt like a lead weight in her chest. She leaned closer to the window when she caught sight of Angus striding to his horse in the courtyard below.

Thoughts flitted through her mind, one after another. He was really leaving, but then, she had never doubted otherwise. Mayhaps she should have gone below, but it would have been a lie to stand there and bid her husband Godspeed. She should pray. She could not.

The door to her chamber opened quietly, but she did not hear. She felt a presence beside her and knew instinctively that it was Vail, but she did not look at him. Her gaze never left Angus as he shouted orders to his men. The hate she expected to feel for him wasn't there. She was dead inside.

A soft breeze reached her, ruffling some strands of hair. Her eyes burned with unshed tears. She felt as if the earth had opened up to swallow her into the depths of a black pit. She was devoid of all emotion. Was she going mad, or did she yet hate Angus so much that she could feel nothing?

She watched as Felix took his place beside his nephew, and together they led their men from the castle. Her eyes blazed as she stared at her husband's uncle. There was one she could truly hate. What he had convinced Angus to do was wrong, and she hoped that he would meet a swift end at Archibald's hands.

"Angus won't let me go," Vail said.

"What?" Claudia asked distractedly, straining to keep her husband in sight.

"Angus forbade me to go."

Claudia turned to her brother as the last men rode through the gate. She took in the unshed tears of disappointment brimming in Vail's eyes. He looked so forlorn.

"Oh, sweeting," she murmured, placing a comforting arm around his shoulder. She led him to the bed and sat him down beside her. Was this to be her salvation? Was Angus saving her brother the sight of the coming destruction in order to appease her? She felt a great weight lifting from her shoulders, grateful that her husband spared her brother from the coming debacle.

"Tell me what he said," she urged him.

"He ordered me to remain behind. He said that I must protect you and Orgueilleux. He tried to make me believe that that is more important than what he is doing, when in truth he does not want me to be underfoot."

"Now, you know that is not true," she said, hugging him to her. "Has he not taught you a great deal in the past months, and only because you would not rest until you had his word on it," she added teasingly. "Mayhaps he feels you will be the most help here," she amended when a tear escaped Vail's eye.

"But I am his squire. My place is with him. Oh, Claudia, I yearn for my first battle, and Angus is treating me like a babe."

Claudia's heart raced at her brother's words, but she managed to reply calmly, "Angus is your lord. You must not question his orders. Now, take yourself out of here so that I can dress. I'm sure you have some tasks to perform."

She watched as Vail left the room dejectedly, unable to join in his sorrow.

Vail lay in his bed feeling heartily sorry for himself, engulfed by the humiliation at being left behind. He gritted his teeth and clenched and unclenched his small fists. He was not a babe. He was not! How had he failed Angus? What had he done that Angus found it necessary to punish him so?

He went over in his mind all the possibilities for this chastisement, but could not remember anything he'd done wrong. He was a fast learner. Even Angus said so, and he'd seemed very pleased with his progress.

Vail's little chin jutted out. There was only one way to show his lord that he could stand the rigors of battle, but Angus had robbed him of the chance to prove himself. He just knew that if he were with Angus, he could show him how strong and brave he really was. Instead, he'd been restricted to the castle like some old woman. Claudia could take care of things here. He wanted action.

It must be very late, he thought. It'd seemed like hours since he'd bid his sister good night.

Vail slid from the bed and burrowed beneath it to retrieve a knapsack. He crept to the door and opened it quietly to peek out into the corridor. After looking both ways to be certain no one was lurking about, he stepped into the hall and eased the door shut behind him.

He breathed a sigh of relief when he reached the stables without being discovered. He saddled his horse, all the while speaking in a hushed, soothing tone to keep it quiet. Then he led the beast outside, and skirting the walls of the castle, coaxed the animal to the postern door. Vail unhooked the latch and slipped through to the outside, and freedom, keeping a tight hold on the reins.

He would show Angus how courageous he was. He would show everyone.

Angus stepped purposely through the tent flap and regarded his uncle, who was stuffing a large piece of roast chicken into his mouth. Felix looked up, and Angus strode forward to face him. "Uncle, we've not yet finished setting up all the tents, and already there is trouble brewing."

"Eh, what's that you say?" Felix asked between bites.

"A fight broke out between one of your men and one of mine."

Felix shrugged, paying more attention to the drumstick he devoured than to his nephew. "These things happen."

"Nay, they do not. Not where my men are concerned," Angus said, shaking his head grimly. "They know the penalty for fighting among themselves."

"So discipline the man," Felix drawled offhandedly.

"It was your man who instigated the trouble. Might I suggest that he be punished as well?"

Felix threw down the chicken leg and dipped his fingers into a nearby bowl to wash them, annoyed by this turn of events. "I cannot be bothered by every little squabble among the ranks. When this many men are thrown together in such close quarters, fights are bound to break out."

"And if we allow it, how can we expect to have any control over the men during the real fighting?" Angus asked heatedly. "We came here with a common purpose in mind, or so I thought, and I expect a certain code of discipline to be maintained. I will not allow my men to enter into any brawls out of boredom. I will return to Orgueilleux before that happens. I may do that anyway, after what happened today."

Angus turned on his heel to leave, but before he got to the entrance of the tent, Felix was after him like a shot. "Wait!" he cried, running after Angus and putting an arm around his shoulder. "Now, wait, nephew. Do not be too hasty. I think all the men are itching for battle and simply cannot contain themselves."

Angus's eyes glittered in anger. "Is that why your man shot Archibald with that arrow?" he asked scornfully. "I gave my conditions under which I would join you. I expected to talk to Duke Theo first, yet your man flagrantly ignored the flag of truce."

"I explained that to you," Felix said heatedly. "The man thought that someone on the wall was getting ready to shoot you. Would it have satisfied you to have an arrow pierce your heart instead?"

"It almost did," Angus retorted, remembering how he had had to dodge the flurry of arrows from the wall as he retreated to his own troops. "It is a good thing that Archibald's is only a flesh wound. I find the actions of your men reprehensible, and if you have no more control over them than you do, I do not want any of them at my back."

"You are right, of course," Felix said, grabbing Angus's arm when he once again tried to leave. "The men should be punished as an example for all to see so that this does not happen again. I will see to it."

Angus studied his uncle's worried features, puzzled by the sudden outbreak of perspiration on Felix's forehead. It was obvious that Felix was afraid to face his adversary alone and needed his help. Angus struggled with ·his conscience for a moment before muttering, "Very well." He could not throw Felix to the wolves. The man was family.

Felix's face split into a relieved grin. "Come now, let me show you the plans I've worked out for felling our enemy," he said, leading Angus back to the table where charts, that he'd been poring over while he ate, were spread out.

It was very late when Angus reached his tent. After going over the battle strategy for most of the night with Felix, he was ready to collapse in exhaustion. A frown marked his forehead as he pushed aside his tent flap to enter. It was unlike Owen to forget to leave a light burning for him, but he was too tired to be overly concerned about it. All he wanted to feel was the cot at the other end of the tent under him.

He moved forward, removing his sword and sheath as he went, when his foot struck something, and he had to catch himself to keep from tumbling. He heard a pained cry.

"What in blazes..." He fumbled in the dark until he found a candle and lit it. He turned and sucked in his breath at the unexpected sight that greeted him.

Vail sat hunched on the floor of the tent with his arms folded over his head as if to ward off a beating, his eyes squeezed shut.

"What the devil are you doing here?" Angus hollered.

Vail's heart pounded frantically as he raised his head to stare at the demonic giant standing over him. He'd never seen Angus look so fierce. It was enough to make him swoon. Mayhaps it had been a mistake after all to come here. He'd simply not considered the consequences of his wild scheme. Claudia often reprimanded him for his rash actions. Now he was really in for it. He swallowed convulsively, but no sound would come.

Angus reached down and grabbed Vail by the collar, hauling him to his feet. "Answer me, boy. Why are you here?" he growled, shaking Vail as though he were a rat caught tight between a dog's teeth. "Has something happened to Claudia? Is something wrong at Orgueilleux? By God, only the direst catastrophe had better have brought you to me."

"Na-nay, my lord," Vail whispered, frightened out of his wits by Angus's temper. He suddenly found himself flung across the tent to land on the cot in a heap.

"Sit! Now, you had best find your tongue and tell me why you came here against my strict orders to remain behind." Angus stood with his arms akimbo, glowering at his brother-by-marriage.

Vail quaked under the scathing look. "I—I meant no harm," he stuttered, tears of fright filling his eyes. "I wished only to prove to you that I was brave." He dashed the teardrops from his cheeks. "I did not mean to make you angry. I wanted so much to be with you. How can I learn to be courageous if I am left behind to tend the women?"

Vail spoke with such disgust, Angus was hard pressed to keep from laughing. Instead, he turned away abruptly. The lad looked so pitiful, it tore at his heart. He poured himself some wine before looking back at Vail.

"Does Claudia know you are here?"

Vail shook his head slowly.

"You disobeyed me."

"I—I am sorry," Vail answered meekly, hanging his head.

"That is not good enough," Angus said, slamming his cup down on the table. "The first lesson of a good warrior is to follow orders. You have already broken your training with this misconduct."

"What will you do to me?" Vail asked fearfully.

Angus stared hard at the boy and grimaced. "Do not worry. I will think of a suitable punishment."

"Will—will you send me home?"

Angus shrugged and sighed wearily. "You are here now; you may as well stay."

Vail could hardly believe his ears. He'd accomplished his mission after all. He grinned as he scrambled from the cot. "You won't be sorry for your decision," he said, beaming up at Angus.

"Do not be too sure of yourself, young man," Angus answered dryly. "You are going to work very hard. Now, get to bed. It is late."

"Aye, my lord," Vail said, still grinning as he curled up on the bedroll on the floor. He would work, and work, and work. Just so long as Angus kept him at his side.

Claudia strode through the stable door purposefully. Her heart constricted with fear, and she fought hard to control the rising panic that threat-

ened to overtake her. She'd not been able to find
Vail all morning, and all her inquiries as to her
brother's whereabouts received the same negative
answer from everyone. It was unlike Vail to hide
himself away and shirk his duties.

Only moments earlier Hugo had come running
to tell her that the head groomsman, Rolf, had
something of importance to tell her. Claudia walked
between the mostly empty stalls to where the man
stood, shuffling his feet nervously. She was gripped
by a sense of apprehension when she saw the
worried look on Rolf's face.

"My lady," he greeted her timidly, "I heard you
were looking for Lord Vail."

She clutched the man's sleeve hopefully. When
she found that little scamp, she'd flay him. "Do
you know where he is, Rolf?"

"Well, m'lady, I can't say that I do."

"Then why did you wish to see me?"

"I—I thought you should know, his horse is
gone," Rolf said, indicating the stall beside him.

Claudia shifted her gaze to where the man
pointed, and saw the truth of his words. Vail's
horse was indeed gone.

"I did not think it important when I saw, first
thing this morning, that the horse was not in his
stall. You know that Lord Vail sometimes likes to
ride out at first light. But when I heard that you
were searching for him, that he could not be
found . . ." Rolf let his words trail off at the stricken
look on Claudia's face.

"He was not here when you came in?" she

whispered, unable to drag her eyes away from the empty stall.

Rolf shook his head. "Nay, my lady."

Claudia's mind skipped in circles. Where could he be? She knew how upset he'd been at having been left behind by Angus. Was that reason enough to run away? Was he just hiding from her out of spite? Mayhaps he'd gone to the northern lands, but to stay there for so long...

Her mouth in a firm line, she whirled and almost ran out of the stables. "Saddle my horse, Rolf!"

It took Claudia only minutes to round up a small search party, but to her it seemed like hours before they rode through the gate. All the way to their destination she fumed over what she would do to Vail when she found him, alternately thinking up a gruesome punishment for him and praying for his safety.

The serfs on the new farmland had not seen Vail, nor did the little search party find him as they skirted the outlying areas on their way back to the castle. Claudia finally faced the one thought she'd tried so hard to suppress. *Her brother had gone to Angus.*

Dear God, Vail had disobeyed her husband! What would greet him at Angus's hands? Mayhaps he would get the sound beating he deserved.

She shook her head as though to clear it. Somehow she could not believe that. Angus would not harm her brother. No doubt Vail would be punished, but Angus would not hurt him. If that's where he was.

She prayed fervently that Vail had reached Angus safely. Angus would protect him. Claudia's heart lurched suddenly as another thought crept into her mind. But who would protect Angus? Her husband was soon going into battle. She was certain of it, for it was his uncle who had persuaded Angus to join him in his quest to destroy Theo. Claudia knew without a doubt that Felix would not be satisfied with Angus's demands to speak to Theo first. Nay, somehow she knew Felix would contrive to attack first. She just hoped that Angus would be able to fulfill his promise before Felix could carry out his scheme, as he had with her father. And knowing that Vail had thrust himself into the middle of all the trouble alarmed her. Now she not only had Angus to worry about, but Vail as well.

She was shocked by that thought. The idea of actually being worried about Angus had never crossed her mind before, but it was true. She was worried for his safety. So many things could happen. She could very easily lose both her husband and her brother in one moment, and she was suddenly seized by such panic that she felt physically ill.

Hugo grabbed her as she swayed in the saddle. "My lady, are you all right?" he asked, a frown of concern creasing his forehead.

She could only nod in answer.

"Mayhaps you should ride with me," he offered.

She shook her head resolutely and tightened her hold on the reins. "I am fine. Orgueilleux is in sight."

A disheartened group rode through the gate and into the courtyard. Claudia shut her mind to all the shouts coming from the watchtower. Only when she heard a gleeful yelp at her side did she jump to awareness. She turned frightened eyes on Hugo, who was grinning from ear to ear.

"My lady, Lord Vail is safe!" he shouted in her ear.

"How..."

"A messenger is within."

She leapt from her mount and fairly ran into the castle.

A young boy, not much older than Vail, sat at a lower table. His head rested on his arms. He was fast asleep.

Claudia tentatively approached him, and as she reached out to touch his shoulder, the boy was on his feet instantly.

He stared at her with wide, frightened eyes. "I—I was only resting," he stammered.

She smiled to put his fears to rest. "It is all right. You have a message?"

"You are the lady Claudia?" he asked distrustfully.

She inclined her head. "I am."

"Lord Angus bade me tell you not to worry about your brother. He is safe with him."

Claudia's face showed her relief. "Was there nothing more?" she asked.

The boy shuffled his feet uncomfortably. There

was another part to the message. If he could just remember it. He scrunched up his face, thinking hard. He would be beaten if he could not remember, but he could not. "Nay," he answered slowly.

Claudia's face fell in disappointment. Angus had not thought to send word as to how he was. She had to know.

"How does my husband fare?" she asked quietly.

The boy's face suddenly brightened. "That is it! Lord Angus is well, and the fighting has not started," he stated proudly, grinning hugely at his accomplishment.

Claudia blinked disbelievingly and just stared at the boy. He was not one of Angus's.

The grin left the boy's face at the lady's serious countenance, and he shuffled his feet, now completely unsure of himself. He was sure that he'd remembered it correctly. Why was she looking at him so strangely? He was going to be beaten. He knew it.

Claudia saw the mistrust in the boy's eyes. If he was not from Angus, then who sent him? "How is it that you know my husband?" she asked.

Did he dare tell the truth, or would he be punished for it?

"Can you describe Lord Angus?" she asked suddenly.

The boy looked at her as if she'd gone mad. Of course he could describe his savior. That was easy. His face lit in a quick grin. "He is tall, taller and broader than a giant even, and he has hair the color of fire."

Claudia smiled wryly at the boy's assessment of her husband. "Aye, that is Angus. But, I am sorry, I do not remember you as a member of this household."

"Oh, I am not. Th-that is, Lord Angus said I could be if you would find a place for me."

Claudia's brows rose in surprise. Angus was now sending home stray boys to her? "What is your name?"

"Leon."

"Have you eaten, Leon?"

The boy shook his head, and Claudia took his shoulder and pushed him down on the bench.

While the boy ate, Claudia coaxed him to tell her of his acquaintance with Angus, and how he'd come to be sent to her. As Leon's tale unfolded, her anger flared at the cruel treatment the boy had undergone.

He'd been little more than a slave under Duke Felix's rule. The butt of many jokes by the men and brutally punished for his slowness.

Angus had come upon the boy in the camp when one of Felix's men, in a drunken rage, threw a bowl of scalding soup on the cowering Leon for no apparent reason, then started kicking the boy. Angus was so outraged at the mistreatment, he beat the man senseless. Then he took the boy to Felix, thinking his uncle could protect the lad. But Felix wasn't interested. Instead, he told Angus to take the boy off his hands. He'd yet to give Angus and his bride a wedding gift. Leon was it.

The boy beamed at Claudia, thinking of his

importance at being bestowed as a gift to such a
great lord and such a kind lady. He knew he would
like it here. The food he wolfed down was not only
delicious, it was plentiful as well.

Claudia was appalled at the treatment meted
out to Leon, and grateful to her husband for
rescuing the lad. "You need have no fear of being
beaten, Leon," she assured him. "As long as you
work hard and are honest, you will be treated
kindly."

He nodded solemnly. He believed the lady.
After all, had not Lord Angus rescued him from
hell?

The days flew by quickly as Claudia oversaw the
cleaning of the castle for the coming winter. Walls
were scrubbed free of accumulated grime. Old
rushes were swept up, and the floors, too, were
scrubbed before new rushes were laid upon them.
Storage bins were filled to capacity with the serfs'
labors in the fields.

Claudia silently thanked her husband for sending Leon to her. The boy was truly a godsend, for
he worked hard and uncomplainingly at any small
task she set him to.

Leon worked willingly because he quickly learned
that to do so brought praise instead of harsh
words, and he realized that as long as he did so,
no beatings would come his way.

The atmosphere at Orgueilleux was one of light-
hearted industriousness. Claudia went about her
daily tasks humming under her breath, more often

than not with a ready greeting and a smile upon her lips. And because of the mistress's high good spirits, the servants found themselves smiling for no apparent reason. The air at Orgueilleux was once again as it had been under Duke Robert's rule.

Claudia attributed the change in herself to the stark realization that she loved her husband. It had been a shock to learn that what she felt for Angus went deeper than the shameful lust she'd first thought was all they shared. When she worried for her brother, Angus's face came to mind, and she found herself worrying over his welfare also. She was unable to separate the two, until Angus became uppermost in her mind. Once she looked into her heart and was able to admit her true feelings, it was as though the chains of suppression that had imprisoned her for so long fell away, freeing her. Now she eagerly awaited Angus's return, praying for his safety as well as for Vail's, and hoping that once they were together again she could show Angus what she had discovered.

Claudia was too busy with the running of the castle, for she wanted everything to be in order upon Angus's return, and too worried about her husband to have much concern for her own welfare. But there were many mornings when she awakened to a queasiness in her stomach. If she moved too fast, she had to make a headlong dash to the chamber pot in the corner of the room, where she heaved out her insides. She ignored the nausea that overtook her, putting it down to her distress for her loved ones, for it passed quickly once she was dressed and involved in the everyday household chores.

After one particularly grueling morning spent in her chamber, she descended to the hall late to sit at the table. She sat at the table, her face white, her hands clasped tightly in her lap. Marian placed her breakfast before her, glancing at her mistress questioningly. The smell of the food sickened Claudia further as she fought to control her cavorting stomach. She finally lost the battle and jumped to her feet, knocking over the bench in her haste to leave the hall.

She was standing over the chamber pot once again when Marian rushed into the room to aid her. Marian held a cool wet cloth to her forehead and clucked soothingly.

"Do not fight it, love. 'Tis the way. Just let it run its course."

Claudia's stomach ached and her throat burned. When at last she was quiet, Marian led her to the bed and gently pushed her down. "How long has the sickness been upon you?" she asked.

"Since Angus left. It will pass," she said weakly, trying to rise.

Marian placed a firm hand on Claudia's shoulder to hold her down. "Aye, it will pass, but you should have told me right away. You have been doing too much heavy work around here that should have been left for others. You don't want to hurt the child."

Claudia turned her head away and sighed. "I

did not wish to worry y—" Suddenly the import of Marian's last statement hit her and she turned wide-eyed to stare at the woman. "Child?"

"Of course. What did you think?"

"But I—I did not...I mean, I never even thought. I have been so worried about Angus and Vail, and I assumed it was affecting me physically."

Marian quirked an eyebrow. "Your worries do not help your condition, but you are stronger than that. You have never been one to swoon at the slightest provocation."

"Angus going into battle is not the slightest provocation," Claudia said hotly.

"Nay, I suppose it is not," Marian answered, "but now that you know the reason for your illness, you must take care. Lord Angus is strong as a bull; you need not worry about him. You just worry about you so that you can present your husband with a strong, healthy babe."

Claudia's hands caressed her belly protectively where a new life had been formed. Her eyes became frightened as she asked, "But what if something happens to Angus?"

"It will not. He will return, and he will not take it kindly if something happens to you or to his child. So, the first order of business is to see that you are well tended, and you will start by leaving the heavy tasks for others. It is my duty to see that you do as you are told."

A tiny smile played at the corners of Claudia's mouth as she gazed at the stern countenance of her old and trusted servant. It seemed that Marian had every intention of doing as she said. At last there would be another babe for her to coddle.

When Marian saw she would receive no resistance, she said, "Now, you lie abed until I bring you something to settle your stomach."

Claudia lay in bed smiling to herself after Marian left the room. A babe. Angus's child. She was awed that their love had formed a new life.

She suddenly frowned. Love? Aye, it was love on her part, but she'd only just discovered that. She had been too full of pride, too stubborn to realize it before. But what of Angus? He had never said he loved her.

But she was his wife. She was going to have his child. That would be a tie that bound them together no matter what. She had to let go of her pride. She had to tell Angus that she loved him. Mayhaps he would laugh at her and scorn her, but she would take that chance. She would fight for her husband with every fiber of her being.

CHAPTER 13

Angus rode around the outside walls of Archibald's castle on his great black steed, inspecting the progress of the men in their attempts to gain access to the inside. He kept as close to the walls as he could without impeding their work, but not so far away as to allow a stray arrow from above cut him down. He'd been heartily discouraged by the defense that Duke Theo dealt them and was beginning to think that the effort to take Monticule was not worth the price they were paying.

Secretly there were times during this two-week siege when Angus thought of going home, but he'd never been one to run from a fight, even if it was a fight his uncle had instigated. He blamed Felix for starting this whole thing. And he blamed Archibald for letting Felix push him to this point instead of listening to reason. But every time Angus had sent a message to Theo to talk, he'd been spurned. Mayhaps Felix was right. Archibald's adamant refusal to sit down and talk face-to-face made Angus wonder if the man wasn't the one behind the attacks on his land. He most certainly intended to find out.

His mouth was set in a grim line of determination as he surveyed the men digging a tunnel along the west wall. He rode on and watched the strongest attack taking place at the east wall, where men were using ladders to climb to the top of the broad stone wall, only to be pushed back to try again. At the huge wooden doors of the stockade, troops used battering rams to gain entrance—to no avail.

No castle could be as impregnable as this one.

Angus scanned the north wall above him. It was the back of the stronghold, and it seemed to him that the least amount of manpower had been retained there. An idea formed in his head and he rode furiously away to find his uncle.

He and Felix were discussing the merit of starting a series of small fires along the east and south walls to draw the attention of Archibald's soldiers when Owen entered the tent.

"My lord, there is a messenger..."

As Angus and Felix straightened, a man burst into the tent and saluted them. "I come from my lord Fulk Nerra, Count of Anjou, who demands your presence immediately."

"The Count of Anjou? I've never met the man," Felix stated, puzzled.

Angus threw down the stick he'd been using as a pointer on the map spread out on a table before him. "I have," he replied in a matter-of-fact tone. He placed a hand on Felix's shoulder. "Uncle, I think it would be wise to hold off on an attack until I return."

"My lord wishes to see both of you."

Felix and Angus exchanged glances. "Very well," Angus replied. "I will leave Owen in charge. He will see to it that the troops remain in control," he added, staring meaningfully at Felix. He turned to the messenger. "I will get some provisions for the trip and then we will be on our way."

"That won't be necessary, my lord. The count is only a few miles from here with his house guard." At the startled expression on Angus's face, the man added, "We shouldn't be too long."

A guard on each side of the entrance to the count's tent held back the flaps as Angus and Felix were ushered inside. There were several men in the tent, but only one that Angus recognized.

Fulk Nerra glanced up as his guests entered. "Ah, Angus McMahon of Orgueilleux. We meet again. And this must be Felix Perrin of Talus," he said, remaining seated.

"I am honored that you have heard of me, my lord," Felix replied, flattered that he had come to the attention of such a powerful man. This was indeed a good omen.

The count's smile did not reach his eyes as he answered. "I am well acquainted with what goes on in Brittany, as I have many interests here." Nerra's attention turned back to Angus. "So, what is the reason for the attack upon one of your neighbors, Angus of Orgueilleux?"

"There is reason to believe that the man has been attacking Orgueilleux, my lord."

"What's this you say? Why would Theo Archibald have cause to do such a thing unless he was provoked?"

"There was no provocation on my part, my lord," Angus said stiffly.

"Theo Archibald is one of the most peaceable men I know. I have had the fortune of calling him friend for many years. He is a master at words, not war."

"That may be true, my lord, but Orgueilleux is a rich estate and I have suffered great losses since it came into my hands."

"Since it came to you through a siege that you instigated."

"Only because my uncle, here, said that his land was attacked by Robert Cherveny."

The count's gaze wandered back to Felix. A long moment of silence passed before he murmured, "I see. What proof do you have of Archibald's attacks?"

"None, directly," Angus answered, irritated by this examination. "However, he did enter my castle in subterfuge to meet with my wife without my knowledge—"

Felix broke in. "And when we approached Monticule with a flag of truce, my lord, he set his troops upon us."

"He attacked you?" Nerra asked in surprise.

"Yea, my lord, he did."

The Count of Anjou leaned back in his chair. After a pause he said, "It is not normally my practice to interfere in the disputes of others. However, in this case I find that I will have to. Angus of Orgueilleux, did you mean what you said in Noyon about coming to my aid should I need you?"

"Yea, my lord, I did."

"Then I must ask that you put aside your own quarrel with Theo Archibald for the moment and help me. The Count of Rennes has attacked Nantes, and Eudes of Blois has gone to his assistance. I find that I must stop them, and I need you to join me."

"I gave you my word of honor in Noyon, my lord. I will accompany you," Angus replied without hesitating. "Uncle?"

Felix looked from his nephew to the Count of Anjou. "I will fight."

Nerra smiled and stood. "Good. I will let you return to your homes so you can make the arrangements that are necessary in order to join me. Can you make it to Redon three days from now?"

"With a lot of hard riding, my lord," Felix said.

"Excellent." As Angus and Felix turned to leave, the count stopped them. "There is one other matter. I am asking Duke Theo to join us also. If you feel that you cannot suppress your desire for revenge against the wrong that you feel has been done to you by this man, Angus or Orgueilleux, tell me now."

"My lord, I have given you the word of a McMahon. My own grievances shall be put aside— for now."

The count nodded. "Very well."

* * *

Claudia sang softly as she strolled through the castle, inspecting the work that had been done. She was supervising the hanging of one of the tapestries that had been removed to air when Hugo burst into the hall to inform her that Angus was approaching. She hurriedly put the servants to work getting water heated for his bath and food prepared, and rushed up the stairs to her chamber to change from her coarse brown woolen garb into something more presentable. Angus hated the gown she chose to wear when there was heavy work to be done, telling her that he had trouble distinguishing her from the rest of the serfs. Claudia knew he was teasing her, but with her newfound discovery that she loved Angus, she wanted desperately to please him.

The two weeks that Angus had been gone had stretched into an endless abyss of time for Claudia, and the waiting had been unendurable. Now, at last, she could find out if her feelings would remain steadfast in the face of what Angus had to tell her. Running down the stairs to greet her husband, she fervently prayed that Theo was safe and well.

Standing just outside the huge oaken doors of the castle, Claudia watched her husband ride through the gate. He immediately started bellowing orders to the men to get supply carts loaded, and her heart plummeted. So, it was not over.

She had to force herself to remain where she was as Angus rode toward her and dismounted.

She hardly noticed Vail take the horse's reins and run off to the stable after shouting a greeting to her.

Angus mounted the stairs, removing his helmet. He halted on the step below Claudia and smiled tiredly at her. The smile slowly left his face when he saw her icy expression. He grunted. "So, you are still angry with me?"

"What did you expect when you come back here to arm yourself for a full-scale war with a man who has been like a father to me?"

"If you had bothered to welcome me as a proper wife should instead of throwing accusations at me, you might have found that it is not Archibald that I go to fight," Angus threw at her on his way inside.

Through Claudia's anger, Angus's words penetrated her mind. She whirled around to run after him. Reaching him just as he placed a booted foot on the first step of the winding stair, she grabbed his arm to stop him. "Uncle Theo is all right?" she asked, hardly daring to breathe.

Angus caught the anxious note in her voice and replied softly, "Aye, he is well."

"What happened?"

"He was saved."

"What? I do not understand."

"We laid siege to Monticule and almost had it within our grasp when the Count of Anjou intervened."

"The Count of Anjou," she breathed. "You are going to fight the Count of Anjou?"

Angus laughed at the mixture of puzzlement and fear on his wife's face. "Nay, my little pigeon, not fight him. I am going to fight *with* him."

She shook her head. "I do not understand."

"The count has asked Felix and me to join him in his fight against the Count of Rennes and the Count of Blois at Nantes. That is why I must get the men and supplies ready. We are to meet him in three days at Redon."

"Three days!"

"Aye, I must leave immediately."

"Can you not even stay the night?"

At the forlorn expression on her face, Angus drew her to him and kissed her tenderly. "Nay, my sweet. We must hurry."

"How long will you be gone?"

"I do not know."

Nestled in his arms, she whispered, "Angus, be careful.'

In answer, Angus buried his face in her sweetly scented hair and crushed her to him.

The days passed into weeks, and the weeks into one month, then two as Claudia anxiously awaited word from her husband. Marian kept an eye on Claudia like a faithful watchdog, smothering her with attention until she felt she would scream. She wasn't allowed to lift anything heavier than her stitchery, and any time she protested, Marian answered pertly that she was not going to be the one left behind to explain to Lord Angus should something happen to his wife. Besides, Claudia had enough sewing to do before the babe was born if she expected to clothe the poor wee thing.

Claudia just smiled and shook her head in resignation. The other servants picked up their cues from Marian, and Claudia found that all she had to do was indicate a fondness for something, and it would appear as if by magic. The only respite she got from all the pampering was when she took her daily stroll. She faithfully went to the wall every afternoon—even, much to the horror of the men-at-arms, when she became ungainly—and stared across the vast expanse of land, hoping for a sign of Angus's return.

One day after Angus had been gone for more than two months, she made her way to the stairs, ready to take up her vigil, when Rodney let out an excited shout from the watchtower.

Claudia paused in her climb as men took up their positions, then hurried the rest of the way up to peer over the edge of the wall at the lone rider approaching. Her heart beat frantically for a moment before she cried out in despair. The rider wore no colors recognizable to her.

"My lady, please go back to the hall."

Claudia turned snapping eyes on Norbert, Angus's master-at-arms, who'd been left in charge of the defense of the castle in his absence. She opened her mouth to retort sharply that even in her condition she could probably take care of one attacker. But when she saw the concern on Norbert's face, she gritted her teeth and left. Everyone treated *her* like the babe!

She stormed into the hall, whipping off her heavy mantle, for winter had come to the land. Stalking to her chair by the fire, she picked up the tiny nightdress she'd been working on and resumed her task irritably. It wasn't long before Norbert came running to tell her that the rider was a messenger.

"From Angus?" she asked breathlessly.

"Nay, my lady. It is my little brother Harlan, come from Lord Duncan in Erin," Norbert answered, beckoning the messenger forward.

Claudia stared at the stranger uncomprehendingly. "You come from Angus's home?"

"Aye, my lady," Harlan said, bowing at the waist.

"Your message must indeed be urgent if you've traveled so far. But I am afraid that my husband is not here."

"Norbert told me. If I have your leave, my lady, I will remain here until Lord Angus returns. I have orders not to depart from Brittany until I have spoken with him, but I would like to visit with my brother as well. With your permission, of course."

"Of course, you are welcome. I trust that all is well in Erin."

"Aye, it was when I left, but if I do not deliver the message entrusted to me, the lady Dorcas will flay me alive and feed me to the dogs."

Claudia's face went white at the mention of that one's name, and she strangled out in a bare whisper, "Who?"

"The lady Dorcas, and I dare not leave here

without imparting her message . . ." Harlan's words trailed off as he watched Claudia grip the arms of her chair and arise unsteadily. "My lady, are you ill?" he asked in alarm, reaching out to steady her.

"Nay," she whispered. "The servants will see to your needs. I—if you will excuse me." With halting steps she ascended the stairs to her chamber.

She stood leaning against the door, her eyes squeezed tightly shut to hold back the tears that threatened to spill forth. So, it had started. Was she never to be free of Angus's true love? Would the shadow of Dorcas always stand between them? What message could be of such import that the woman had to seek out Angus clear across the sea? Was she on her way to join him?

Claudia's heart pounded in her chest. What was to become of her? Her hands flew to her softly swelling belly. What would become of this child? She loved Angus. For their sakes, Angus's and hers, and the babe's, she somehow had to win her husband's love.

Angus leaned back against the tree trunk and watched Vail clean his sword. It felt good to relax for a while, and Angus had every intention of taking advantage of the few moments rest he was allotted.

In the six months since he'd joined Fulk Nerra, as winter raged across the land, he had been in one battle after another all across the countryside. They'd started out in Nantes, managing to scatter the Count of Blois's forces before he could come to the aid of Rennes, but were unable to save Guerech, Count of Nantes, from assassination. Since that time, Nerra had been bent on routing the enemy with a vengeance, and had spent his time in protecting not only Nantes, but his own province of Anjou as well.

Angus was tired. He missed Claudia and wanted to go home, but his conscience would not allow him to leave in the middle of a fight.

Now they were on the Count of Blois's doorstep and tomorrow would try to do what damage they could to the town.

"Is this all right, Angus?"

Angus looked over to where Vail sat holding up the sword for inspection. Angus smiled at the expectant look on the boy's face. "Aye, Vail, that is just fine. You'd better get something to eat now, then turn in early. I will have to leave at first light and you must assist me." He watched Vail scamper off, thinking that the boy would be spared from tomorrow's fighting. Angus was thankful for that. He would leave Colin behind with Vail. If anything should happen to him in the coming battle, Colin had orders to return Vail to the safety of Orgueilleux and his sister's arms.

Angus's sword slashed left and right as he cut a path through the throng of fighting men, striking down any who opposed him. They had breached the Count of Blois's defenses and were now battling through the town. He heard someone shout his name and turned to see Owen running toward

him. Out of the corner of his eye he saw the flash
of steel and turned to ward off the blow, but
slipped in a pool of blood and stumbled to his
knees. He let himself fall and rolled away as the
sword struck harmlessly the spot where his head
had been only seconds earlier. He heard a scream
and watched his assailant tumble to the ground.
Owen helped Angus to his feet, a grim expression
on his face, then turned away to cut through
another enemy.

For the next hour Angus was busy struggling to
hold on to his life. When he spotted Archibald
pinned down in the entrance to an alley, he fought
desperately to reach the man. He would protect
Archibald himself if that was the only means he
had to find the answers he sought. His arms ached
from wielding his sword and shield. Perspiration
dripped from his forehead into his eyes, almost
blinding him.

At last he reached the alley and looked around
frantically. His breath caught in his throat as he
saw Felix engaged in a fierce battle with Archibald.
Angus fought like a madman to reach his uncle's
side, cutting down anyone who opposed him. There
were too many questions that had to be answered,
and Angus was determined to talk to Theo first.
His uncle had promised him as much.

He felt as though he were in a slow-moving
dream as he watched Felix at the advantage, back-
ing Archibald toward the stables, slashing at his
opponent in a frenzy. A bellow of rage rent the air.
Unaware that the sound had come from him,

Angus watched the point of Felix's sword rip Archibald's abdomen open. The man's glazed eyes stared at his longtime enemy as Felix laughed demonically. The sword fell from Theo's hands, and he clutched his stomach as if to staunch the flow of blood gushing forth, then he fell to the ground dead.

Angus ran forward and whirled a still-grinning Felix around to face him. "Why—when you promised to let me talk to him!" he shouted, livid with rage.

Felix calmly pried his nephew's fingers from his arm. "I never promised him to you," he said coldly. "Besides, he has had that coming for a very long time. What matters if it happens here or at Monticule? I have attained what I set out to do."

Angus's chest heaved in anger as he glared after his uncle sauntering casually away. But I haven't, he thought bitterly.

Claudia sat before the hearth in her chamber, staring into the depths of the flames. In the four months that Harlan, the messenger sent by Dorcas, had been there, she had not been able to pry from him the nature of his message for Angus. Even the servants, with their knack for gossip, could not find out anything. The man was tight-lipped, and totally loyal to his lady.

What was to happen to her and her child, Claudia wondered for the hundredth time. Would Angus's paramour always stand between her and her husband? Was the woman on her way even now to join Angus? The questions kept running round and round in her head.

Claudia's heart felt like a dead weight in her chest. How could she stand aside when she'd so newly discovered her love for Angus? A little voice nagged at her that Angus did not love her. He had never said that he did. Would she never be able to win his love?

It seemed that he'd been gone for ages. She had received only one message from him in all these months, and that had been a terse note telling her that he was well and did not know when he would be home. He'd not said that he missed her. If only he would come home so that she could look upon him. If she could just see him, mayhaps...

There was a knock at the door. Marian burst into the room. "Rodney bade me tell you that Lord Angus is on his way. Come, I will help you change," she said, choosing a fresh gown.

Claudia didn't move from where she sat, staring at Marian uncomprehendingly.

"Well, come, child, you don't want to greet your husband in that old thing, do you?" Marian asked distastefully, indicating the faded russet gown Claudia wore.

"Angus is really here?" Claudia asked breathlessly.

"Aye, that he is, and you must prepare yourself."

Claudia needed no more urging, and she hurriedly donned the blue gown of soft wool that Marian held out to her. She ran a brush through her curly locks before donning her veil, then she fairly flew out of the room as fast as her condition allowed her.

By the time she reached the stairs, she could hear the men entering the hall. She stopped and stared at her husband, surrounded by those left behind as they questioned him eagerly about his battles. She took in his form hungrily. He was bigger than life, and more handsome than she remembered.

Smiling, as he answered one of Hugo's questions, Angus raised his head, and his eyes locked with hers. His breath caught and his mouth dropped open at the sight of her. He ignored all those around him and climbed the stairs to where Claudia stood, his eyes never leaving hers. He lowered his gaze to her round belly and reached out tentatively to touch her there. Then he raised his eyes to look at her wonderingly, and his face split into a huge grin.

Claudia thought her heart would stop at the joyous expression on his face. She was so close, she could see the laugh lines crinkling his eyes, and her own reflection in the depths of his emerald eyes. Without speaking he lifted her in his strong arms and carried her up the stairs.

They passed Marian on the way to their chamber, but neither one saw her. Angus kicked the door shut behind him without releasing his hold on Claudia. Then his mouth devoured hers hungrily, showing her his aching need for what he'd missed so terribly in the past months. He lifted his head to look at her and smiled.

She smiled back timidly. "Mayhaps you should put me down, my lord. I must be very heavy," she murmured shyly.

His grin widened, deepening the dimple in his left cheek. He wondered how the beautiful creature in his arms could possibly think that. She weighed no more than a tiny little pigeon. "Nay. A child," he stated wonderingly. "My child. My son!" he cried joyously, whirling Claudia around. He stopped abruptly and asked with concern, "I did not hurt you, did I?"

She smiled and shook her head.

Angus suddenly sobered as memories flooded back to him of Claudia's outburst about bearing his child. She'd not wanted any part of it. Would she hate him now for all time?

Claudia's heart skipped a beat as she watched the change of expression on her husband's face. Mayhaps he did not want her to have his child after all. The thought flashed through her mind that he might prefer his Dorcas to give him a son instead, and then another thought replaced that. What if she already had? What if that were the reason for the messenger she'd sent? Claudia's eyes darkened in anger at the idea that Angus's mistress should always come between them.

She was his wife. She was going to have his child. And someday his love, she thought determinedly.

Angus caught the glint of fire in his wife's eyes. She was angry, but it was too late. But . . . What if she took her anger out on the child? He suppressed the thought quickly. Surely she would not go that far, no matter how much she hated him. She seemed in good health now, but it wouldn't hurt to keep a close eye on her.

He wondered irritably why she hadn't told him and asked aloud, "Why did you not let me know?"

"Why should I have?"

"Why? Why indeed! You are with child," he sputtered. "I should have been informed."

She laughed. "I do not see why. You could not have changed the situation." At the scowl on his face, she lowered her eyes. "I—I did not know until after you'd left for Monticule and when you returned, I decided not to tell you. You wouldn't have stayed anyway, and I feared you would only worry needlessly. I thought you would return to see me at some time, but when you did not come, I expected you would be here any day. It would have been silly for me to send a message and worry you over nothing."

"Nothing? You call my child nothing?" he asked incredulously, setting her on her feet.

"I did not mean that. I meant only that I am not ill; I am merely with child. I am in good health, my lord."

"Aye, you look well, and I intend to see that you remain so." He frowned. "Shouldn't you be in bed or something?"

She laughed again and shook her head. "Nay, I should not, and if you try to pamper me any more than the servants have, I swear I shall scream."

Relief flooded Angus at her words. Apparently

she had been well taken care of in his absence, and she did not seem upset now.

She raised her arms to help him divest himself of his armor, but he stopped her when her hands grazed his chest. He didn't think he could bear having her so close and be unable to touch her. His need was great, and not to be able to hold her and love her was agony. But in her condition, he dared not.

Claudia bit her lip in consternation. Angus did not want her. He could not bear to look upon her in her present state. She felt a surge of anger at his rejection, but quickly stifled it. Instead, she smiled tremulously and said that she would see about having a bath brought up to him.

Angus watched her leave the room to call the servants. Was that relief in her eyes at not having to touch him?

Each one avoided the other's eyes while the tub was placed in the room and filled.

Angus stared into the fire, a cup of wine in his hands, brooding on the recent events of the battle. Thoughts filled his mind of how he would be able to break the news to Claudia about Theo.

Her soft voice intruded on his thoughts, making him start guiltily. "Angus, let me help you with your armor."

He set the cup down and sat on the bench before the hearth. At least from her position behind him, he did not have to look her in the face. He'd never considered himself a coward before, but to have to tell her that he had failed in his mission, especially in her condition...

As if reading his thoughts, she asked, "Was your undertaking successful?"

"Yea," he muttered distractedly.

She walked around the bench to face him. "Angus, did you have a chance to talk to Theo? He confirmed what I told you, didn't he? He was not behind the attacks."

He stared at her in silence, and her heart raced.

"Angus?" The word came out in a half whisper.

He winced at her reproachful look.

"Angus, please tell me that you talked to Uncle Theo, and that he is all right."

Holding her steady gaze, Angus expelled his breath. "I wish I could."

Her face drained of color. "You promised!" she cried.

Angus ached to see her pain. He reached for her, but she quickly stepped away. She stumbled to the bed and sat down heavily.

"I tried, Claudia. God knows, I tried."

"How?" she asked in a flat tone.

He turned to face her. There was no point in holding back the harsh truth from her. Taking a deep breath, he answered, "Felix killed him during the last battle at Blois."

At Felix's name, Claudia's head jerked up. "How convenient for Duke Felix that Uncle Theo was in such easy reach," she said, unable to keep the bitterness out of her voice. "Where were you while your uncle was murdering the kindest, dearest man I have ever known, save my father?" she asked scathingly.

"I was close enough to see it all but too far away to save Archibald," Angus replied in a dead tone. As it was, he blamed himself for what had happened. He had known how much Felix hated Theo Archibald. If only he had been able to get to the man first. "Claudia, I'm sorry," he whispered.

Claudia was vaguely aware of the anguish of her husband's voice, but she was too filled with a gut-wrenching agony of her own to care. "Sorry! What good is that now?"

Angus stood up abruptly and paced back and forth in front of her. "I will not make excuses for myself," he said tightly. "Don't you think I know how much you are affected by this? If I could bring Archibald back, I would, but I cannot. Don't you think I have asked myself if there wasn't something I could have done to change things? There was not. What's done is done. Would you rather it were I whose body was carried home?" he asked, his voice rising with each word he spoke.

Claudia's head moved from side to side in denial. Tears streamed down her face. "I did not mean that," she managed to gasp out between sobs.

"Nay? There was a time when you would have been overjoyed at the news of my death." He was angry with Claudia's assumption that he had willingly let Archibald be killed. But mostly, he was angry with himself for having been unable to prevent what had happened.

Claudia brushed her tears away fiercely and looked up at him. "Once that was true. But you are my husband, the father of my child. I looked upon Theo Archibald as my uncle. Am I not allowed to mourn for him?"

Angus sank down on the bed beside her and pulled her to him. He brought her head down to lay against his chest. "Aye," he whispered, "and I will mourn with you."

Thankful for the comfort of Angus's arms around her, Claudia broke down and wept. The tenderness he displayed was a soothing balm to her misery, assuaging the grief she felt. Deep down inside her she had known what the outcome of her husband's going to Monticule would be. And once again it was Felix Perrin who was responsible. She could not, in good conscience, blame Angus for what had happened.

When she'd cried herself dry, she pulled away and wiped her eyes. "Your water is getting cold," she said softly.

Angus brushed some wisps of hair from her face. He kissed her forehead before getting up to finish undressing and climb into the tub. As he sat in the bathwater, he watched Claudia move about the room gathering clean clothes for him.

"You do not have to do that if you do not want to."

"I need to keep busy," she replied tonelessly.

Sensing that his wife did not want to talk, Angus lapsed into silence. He covertly eyed her, wondering if the recent turn of events would set them further apart. He wanted Claudia so badly. He felt that in the months before the siege they had become closer, and that it would have been only a matter of time before she admitted her love for him. Would she now hate him forever?

She was more beautiful now, if that were possible. Memories assailed him of another bath, one that she had shared with him. She had been more than willing, shyly exploring him until their passions could no longer be ignored. Angus swore silently. How could he even think of that time when she was so aggrieved? He must not let his passion for his wife rule him, but rather control himself in her presence. He was not a beast of the field!

He stood up abruptly, sloshing water onto the floor, and was dismayed to find that that last thought had not cooled his ardor. Claudia was beside him instantly, and he roughly grabbed the cloth she held out to him. He stepped from the bath to dry himself briskly before the fire, angry that he wanted his wife so badly and could not have her.

Claudia had not missed the proof of Angus's need when he stepped from the tub. He wanted her, she was sure of it. And it would be so wonderful to have his arms around her once more. She needed his closeness. She had lost her family, and now Uncle Theo. She could not bear it if she lost Angus too. She moved to stand behind him and brushed her lips lightly across his back.

Angus jumped at the contact and shrank away. "Do not touch me," he whispered hoarsely.

Claudia was struck mute. She stared at him in disbelief. Mayhaps he'd not been thinking of her after all. A sob tore from her throat, then she whirled and fled from the room.

"Claudia!" Angus shouted, but she was gone. He let loose with a string of epithets as he struggled into his breeches. God's teeth! What had he been thinking of? To have been so harsh with her was stupid and uncalled for. He had to find her, for if anything happened to her, he would never forgive himself.

CHAPTER 14

Claudia ran blindly down the stairs and through the hall, ignoring those who lingered there. She brushed past a figure coming through the door, not seeing him clearly, and rushed outside to stand inhaling great gulps of air.

A startled Harlan moved aside quickly to keep from being knocked down. He started to call after her, seeing how upset she was, but she'd already disappeared through the doorway. He shrugged and kept on walking. Right now he was more concerned with his mission.

Tears streamed down Claudia's face unheeded. Angus truly did not want her. Where was she to go? What was she to do? Orgueilleux was all she had ever known. The pain of having to face her husband day in and day out was like a knife stabbing at her heart. She sobbed with the knowledge that theirs was a forced union, and one that Angus bore grudgingly. Once he'd had time to consider the situation, his seeming joy that she was to have his child had been replaced by the belief that they shared only the desire of a man and woman, instead of the love of a husband and wife.

She was appalled by his violent rejection, ashamed that she'd been carried away by her fantasies of what could have been. There was nowhere for her to return. The only person who loved her was Vail. She found that thought comforting as she wiped the tears from her eyes. She'd not greeted her little brother yet and suddenly had a strong urge to seek out the security of his companionship and consolation. She headed for the stables.

Angus was still muttering under his breath as he descended the stairs hurriedly. He'd not meant to frighten Claudia, but considering the hurtful condition he was in, her closeness was a terrible strain on him. She was so beautiful, and made even more so in his eyes by her pregnancy. The idea of assuaging his physical needs on one of the serving girls fleetingly entered his mind, but he quickly dismissed the thought. He wanted no one but his wife. Only she had the power to arouse him until he thought he would go mad.

His gaze roamed the hall searchingly, and not finding Claudia about, he swore again and strode angrily to the door. But before he reached it, a hand came out to grasp his arm. He scowled blackly at the restraining hand, his mind still intent upon finding his wife, when the object of his delay spoke.

"My lord, I realize that you've just returned,

but I am most eager to speak with you, for I have been waiting for some time."

Angus raised his eyes to stare blankly at the man, his mind elsewhere.

"Do you not remember me, my lord?" the man inquired uncomfortably.

Angus looked at the man as though he were an idiot. Naturally he knew everyone in his father's household. "Of course I know you, Harlan," he answered irritably. Awareness suddenly lit Angus's eyes. The man had remained behind to serve his father. "Harlan! What are you doing here?" He grabbed the man's arms and shook him, panic seizing him. "Has anything happened to my father? What is amiss?"

"Everything is fine," Harlan said quickly, sure that Angus would loosen all the teeth from his head.

A frown creased Angus's forehead as he stopped shaking the man. "Then why are you here?"

"I have a message for you from the lady Dorcas."

"Dorcas?"

"Aye, she bade me seek you out to deliver her message for your ears alone."

The frown deepened as Angus led Harlan to a quiet corner, away from prying ears, thinking that the missive could be anything from an appeal to let her join him, to informing him of the most dire danger that threatened his family. He knew how impulsive his sister was.

"Now, what is it?" he asked as calmly as he could.

"The lady Dorcas bade me to extend her wishes for your continued good health, and—and to inform you of her impending marriage."

Angus blinked. His mouth dropped open to form a word silently. He was not quite sure what he'd expected, but he was certainly not prepared for this revelation. His sister had always been adamantly stubborn concerning the subject of marriage. She would never marry, she had sworn.

What had changed her mind? There had been swains enough as Dorcas's childish body developed into soft, womanly curves. Some of her suitors had been most handsome, but she'd contemptuously shunned them all.

This was not a mere whim on his sister's part. Angus recognized the message for what it was—a plea for his help.

"You'd better tell me what has happened," he said grimly, "and do not leave anything out. But first tell me, how does the rest of my family fare? How is my father? Does he approve of this union?"

"It—it is by Lord Duncan's demand that Lady Dorcas is to be married."

Angus stared in astonishment. How could this be? For years his twin had successfully evaded that state. How could Duncan force her against her will? It was against everything they believed in. "Tell me," Angus demanded.

Harlan shuddered at the hardening of Angus's eyes. He hoped that his tale would not bring Angus's wrath down upon his head. He would not wish to cross any of the McMahons.

"Your father," he began, "has entered a contract for peace with Cedric McNeil, head of the McNeil clan."

Wrath blazed in Angus's eyes. Harlan faltered, but Angus prodded him to continue.

"As you know, my lord, the McMahons and the McNeils have been bitter enemies since Cedric returned from Norway with a Viking bride and built a stronghold near onto the McMahons'. There has been raiding and battles on both sides all these years, but now your father and the McNeil say they are tired of fighting. Your father has said that too many young men are dying, leaving their wives and babes bereft."

"I know all this," Angus growled. "Get to the point, man."

"It was Egan McNeil," Harlan said quickly. "He is Cedric's cousin, and he came to Lord Duncan with the proposal that the McMahons and the McNeils declare peace, and that a marriage between their clans would seal the agreement. It was Dorcas who was chosen over Thalia and Gwendolyn as bride."

Angus swore long and angrily. How could his father think to sacrifice Dorcas for the good of the clan? And to a Viking no less! A traitorous dog who'd turned against his own country and gone over to the enemy. He said as much to Harlan.

The man's surprised expression stopped Angus's diatribe in mid-sentence.

"Nay, my lord, it is not Cedric McNeil to whom Lady Dorcas is to be joined, but his son, Neil."

That barely appeased Angus. "At least she will not have to put up with a fat old cob drooling after her and scaring her half out of her wits." He suddenly frowned. "What of the son?"

"I—I do not know. I've not seen him myself, but it is rumored that he is a savage as tall as a giant. He's spent the last five years in Norway, and it is said that he will return there once—once he does his duty," Harlan finished lamely.

"Will Dorcas accompany him?"

Harlan shrugged and shook his head. "I do not know. It is said that McNeil is as unhappy about the situation as Lady Dorcas," he replied candidly. Angus had asked to be spared nothing, and Harlan was only too pleased to comply. He knew how upset his mistress was, for he had seen her eyes red from weeping. He'd been shocked to learn that the lady Dorcas was so vulnerable. He'd never thought of her in those terms before and found himself wondering why. She was indeed a beautiful woman. Mayhaps it was because she was such a fierce warrior. She'd always seemed so capable in any situation, but this was completely out of her realm. Mayhaps Angus would be able to help his sister when no one else could.

Angus was thinking along the same lines, only he was not as hopeful. How could he help Dorcas? He felt impotent. He could not leave Claudia in her present condition. He would not want to even if he could, and she was not able to travel. He was overcome by a helpless rage at Dorcas's predicament and at being too far away to do anything.

Angus had no doubt that Duncan loved all his children. How could he treat his eldest daughter, who was precious to him, so callously?

"My lord," Harlan said hesitantly, "I know that this comes as a great shock to you, but I promised Lady Dorcas that I would impart her message and return posthaste. I was delayed coming here, since I was set upon by thieves soon after reaching this land, and was badly hurt. I lay in a fever for weeks, and I have been here awaiting your return for months."

Angus glanced distractedly at the man. "You must return without delay. When will the wedding take place?"

"I do not know. Lady Dorcas has done her best to postpone the nuptials, but I fear I may have been overlong bringing this message to you."

Angus's lips compressed in a tight line. "Then you must not waste any more time here than necessary. Give me a moment to pen missives to my father and to Dorcas for you to take with you."

Angus returned to the hall sometime later. He'd found it difficult to control his anger so that he could write a sensible, pleading note to his father and another soothing one to Dorcas. He handed the messages to Harlan, telling him to be careful with them. "I will guard them with my life, my lord," replied the man solemnly. "If only I were a brave man, I would cut out that black Viking's heart for the lady," he added feelingly.

"I know you would," Angus said, smiling at the man's fierce expression. "Come," he added, clap-

ping the man on the back, "I have something I
wish you to take back to Erin."

He led Harlan outside to the stables. The men
entered the dimly lit building, and Angus led the
way to a stall housing a white stallion. The horse
perked its ears and tossed its head at the intru-
sion. His nostrils flared and he snorted, pawing
the ground.

Angus ran a soothing hand over the horse's
neck. "I won this prize during my last 'conquest,'"
he said dryly. "This is a devil stallion, as beautiful
and free as Dorcas. But he is not so wild that he
cannot be tamed by a gentle and loving hand,
given enough time. Tell her that, Harlan. Tell her
that I make this gift to her, for I know that with
her gentle persuasion she will be able to mold this
noble beast to her liking."

Harlan stared disbelievingly at the prancing stallion. How did Angus expect his sister to handle
such a powerful, and what looked like to him, very
disagreeable animal? He could only nod in answer.

"Tell her—tell her also that she is in my thoughts,
and that I will come to her just as soon as I am
able."

Harlan nodded solemnly. "Aye, my lord, that I
will."

Angus clasped the other man's hand in a warm
farewell. "I will instruct my men to escort you to
the coast. God go with you."

"And with you, my lord," Harlan replied before
leading the stallion out of his stall.

Angus felt as though something were not complete as he watched Harlan's retreating back. He called after the man, "Harlan." The man turned and looked back. "Tell Dorcas that I love her. If anything should happen to her..."

He was interrupted as Harlan said quickly, "Never fear. We will watch over her, and protect her."

Claudia sat like a stone statue against the pile of hay, paralyzed by what she'd heard. She knew by the silence surrounding her that she was once again alone. Her chest heaved with sobs as tears flowed down her cheeks. All that she'd been so afraid of was coming to pass.

Angus did not love her. He never had, and he never would. His ardent declaration of his love for Dorcas echoed in her ears, and her dream of winning her husband over this unknown woman went up in smoke. What a fool she'd been to lose sight of reality, she thought bitterly. She must have been mad.

She got to her feet, numb with shock, and had to hold tightly to a post to steady her shaking limbs. She tried to move, but found herself trembling so badly that she sank to the ground once again. It would be safer to stay where she was until she gained control.

Angus stalked toward the castle. What could possibly happen next, he wondered. He was concerned for his twin and her predicament, but he had a more immediate problem to attend to. He must find Claudia. In her state of mind, there was no telling what she would do.

He hurried across the yard, but before he could reach the door to the castle, Owen was upon him.

"Angus, I must speak with you," he said, falling in stride beside his young friend.

"Not now," Angus growled. "It will have to wait."

Owen stopped dead in his tracks. He'd found the answers he searched for. Now Angus must know the truth. "Can your life wait?" he called after Angus.

Angus came to a sudden halt and turned to face Owen. "My what? What are you talking about?"

"There have been too many accidents since we came to Brittany, Angus. Too many attempts on your life."

Angus's face cleared as he laughed. "Are you turning soft in your old age? What is the matter with you, Owen? Wounds are the fortunes of war, and we both know that death can come at any time."

"But not the way they've come about to you," Owen said, stepping forward.

"What are you talking about?"

"I am talking about your two brushes with death almost a year ago, and again last week at Blois. I am talking about your imminent murder!"

The startled look on Angus's face was enough for Owen to press on. "That's right, your death, at your uncle's hands."

Angus drew in his breath sharply. "You must be mad."

"Nay, I am not mad. I have carefully assembled my facts, and they are very grim indeed."

"Why would Felix try to kill me? For what purpose?"

Owen shook his head. That was the one question that plagued him also. "I do not know. I know only that I speak the truth. Remember when Dennis said that he knew the man who shot you in the woods, but couldn't recall from where?"

Angus nodded mutely, unable to find his voice.

"Well, he finally remembered. It was right here after we took Orgueilleux. The man was one of Felix's. And in the battle at Blois when you were almost cut down in the street, the man I killed to save your life was also one of Perrin's men. He'd come through the gates with us. I suppose that in the madness of battle, he thought that your death at *his* hands would not be discovered."

Angus stared dumbfounded at his longtime friend, unable to grasp the meaning of what he said, yet knowing that Owen would not lie to him. If Owen said his uncle was trying to kill him, then he must have the facts to back up his accusation. But why?

Owen went on. "I was right behind you in the middle of the town when another of Felix's assassins tried to do his master's dirty work. I cut him down but did not kill him right away. Instead, I dragged him off and interrogated the whimpering cur, and found out that Felix has put a price on your head for the one who would slay you. It was also he, and not Duke Theo, who set fire to Raymond's hut."

Angus's face turned a mottled red in his fury. Why did Felix seek his death? There was no sense to it. The man was family. How could he think to harm his own flesh and blood?

Angus was assaulted by a great sense of hurt and rage as he whirled and strode angrily into the castle, throwing over his shoulder an order for Owen to see that his destrier was saddled. He had not believed that the day could get any worse, he thought as he grimly donned his armor. A pang of guilt and remorse swept over him as the image of Claudia filled his mind. He wished she'd not run away as she had, and vowed that upon his return he would make things right between them. But at that moment he was driven to find out why his uncle wanted him dead.

He rode for Talus with a grim determination— alone. He'd been adamant in his refusal to allow anyone to accompany him, rejecting all of Owen's arguments in favor of his companionship. When Owen saw the furious glint in Angus's eyes, he'd backed down. He knew that this was something his friend had to do on his own. He was not too worried, for Angus now knew of Felix's treachery and would be wary. In truth, in Angus's present frame of mind, Owen felt that Perrin was the one who should beware.

Angus entered the castle at Talus as grimfaced as when he'd left Orgueilleux, to find his uncle lounging comfortably before the fire. Felix did not bother to rise as Angus strode into the hall, but merely turned his head to see who was approaching.

He raised a surprised eyebrow. "Well, nephew, to what do I owe the honor of this visit so soon after our last meeting?"

"Some disturbing information has reached my ears," Angus replied in a deceptively calm voice.

"And what might that be?"

"There is treachery afoot, *uncle*."

Felix stopped the goblet of wine halfway to his lips and glanced at Angus. "Oh? What sort of treachery?"

Angus's mouth curved in a mockery of a smile. "Are there different kinds?" he asked blandly. "This is the kind that stinks of putrid flesh."

Felix toyed with his goblet. "Mayhaps you'd best tell me what is eating at your insides."

"Paid assassins. Fire. The death of innocent people. Need I say more?"

Felix stared at him, all pretense of friendliness and warmth gone from his cold blue eyes. "Nay," he answered simply.

"Why?" Angus spat out.

Felix's lips curled in a snarl. "My sister betrayed her home and family. She turned her back on all those who loved her to run off with a foreigner. I swore when she left that Duncan McMahon was going to pay. 'Tis a pity that it wasn't with his firstborn, but when I saw the love bestowed upon all his children equally, it did not matter."

Angus stared disbelievingly at his uncle. Felix was mad. His mother and father loved each other dearly, and as for his mother "running off" with Duncan—it simply wasn't true. Angus had been weaned on stories of how his mother had saved the stranger shipwrecked off the shores of her homeland, of how their love had grown. Her father had given his blessing to their union. Felix was insane to think that Heloise had been stolen from the bosom of her family and in turn would steal what was so very precious to Duncan.

Felix tossed off the rest of his wine. "What better way to revenge my sister's death at that barbarian's hands than to kill in return? But only after you helped me attain my goal of the land I wanted."

Angus was startled by his uncle's words. What was the man talking about? His mother wasn't dead. Felix had seen her alive and well, and happy during his visit to Erin.

"My mother is not dead. You saw that for yourself."

"To me she died the day she left Talus. If she had done my bidding, I would have attained my rightful place at court. I could have been wealthy beyond my wildest dreams had it not been for my *dear sister*. I have waited patiently all these years to avenge myself against all those who ever betrayed me. The lady Jeanette spurned me in favor of Robert Cherveny because he had more money and power. A lot of good it did her in the end."

Angus watched the light in Felix's eyes with a horrified fascination. His uncle was clearly mad, and Angus felt the bile rise in his throat at the thought that he'd been a pawn in Felix's insane scheme.

"Imagine my lovely sister's grief at finding her beloved son has died. How she will mourn. You know," Felix said smoothly, cocking his head to one side, "you really have been very difficult to kill. It is almost as if you have the nine lives of a cat. I was very disappointed that all those set to the task failed so miserably. Even that slut in Noyon was unsuccessful. I detest bumbling fools. But I regained all that she took from me, plus more when I killed her, and now I shall have everything that I ever wanted. I have Archibald's place. Now I have Orgueilleux." Felix's smile widened. "Orgueilleux and that delectable bit of flesh that you call wife are mine at last, and I did not have to lift a finger to complete the construction. You finished it for me. For that I thank you," he said, raising his goblet to Angus.

At the mention of Claudia, all reason left Angus. He grabbed Felix by his tunic, pulling him to his feet. The goblet flew from Felix's hand as Angus shook him. "Do not soil Claudia's name upon your lips," he growled.

Felix shook himself free and laughed. "I have soiled more than your *wife's* name. Why do you think I did not give her to you immediately upon her capture?"

Angus's teeth bared in a feral snarl as he lunged forward, but Felix was expecting the move and easily sidestepped him. The grin left his face to be replaced by a hard glint of hate as he shouted, "Guards!"

At once Angus was seized from behind. It took five men several minutes to drag him to the floor, where they bound him. He was pulled roughly to his feet to stand glaring at Felix.

"Take him to the dungeon," his uncle said, dismissing them with a wave of his hand.

Angus was thrown into a cubicle where only a small opening high on the wall allowed any light into the room. He surveyed his surroundings ruefully, noting that the room was totally bare. Slumping down against the wall, he contemplated his situation. Mayhaps he had been foolish in coming here alone, but he'd been so angry. He was not dead yet. Where there was life, there was hope. Somehow he would make Felix pay for all the hurt done to him and his.

His heart lurched at the thought of Claudia. He hated to imagine what Felix would do to her if he got his hands on her. The idea of his wife in his uncle's clutches made him shudder.

He sighed. How could a day that had started out so joyous turn so sour? He'd never had a chance to tell Claudia of his feelings for her. Angus silently vowed that he would find a way. He would get out of this somehow. Then he could set things aright.

Claudia entered the castle like a sleepwalker. The men greeted her respectfully. If they noticed that her eyes were red and swollen from weeping, they did not let on. Angus was not about, and for that she was grateful. She did not think she could face him just yet. Her worst imaginings had been confirmed by her husband's words. All hope for a peaceful union between them was shattered, as was her heart. The chains of bitterness wrapped themselves around her once again as she silently vowed to hold herself from Angus. Never again would she be hurt.

She was sitting before the fire in her chamber when the door opened. Vail sat down on the bench beside her. His shoulders slumped and he sighed dejectedly, waiting for his sister to notice him. When she did not, he said, "Angus is gone."

Claudia showed no sign of having heard him other than a stiffening of her spine.

"Owen said that he had a mission of great importance to attend to. I wonder why he did not take anyone with him?"

Because he did not need assistance in meeting his whore, she thought bitterly. "Do not meddle in matters that do not concern you."

Vail was taken aback by her sharp tone. "It is dangerous to ride around the countryside alone," he said stubbornly.

Claudia jumped to her feet and whirled on her brother like a spitting cat. "Enough! Do not speak to me of that mangy cur. 'Twould benefit all if he never returns."

Vail's mouth dropped open in surprise. For the first time he noticed his sister's condition. A slow smile broke out on his face as he breathed, "Oh, Claudia. I am soon to be an uncle."

She took a threatening step toward him. "Do not remind me, for it would be better if this child of our enemy had never been conceived. I hate him, and I hate this seed he has planted within me!"

Claudia was horrified by her own words, but she could not keep them from spilling forth. She turned away, tears stinging her eyes. "Leave me," she said raggedly. She continued to stare into the flames even after she heard the door close behind Vail. She had not meant what she said about the babe. It was part of her, too, and that was the part she would nurture and love.

CHAPTER 15

Angus reclined against the wall, his arms propped on his bent knees, his eyes shut as if he were asleep. He was not. His mind had been busy devising ways to escape ever since he'd been thrown into his prison. Unfortunately, he'd not had a chance to act upon any of them, for he'd been left totally alone.

There was no point in opening his eyes. Darkness had descended hours before. No one had thought to bring him a light. For that matter, no one had thought about him at all, for he was not even provided with nourishment.

His lips curled in contempt. If Felix expected to starve him to death, he was in for a great shock. His men would be here long before that happened, since Owen was aware of his whereabouts. Though he'd ridden off by himself, Angus agreed with his friend that if he was not back before the moon was high, Owen was to follow with his men.

He'd not had time to inform anyone else, nor had he intended to. He was reminded of Vail sneaking off to join him at Monticule and did not want a repeat of that situation. The boy was tenacious in his stubborn belief that where Angus went, he had to follow.

A slight smile touched his lips as he recalled how diligently Vail had performed the duties that were his punishment for disobeying orders. The grin deepened as he thought that he'd somehow lost that battle, for Vail had been of a much too cheery disposition the whole time. The only real victory he'd won was in keeping his brother-by-marriage out of the actual fighting. He would never have been able to face Claudia if anything happened to the boy.

A pang of remorse filled him at the thought of his wife. He'd not meant to be so sharp with her. He should have remembered from his mother's time, when she carried his little brothers, how sensitive a woman could be. Women underwent mysterious changes during their time. It seemed that Claudia was no different.

He had no doubt that he would soon be out of here, then he could apologize properly. Once he had the time to spend with her, he could concentrate on wooing her. Then, mayhaps—

Angus's thoughts were interrupted by the sound of a woman singing. His eyes shot open, and he listened intently to the plaintive melody. He looked about cautiously, but there was nothing to see. Everything was shrouded in darkness. It was as though the haunting strain floated on the night breeze, and he began to wonder if he was going mad.

The sound came closer, and he arose and stood listening. It was so near. It seemed to be coming from the wall of his cell. He ran to the window, but the opening was too high for him to see through.

The songstress was just outside.

He stretched his tall frame, and placed a hand on the windowsill, as if willing whoever was there to turn their attention to that space.

"Lady," he called frantically, "kind lady."

The singing stopped abruptly.

Angus tried again. "Who is there?"

The woman did not answer, but started humming tunelessly.

Angus knew that this was no figment of his imagination. He tried a third time. "Good lady, your voice is as sweet as an angel's, but can you not find it in your heart to speak to me?"

He heard a movement and panicked, thinking that whoever it was had moved on.

"You are a knave, sir!" snapped a hushed voice from the outer wall. "One does not speak to strangers."

Angus was afraid that the woman would leave. He was desperate to keep her talking. Mayhaps she could help him.

"How do you know that I am a stranger?" he asked.

"If you were not, you would not ask such a silly question."

"But I cannot see you, nor you me, for it is pitch black."

For a moment silence greeted him and he thought she was gone.

"Everyone knows who I am," came the peevish reply.

Angus racked his brain trying to find the answer she sought.

"Everyone knows me and my song," she said in a singsong voice.

Damnation! Why couldn't she simply give her name? Mayhaps she was mad, or mayhaps she'd been sent here by his uncle. It did not matter. He had nothing to lose.

"Why are you in the dungeon?" she asked so abruptly, she caught him off guard.

If this were a trap, it just might set things in motion to end the waiting. If not, then she might be able to help, he thought.

"I am a prisoner," he answered honestly.

"A prisoner," she whispered. "Oh, my, it has been ever so long since we've held anyone."

Angus grimaced at the awed tone of her voice. "I am Lord Angus of Orgueilleux, and I am being held against my will."

"You lie!"

He was taken aback by the hostility of her accusation. "My lady, I do not lie," he said, trying hard to keep a rein on his temper. "I am Angus of Orgueilleux, late of the clan McMahon on the isle of Erin."

"Nay! It is not possible," she cried. "Though it

has been many years since I've seen him, I know that Robert Cherveny is the master at Orgueilleux. You are an impostor, and I will not listen to you any longer."

"Wait! Duke Robert is dead," Angus called desperately. He held his breath, but only silence greeted him, and he sank against the wall in despair.

"How?" came a hushed whisper.

"He was killed in the taking of his castle."

"He was a good man, so kind and generous to all," the woman said in a plaintive voice.

"Aye, so I've been told. I now regret not having known him." Angus breathed a sigh of relief that the woman had not left.

"But if he is dead, and you are now lord—"

"I do not disclaim having helped to destroy him," Angus interrupted. "Nor do I regret all that I have gained," he added, thinking of Claudia. "But Orgueilleux was given to me in payment of the bargain struck with my uncle."

"Your uncle?"

"Felix Perrin," Angus spat out. "Lady?" he questioned as silence once more greeted him.

"You think I am a fool!" the woman snapped. "Everyone thinks I am a fool." She suddenly giggled, and chanted in a singsong voice, "I've caught you again. You should not lie. My husband has no kin here."

Husband! Angus's heart beat faster at her words. He'd forgotten all about his aunt. Felix had mentioned her only briefly, once long ago. What was her name? Had he even used it? Ethelda. Enid. Nay. It was more like Aurora. Eudora! That was it!

"Aunt Eudora, it is I, Angus, Heloise's son from Erin."

"Heloise," Eudora gasped.

"Aye. Felix came to my father, Duncan, to ask for his help in subduing other lords. Though my father could not leave his people, he allowed me to accompany Felix with my men, thinking that my uncle was an honorable man. But he betrayed me, and now I find that I am in trouble because of it."

"I remember Heloise," Eudora murmured in a far-off voice. "She married the man of her choice."

Angus frowned. Either his aunt had not heard him, or she did not care. Hadn't Felix said she was ill? He'd been almost embarrassed to discuss his wife with Heloise, and had quickly changed the subject. Mayhaps she *was* mad, Angus thought.

"You were brought here by the devil!" Eudora said with such venom that Angus was once again taken aback.

"Aunt Eudora, I need your help. Can you unbar the door so that I may be free?" he asked hopefully.

"I have no family, you know," she whispered. "It is nice to be called aunt."

Angus was beginning to wonder in earnest if she were truly mad. She seemed to lose track of their conversation so easily. Desperately he pleaded, "Will you help me?"

"You have such a nice voice. I would very much

like to see you. We can have a lovely visit, and you can tell me how your mama fares."

Angus sighed in exasperation. He was frantic to be released so that he could avenge himself, and his aunt wanted to gossip!

"Aunt Eudora."

Silence greeted him.

"Aunt—" He knew it was of no use. She was gone. He didn't know what to think. She may have put him from her mind as easily as she had come upon him. Then again, mayhaps she was on her way to him now. It was hard to tell what a mad-woman would do.

If she did come to him, he felt that he could easily overpower her to gain his freedom. She'd not said a word about helping him, but only that she wanted to see him. His thoughts were racing erratically when he heard the bar being lifted from the door. He stood poised to spring, barely breathing, waiting for whoever would enter. He hoped it was Eudora and not someone else.

Angus blinked, and his jaw dropped at the apparition in front of him. Eudora was swathed in a high-necked white nightgown. Layer after layer of gossamer fabric swirled about her as she floated into the room. One sleeve was pushed back to reveal a slim arm as she held a torch, bringing light into the chamber. The other sleeve covered her tiny hand completely, and the hem of the gown was dirty where it'd been dragged along the ground. Her hair fell about her in a tangled mass of brown curls.

She, in turn, blinked, then stared at Angus curiously. "Oh, my, you are a big one!" she exclaimed. "You do not look like Heloise."

"Nay, my lady. I have my father Duncan's coloring."

He assessed his newfound aunt as thoroughly as she did him. She was a tiny woman, and so thin he was sure a strong wind would blow her over. Her face was a perfect oval with deep blue eyes framed by dark lashes, a fine straight nose, and a little heartshaped mouth posed in a moue of astonishment. She was by no means a beautiful woman, but if she fixed her hair decently, he thought that she would be quite pretty.

The most arresting thing about her, however, were her eyes. Angus saw a great deal of pain and sadness there, a look of defeat, as though she no longer cared for the world, or what happened to her.

"Aunt Eudora, I wish to thank you for coming to help me."

"Help you?" She cocked her head to one side. "But I thought you were here to visit with me?"

"Nay. Remember, I am being held prisoner."

Her eyes took on the glazed light of one unbalanced. "Aye," she said breathily, looking around her secretively. "There are demons here. They are all demons." She shuddered. "I do not like it here. The devil kept me here once."

Angus eyed her with a puzzled frown. Was she speaking of his uncle, or some imaginary distortion of the mind? "Do you refer to Felix?" he asked slowly.

"The devil is always here. He seeks to destroy," she answered, glancing behind her warily.

Angus took a step forward. "If this room disturbs you, aunt, let us leave it. We shall find pleasanter surroundings to speak in," he said soothingly, taking her by the arm.

"That would be most unwise," interrupted a voice from the doorway.

Angus jerked his head up to stare at the dark visage of his uncle. He felt Eudora trembling at his side as she looked around wildly.

"Well, well," Angus said sardonically. "And here I was beginning to think that I'd overstayed my welcome. Really, uncle, your guest accommodations are atrocious."

"The accommodations are assigned accordingly. You won't be needing yours much longer."

"Do you really believe that you can get away with this?" he asked contemptuously as his uncle sauntered into the room. Felix grabbed the torch from Eudora to place it in a wall sconce. He frowned at his wife as she cowered away to a far corner of the chamber before turning his attention back to his nephew.

Felix's grin reminded Angus of a wolf baring its teeth. "Oh, but I already have gotten away with it. After all, you are the one in captivity, not I."

"And just how do you propose to explain my death?"

Felix chuckled deep in his throat. "It is all very

simple really. You shall have an accident. You see, you never reached me. Alas, you were on the way to see me, but the countryside abounds with thieves and murderers. For one man alone to stave off an attack by a number of men . . . Tsk, tsk. It really is too bad, you know.

"Of course, since that lovely little morsel Claudia will be all alone, I will simply have to take command of Orgueilleux. Yea, indeed, it is my duty."

"The same way it was your duty to take Monticule and murder Archibald?" Angus snarled.

The two men were so engrossed in each other that neither heard Eudora catch her breath, nor whimper with pain when Felix laughed harshly.

"Archibald was killed in battle."

"Nay," Angus said. "You set about to murder the man, and you did it."

"True," Felix said, "but it will never be proven."

Eudora's mind exploded with Felix's words. The pain was too much to bear. Her love had been stolen from her, first by her father, and now by her husband.

It had been enough to know that Theo Archibald was close by. That knowledge had sustained her through her days. But death. That was the final blow.

Her eyes shimmered with all the hate she felt for her husband. She'd suffered so much pain and misery at his hands through the years, and it was only Theo's presence that had insured her from any permanent harm. How she hated Felix. He was the devil incarnate, and it was up to her to send him back to hell.

The conversation between the two men was lost to her as she reached into the folds of her gown. One thought increased in intensity—Felix must die. She pulled out a pair of shears and lunged toward him, striking him in the back of his neck. He emitted a strangled sound as blood gushed out, and he clawed at the wound. But he was too late to grab the weapon as Eudora plunged it into his back.

The sound of tearing flesh echoed as Eudora ripped the shears from his body only to stab him again and again, sobbing, hysterical in her fright and rage. At last he gave up the fight to stay alive, and crumbled to the floor, the gurgling scream turning into a death hiss.

Eudora seemed not to know that he was dead as she continued her assault on the inert form. She was unmindful of the blood that covered her face, her arms, her gown as she repeated, "Devil—devil—devil—"

Angus watched the attack with horror. It was as though everything had slowed to a dream. At last he aroused himself to leap at his aunt and pull her away. In her madness she turned on him, ready to strike, and he had to wrest the shears from her, amazed at the strength in her tiny frame. He placed his arms around her shaking form and held her close, murmuring soothing words to calm her.

At last she stood quietly, panting from her exertion. "I am cold," she said hoarsely.

"Come," Angus said quietly. He took her by the shoulders and led her from the carnage in the room.

Eudora allowed Angus to lead her docilely up the stairs and away from the dungeon, unaware of the blood that covered them both. She waited like an obedient child when he hesitated upon seeing a guard at the top of the stairs.

At the sound of footsteps the man looked down. His eyes widened in astonishment at the sight that greeted him, before being replaced by fear. he took a few halting steps backward, then turned and ran, screaming that ghosts were prowling the castle.

Angus swore under his breath that the guard would alert the rest of his uncle's men. He grabbed Eudora's arm and propelled her into the hall. It was near daylight, and he knew that Owen and his men would be along soon. He had to stop any fighting that might take place until they reached him.

Just as he feared, the master-at-arms came running into the hall, followed by some of Felix's men, their swords drawn. They stopped in their tracks at the sight of their mistress and Angus.

At last the master-at-arms found his voice. "Where is Duke Felix?"

"Your master met with an accident. You now answer to the Lady Eudora if you all wish to keep your positions, and to me as my aunt's protector," Angus said sternly. "My men will be here shortly.

Open the gate to allow them entrance. Now!" he ordered harshly when no one made a move.

One of the men, jolted by the command, ran from the hall to obey. Satisfied, Angus continued. "You and you," he said, pointing to two more, "go to the dungeon and fetch Duke Felix. One of you go find the priest." He turned his eyes on the servants milling around nervously and beckoned one of the women. "Take your mistress upstairs and clean her."

The maid's eyes grew wide with fright, and she started to back away.

Angus grabbed her swiftly and shook her. "Do as I say, woman, and be gentle with her, for she is out of her wits with horror."

As Eudora was being led away, Owen, followed by Colin and Dennis, strode into the hall.

Colin and Dennis stopped and stared, speechless, but Owen hurried forward. "Where are you hurt?" he asked.

"It is Felix's blood you see."

Owen nodded in satisfaction. "You had to kill him," he said matter-of-factly.

"Nay." Angus noted the surprise on his friend's face, and led him away from prying ears. "It was not I, but Aunt Eudora who killed him," he said. At Owen's raised eyebrows he explained the events leading up to and including his uncle's death.

"I do not know what set her off," he concluded. "I've no illusions that it was to protect me, for I'd only just met her, but knowing the cruelty of my uncle, I've no doubt that what she did was in self-defense."

Owen nodded in understanding. "If what you say is true, and the lady is, er—that is, if she is not quite right in the head, how can you expect her to command Talus and protect it? Especially if she is to order those who were loyal to Felix?"

"Eudora has suffered a great shock and is in no way ready to be placed in that position. I will take her back to Orgueilleux with me. Mayhaps Claudia will know what to do to heal the wounds of her soul. In the meantime, you shall remain here."

Owen nodded in assent, accepting Angus's trust in him with the casualness of a fast friend.

Angus laughed at Owen's grave expression and clapped him on the back. "Do not be so quick to acquiesce, my friend. We do not know what lies in store for you."

Together they examined Talus and found that it was a well-kept abode. That the inhabitants worked hard out of fear and not out of any loyalty for their dead master did not escape either man. Angus gathered together all those who'd served his uncle, from the men-at-arms down to the lowliest serfs, and told them what was expected of them, and that until the lady Eudora returned, the castle was under the protection of his men. No one uttered a sound as he spoke, too frightened by all that had happened that morning. The red giant who stood before them was bigger than life in their eyes, and the dark, scowling stranger at his side, who was being left in charge of the castle, made them all shudder, for they knew not what to expect. They knew only that they'd been released from one hell, mayhaps to be thrust into another.

Angus eyed his aunt as she rode beside him. He felt emotionally and physically drained from all that had happened, and was eager to reach Orgueilleux. There was still a matter there to be settled. But out of concern for Eudora, he decided it was best to take his time and not push her.

After he was satisfied that Owen would receive no resistance, he'd gathered twenty of the forty men Owen had brought with him for the return trip home. Eudora had entered the hall, cleaned and gowned, her hair neatly bound and concealed by her veil. Angus had spoken to her soothingly, but she seemed not to hear. She had followed him docilely to a waiting horse and allowed him to lift her into the saddle. She'd not acknowledged anyone's presence, nor had she spoken a word. His queries as to her ability to travel, and his concern for her, had met silence as she stared ahead. So Angus had finally given up and left her in her own little world.

Eudora giggled, but quickly smothered her mirth when she saw her nephew look at her sharply. She thought she saw him shudder. Poor boy. She mustn't frighten him. But it was all she could do to keep from smiling. She wanted to laugh out loud.

She was free. Really and truly free. She had lived in hell for so long that she could not quite believe the truth of it and had to pinch herself.

It had all been so very simple. Why hadn't she thought of murdering Felix years ago? Then she would not have had to slip into a world of seeming madness in order to be safe. But she had not, and now she bitterly regretted that she'd not found the courage. She was free, but at what price? Poor Theo was dead. The man who should have been her husband. The love of her life. But through her father's foolish penchant for gambling, she'd been bartered away, along with all his holdings. She would never forget that fateful night twenty years earlier when she was informed, quite casually, that she was to marry Felix Perrin. From then until just a few hours ago she'd been plunged into a hellish nightmare. She wanted desperately to cry. She mourned her loss and all the wasted years. The tears would come later, in private, she knew. That was as it should be.

Eudora was grateful for her nephew's kindness and generosity, glad to get away from Talus. In time she would decide what to do.

Angus watched Eudora worriedly, wondering if he was doing the right thing. But he could not have left her at Talus. She would have been safe enough in Owen's hands, but having been a bachelor all his life, Owen probably would not know how to bring Eudora out of her lethargy. Besides, it was obvious from her condition that his aunt had not been well treated. What she needed was the calming influence and understanding that another woman could offer. But was it fair to ask Claudia to give her time to a madwoman? Could Eudora be made to realize the world around her?

Angus wrestled with himself. Surely Claudia would not shun this poor woman. But was it right that she, in her condition, should have to try to reach Eudora? What if his aunt were, in truth, mad? Would any in his household be safe from her?

It was too late to change his mind as Orgueilleux came into sight. Angus's eyes lit in anticipation of what awaited him, and he had to curb the longing to spur his horse forward in his eagerness to reach home. Home.

He smiled slightly, wondering when he'd started thinking of the stronghold as such. It had been ever so long since he had thought of his father's house in Erin as home. He missed his family, especially his twin, but it was no longer with a sharp longing that stabbed at his heart. Instead, he found himself with an aching need to be with his wife at Orgueilleux.

Claudia stared out the window at nothing in particular, her arms wrapped around her to ward off the chilly spring air. She'd not left her chamber since Angus rode away. Marian brought her food, and grumbled as she carried away the untouched trays. Claudia did not hear, nor did she care.

Her husband had left her for his true love. He cared naught for her, or for the babe he'd placed in her womb. She shivered. She felt so cold inside. Cold and lifeless.

She heard the clattering of hooves from the lane below and looked down. She saw Angus, and her breath caught. Her heart hammered in her chest as she clutched the windowsill for support. A woman rode at her husband's side.

Claudia felt her heart sink in despair. He was going to shame her by flaunting his mistress in her face.

She turned abruptly from the window and strode to the chair by the fire. Her eyes flashed in anger as she sat down. She thought of all the vile things she could call Angus. She would not greet his whore, nor him for that matter! If he expected her to treat his Dorcas with kindness, then he had a surprise in store.

Her hands clutched the arms of the chair as she fought to control her anger. She repeated to herself that she did not care, it did not matter, when the chamber door opened and Angus entered.

He flew to her side and knelt down beside her. He touched her hand gently, but she jerked it away as though she'd been burnt, clutching it tightly into a fist and burying it in her lap so he could not reach it.

"Marian says you are not well," he said, frowning.

Without looking at him, Claudia replied coldly, "She is mistaken."

"But she says you've not been eating."

"I've not been hungry."

Angus sighed. He was so tired. He wanted the comfort of a bath and his wife's smile. Instead, he was faced with a cold reception. What was wrong with her?

"You must think of the child—"

His words were cut off as Claudia bolted from the chair. "Nay!" she spat out, her eyes shooting sparks of fury. "You have your heir, mighty warrior, but do not tell me what to do or how to live. You no longer have the right. And do not think that you will ever touch me again. You dare to bring your whore into my home and expect me to accept her. Never!" she shouted. "You are my enemy, and you will always remain so."

Angus stared at his wife dumbfounded, trying to make sense of her words. What in blazes was she saying? Whore? He mouthed the word.

"Had this child only been anyone's but yours!" she railed at him. "I hate you! Go have one by your beloved whore and leave me be!"

There was that word again. All of Angus's control took flight as he arose. "Enough, woman! I have had all the castigation I am going to take from you. I have tried to show you kindness, and patience, and understanding, and all I get in return is your scorn.

"Orgueilleux is mine, just as you are mine, and I will no longer tolerate your childish tirades! I do not know what you are babbling about when you speak of my *whore*, but if you'd bothered to greet me as a good and obedient wife should, you would find my aunt below, who needs your tender care, not your vituperation. As for my taking someone else to my bed, it would seem that I could find more consideration from the most common strumpet than I do from you, my wife! And I may just do that to get some peace!"

A sob escaped Claudia at his words. Why was he so angry? He had no right, for she was the one who'd been wronged. Tears of frustration and anger flowed down her cheeks as she whirled and fled from the room. She ran blindly down the stairs to escape him as he bellowed her name. She heard a string of oaths close behind her and turned to see Angus bearing down on her. She took a step forward and felt nothing but air. Her heart lurched as she realized there was no way to catch herself. She plunged forward and heard a scream, heard her name being shouted, then blackness descended over her.

Angus watched in terrified helplessness as Claudia tumbled down the stairs. He ran to her side and pushed a wailing Marian away from her. He lifted her gently and cradled her in his arms, tears gathering in his eyes. Lord in heaven, what had he done? He'd not been in his right mind as he berated her. He was so tired, and Claudia's unfounded accusations had been the last straw. Now he was paying the price of his terrible temper.

Claudia moaned as she regained her senses. She tried to move, but gasped as a stabbing pain shot through her abdomen.

"The babe is coming," a voice murmured behind Angus.

He looked up to find his aunt standing behind,

looking over his shoulder at Claudia with a worried frown.

"Take her to her chamber," Eudora said. "You, woman"—she pointed to Marian—"stop your blubbering and come with me."

When Angus hesitated, Eudora said sternly, "Do you wish to see your son born on the floor?"

He lifted his wife as gently as he could to carry her upstairs, and winced as Claudia cried out in agony.

CHAPTER 16

The hours stretched endlessly as Angus stared into the flames of the fire burning peacefully in the hearth of the great hall. After depositing Claudia in bed, he'd been unceremoniously ushered from the room, and the door was firmly shut in his face. He'd stood uncertainly in the hall, wondering if it was wise to leave his wife in his aunt's care. Strangely, Eudora's strong tone had brooked no argument, and Angus recalled that her eyes were clear as they'd stared unflinchingly into his.

Now he sat in the hall keeping a worried vigil. He'd known fright before, when he'd engaged in his first battles as a young warrior, but it was soon replaced by exhilaration as he fought. Never in his life had he felt such helpless terror as now.

He remembered how pale and still Claudia had been. How white her face became at the pain. And he was to blame. He cursed himself a thousand times over for hurting her. He'd not meant to let his tongue get the better of his head, but he'd been enraged by her outburst. He could make no sense of what she said, except that she wanted no part of him, or his child.

That had cut him deeply, for he loved her so. His every thought was of her and making her truly his. If she lived—

Nay. Angus quickly pushed that thought from his mind. She had to live. If the Lord God took someone, let it be the babe. He whimpered in anguish that the tiny being made out of his love for Claudia might die. He would mourn the child, but he needed his Claudia. They could always make another, and Angus vowed that they would. Somehow he would reach his wife to let her know how great his need for her was. He wanted them both, if it was possible, but dear God, he prayed, if not, please, do not take Claudia.

The servants moved silently around the hall, lighting the torches along the walls and leaving their master to his thoughts. The whole castle was shrouded in sadness this day, as others kept a silent vigil along with Lord Angus.

Colin sat at a table conversing quietly with Father Thomas while Dennis paced the floor. Young Lord Vail went out into the night air to do his pacing, only to return to the hall minutes later to see if there was news. Angus acknowledged no one's presence as he stared miserably into the fire.

Suddenly an angry wail filled the air, and all movement stopped, all heads turned toward the stairs. Angus half rose from his chair, his heart pounding wildly. He took a tentative step forward, but stopped when another cry rent the air. He didn't know whether to laugh or cry as he tore up the steps two at a time.

He pushed open the door to the chamber and saw Marian holding the tiniest infant he'd ever seen by its feet, slapping its backside. The little being yowled with indignation. As she slapped it again, Angus strode into the room and growled, "Stop beating that child."

"We must get air into his lungs so that he can breathe on his own if he is to live," Eudora said from her position at Claudia's head.

Angus turned to his aunt, alarm written on his face. "He?" Angus asked dumbly.

"You have a son. He came prematurely. He is very small," Eudora said quietly.

"Will he live?" he asked, his voice choked.

"If I have anything to say about it, he will," Marian said grimly. At last she nodded in satisfaction. Taking the infant close to the fire, she started washing him.

Angus watched the wee form for a moment, mesmerized. He and Claudia had made another human being. The thought awed him beyond belief as he turned to look at the inert figure in the bed. His heart leapt with fright. She lay so pale and still with closed eyes.

"She has had a very hard time and needs rest," Eudora said. She placed a comforting hand on his arm. "She will be well in time, for she is young and strong despite her size."

Angus dragged his eyes away from his wife to look at his aunt and nodded slowly. Then he left the room. Relief washed over him as he stood in the corridor. God was indeed good. He had spared them both.

Angus paced the length of the courtyard and back again deep in thought, a worried frown creasing his forehead. He was hard pressed to keep his temper in check.

Every day for a fortnight Marian had carried his son to him in the great hall so that he could see for himself the progress the babe was making. At first she'd said that Claudia needed all the rest she could get, and Angus had not questioned her.

He could even understand when Father Thomas was allowed to see Claudia. But it seemed that everyone else in the castle knew better of his wife's condition than he! He heard secondhand from the priest, from his aunt, from Vail, from Marian, and even from the servants as to how Claudia was faring. Still he was barred from her.

Marian said that Claudia was too weak for a lengthy visit. Angus had noted the fear in her eyes and had wondered at it. He'd found out the reason for it a few minutes earlier when he'd overheard his aunt and Marian in heated discussion. Eudora was all for Angus going to Claudia, saying that the depression Claudia suffered would disappear once she saw her husband. But Marian was afraid that seeing Angus would throw her into a worse fit. It would be bad for her and the babe, she'd argued.

Angus swore under his breath at the realization that it was Claudia who'd requested he not be allowed to see her. Damnation! Did she think he meant her harm? He suddenly decided what he would do, and strode determinedly into the castle and up the stairs. If anyone tried to keep him from his wife, he would have them thrown into the tower!

He angrily shoved open the door to his chamber, making the three women within jump in fright. Claudia finished handing her sleeping son to Marian and quickly adjusted her nightgown.

"My lord, you should not be here," she said coldly.

He started to slam the door shut, then remembering the babe, closed it quietly so as not to awaken him.

"It is inconceivable," he said tightly, "that I should be stricken from any part of my home, my lady." Out of the corner of his eye he watched Marian fumbling with his son's covers, ready to explode at her slowness.

Eudora caught sight of the twitching muscle in her nephew's jaw and sensed that Angus was near the breaking point. With a firm hand on Marian's arm, she ushered the servant from the room, shaking her head in warning as Marian started to protest.

Claudia's eyes flickered in fright at their departure. Then she turned her head away so she would not have to look at those piercing emerald eyes.

Angus thought she was more beautiful than ever, if that were possible. Her hair was spread out over the pillows, framing the lovely profile she presented to him. Her hands, so white and frail, nervously twisted the covers.

"Claudia," he croaked. He cleared his throat and tried again. "We must talk. There are things that need to be settled," he said haltingly.

Claudia's heart constricted in fear. The time she'd been dreading was at hand. Angus was going to call her to account for all she'd said to him. She'd given him the out he needed by telling him how she hated him. Now he was going to leave. She must show him that she did not care, no matter what the cost.

She'd forgotten the powerful effect he had on her as he sat down on the bed beside her. She would not be able to stand being so near him. She could not bear the thought of his going, but knowing that he loved another would always cloud any happiness they might find.

"You need not say what is on your mind, my lord," she said in a rush. "I know what is in your heart, and your head, and I—I know that you must leave. It is what your heart dictates, and you must follow your heart."

The frown on Angus's forehead deepened as she swallowed back her tears and hurried on. "We could never be happy as long as you love another. You must seek your heart's desire and go to your love. I—I would ask only one thing of you, my lord..." She hesitated and looked at him fleetingly before lowering her head. Oh, God, he was so handsome. How could she bear to lose him? "Please, I beg of you, show me the respect due as your wife. Do not return here with your Dorcas," she ended raggedly.

Angus stared at her as though she'd lost her mind. "What are you babbling about?"

Claudia let out an anguished sob. Why was he torturing her this way? "I know that it is not I, but—but your Dorcas who holds your heart. If you want to go to her, then do so. . . ."

"My dearest heart, of course I will go to her," Angus said, grinning, "but only when you and the babe are strong enough to travel."

She turned frightened eyes on him, unable to hold back the tears any longer. Was this to be her punishment?"

"Why do you seek to hurt me," she cried.

The smile left his face, to be replaced by a confused frown. "But you just said that we should go to her . . ."

"Not we, you!" she wailed. "If you seek to punish me for my actions, you could not have found anything worse than to shame me before your mistress!"

"My what?" He grabbed her by the shoulders. "Who told you such a vile lie?" he demanded.

Her face paled. "But—but, I thought . . ."

His hands bit into her flesh as he growled, "What? What did you think? That I would stain my own sister's honor?"

"Your sister?" she whispered faintly.

"Yea, my sister. 'Tis true that Dorcas is a part of me, as much as my own soul. I do not know if that is true of most twins, but it is for us."

"Twins?" she echoed.

The anger left Angus's face as he frowned. "You knew that."

"Nay, I did not," she cried accusingly. "I knew only that you had three sisters. You never mentioned a twin." Suddenly her face was suffused with color, and she buried her face in her hands. "Oh, I am so ashamed. I heard you call out to Dorcas in your delirium, and I assumed the worst. And when you brought Vail a present from Noyon, but nothing for me, and—and I found the bolt of green cloth...It was an accident. I swear it. I did not mean to snoop, but I thought that you were hiding it from me so that you could give it to her. Then when everyone extolled her beauty, I became jealous, thinking that you loved another."

Angus grinned at her words. She was jealous. That meant she *did* care for him. He pried her hands away from her face and held them in his own. "My little pigeon, I do not remember anything when I was so ill, and, in truth, I'd forgotten about the cloth. It is indeed for you, but at the time I was too angry with you, so I put it away. I meant to give it to you later." He placed a hand under her chin, forcing her to look at him. "You said that you were jealous. Does that mean you do care for me, a little?" he asked quietly.

She could only stare at him, unable to find her voice.

He placed a gentle hand on her cheek and said, "Mayhaps more than a little? Mayhaps as much as I care for you?"

Her heart stopped a pace, then resumed its rapid beat as their eyes locked.

His hand slipped around to the back of her head to draw her closer. As their lips touched, he whispered, "I love you," before claiming them in a tender kiss.

Claudia shuddered with growing excitement at the sweetness of his caress. He pulled back, and she could see the smoldering embers deep within his eyes. "Angus..."

He did not let her finish as his mouth claimed hers once more, taking her breath away. He released her a second time, and she placed her hands on his chest to hold him off.

"I love you," she said.

He searched her face for the truth of her words, and smiled, seeing it in her eyes. "Now we are complete," he said, his mouth covering hers again.

Claudia's arms went around him to pull him closer. No more would she call her husband enemy, and fight him in his desires, for his desires were hers also. To love and be loved.

All thoughts of what she'd lost were gone, to be replaced by thoughts of what she'd gained. Angus's words echoed in her brain. *Now we are complete*. Aye, they were. A tiny ember of smoldering passion licked at her, building into a flame of ecstasy. She knew it flared within Angus too.

Claudia felt the chains of hate and pain unwind from around her heart as all the ghosts of the past slipped away. They had their newfound love to build the future on.

She sighed contentedly as she gave herself up to her husband. The past became a blur, for there was only now, and tomorrow, and all of the tomorrows to come.